A Song for a Soldier

Emily Darius
2017

Also by

EMILY DANIELS
Devlin's Daughter
Lucia's Lament

Coming Soon
Winnie's Wish

Also from
Phase Publishing

by

Rebecca Connolly
An Arrangement of Sorts

by
Grace Donovan
Saint's Ride

by
Laura Beers
Saving Shadow

A Song for a Soldier

EMILY DANIELS

Phase Publishing, LLC
Seattle

Text copyright © 2017 by Phase Publishing, LLC
Cover art copyright © 2017 by Phase Publishing, LLC

Cover art by Tugboat Design
http://www.tugboatdesign.net

Phase Publishing, LLC first paperback edition
November 2017

ISBN 978-1-943048-43-4
Library of Congress Control Number: 2017958043
Cataloging-in-Publication Data on file.

Acknowledgements

I dedicate this to the brave men and women who
have fought in wars not of their own choosing.
Their dedication to their principles, their steadfast
courage in the face of horrific conditions, and their
strength of will as they return home to try and lead
normal lives are an inspiration to all who know
them. Thank you.

I also dedicate this to my own valiant husband who
never fails to encourage, support, and inspire me.
Thank you, sweetheart.

Prologue

December 27, 1914
Oberste Heeresleitung, Schloss Pless, Germany

"But, General…"

"*Genug!*" General Hugo von Freytag-Loringhoven shouted. "I have heard enough excuses. This fraternization with the enemy must stop now! Our soldiers should not be making friends with the enemy. You will see to it that any man caught fraternizing with the enemy will be court-martialed and serve not less than two years hard labor."

Lieutenant-Colonel Wilhelm Groener stood for a moment, licked his lips, then started to speak again.

"*Entlassen!*"

The interview was over. There would be no quarter given. Never mind that so many of the young men on the front lines had made friendly connections with their British counterparts. Never mind that so many of them now refused to fire on the enemy. Never mind that no one seemed to want this war, except the generals and politicians who declared it.

Now it was up to him to follow the general's orders and pass down the decision. No more fraternizing. He shook his head in frustration.

"I have no idea how we're going to implement this one. It just doesn't make sense," he thought.

December 27, 1914
British Headquarters,
London, England

Meanwhile, in the War Office, two British generals were having a similar discussion.

"This is a fine mess, isn't it?" General sir Horace Lockwood Smith-Dorrien said.

"How did we ever let it get to this point?" Field Marshall Horatio Herbert Kitchener asked.

"We certainly can't expect the boys to begin shooting the enemy when the enemy has become friendly towards them, can we?"

"I should say not. So, what do we do? We can't have a war with soldiers who refuse to fight."

General Smith-Dorrien puffed on his pipe thoughtfully for a few moments, then pursed his lips and nodded. "I see no help for it. We'll have to rotate them out. With new troops in the trenches, we should have no problem convincing them that the Germans are the enemy. As for now, let's issue an order. No fraternizing with the enemy. Anyone caught fraternizing may be court-martialed and may be shot upon conviction at the discretion of the ruling court-martial board." He looked up. "Do you think that would do it?"

Field-Marshall Kitchener nodded and replied, "I should hope so. No one wants to risk summary execution."

With the issue resolved in their minds, the officers returned to duties, fully confident that their orders would be followed and that unfortunate unofficial truce would not be repeated... at least, not in this war.

They were right.

Chapter One

May 15, 1914
Dusseldorf, Germany

Friedrich frowned. Why was it when you were looking for a particular gift, it was nowhere to be found? He picked up a small bouquet of flowers and examined it carefully. No, this isn't right, he thought, putting the bouquet back in the basket.

Moving on to the next basket, he sighed. This bouquet must be extra special, for tonight was their fifth anniversary. Tonight, he thought, tonight is the night we make a baby. They had been trying for three years and were always disappointed when Gerdie found she wasn't with child. But, tonight, he felt lucky. So tonight, the flowers must be just right.

He looked for the proprietor of the flower cart. He saw her flirting with a young soldier standing nearby. Raising his hand and clearing his throat, he tried to attract her attention. She glanced up, barely acknowledged him, then went back to her conversation.

Frowning, Friedrich stepped up to the young couple. "Excuse me, *fräulein*," he said, "do you have any other flowers?"

"*Nein*," the young girl glanced up at him and shook her head, returning immediately to her conversation.

Friedrich rolled his eyes and shook his head as he began walking home, empty-handed. Young love, he thought. Ah, well. His own love was young enough, he supposed.

As he turned down his street, a little flower garden caught his eye. It was a small, carefully tended garden near the front door of a run-down apartment building. In the center was a beautiful rose bush with a perfect pink rose. Just what he'd been looking for.

Perhaps Frau Schmidt wouldn't miss just one flower. He looked around and saw no one, so he carefully stretched over the smaller flowers in front. He didn't want to step into the garden for fear of crushing the other blooms. Bending forward, he grasped the stem of the perfect rose near the main stalk and tried to break it off. It didn't budge. Frowning, he worked a little harder, but jerked back as a thorn pricked his thumb.

He stood up, put the injured thumb in his mouth, and considered his options. He knew if he tried hard enough, that perfect rose would come off in his hands, but it might disturb the rest of the bush or crush the rose and he didn't want that. Bad enough that he was stealing this one flower. He bent down and reached in to try again when a voice startled him.

"What are you doing there?" the harsh voice charged him from a window nearby.

"Um…" he stood up, embarrassed and not knowing what to say.

"I say, Frau Schmidt, he's stealing your flowers," the woman in the window accused.

Friedrich whirled round to see Frau Schmidt standing behind him.

"He's not stealing them, Frau Schultz. He has my permission to take whatever flowers he wants."

Frau Schultz harrumphed and pulled her head inside, closing the window with a loud thunk.

Turning to Friedrich, Frau Schmidt was all business. "I find scissors work better. Doesn't disturb the bush and there's less chance of injury from the thorns."

Guilt filled his heart as he faced the short, white-haired *frau* dressed in a faded flower-print dress with a soiled apron around her plump waist. She wasn't smiling, but her eyes were twinkling as she considered the would-be flower thief before her.

"I'm sorry," he stammered, removing his cap and looking at the ground in shame. "I'd hoped one flower wouldn't be missed."

The *frau* cocked her head and pursed her lips for a moment. "She must be someone special."

Friedrich looked up and nodded. "She's an angel," he said simply. "She's my wife and today is our fifth wedding anniversary."

"I believe there is a flower cart parked not far from here," the *frau* pointed back the way he'd just come. "Why didn't you buy her a bouquet instead of giving her one stolen flower?"

"I looked there," he answered frankly. "None of them were right. They were wilted and sad-looking. My wife deserves a perfect flower, not one that's been sitting in a cart in the hot sun all day."

Considering his answer, she finally nodded, then pulled a small pair of scissors from her apron and stepped into the garden, nimbly treading between the lovely blossoms. She deftly clipped off the one he wanted and handed it to him.

He reached into his pocket for the coins there, but she waved him off. "I remember what love feels like, young man. Go and enjoy your wife. Young love should not be wasted! Happy anniversary to you both."

"*Danke*, Frau Schmidt," he said. "Thank you."

Glancing at the clock, Gertrude shook her head and tried to move a little faster. She'd spent more time at the market than she'd planned and now she was afraid dinner would be late. Friedrich wouldn't scold, but she knew he'd be hungry when he arrived. He always appreciated it when dinner was ready when he came home.

Tonight must be special, she thought. Fifth anniversaries were something to be celebrated, to be sure. But tonight's celebration… well, tonight would be extra special.

Humming to herself, she adjusted the position of the plates on either side of the small table, arranging the glasses just so. The candles in the center were used a bit, but when they were lit, it wouldn't matter. The white tablecloth was pristine. She had spent several hours yesterday washing and scrubbing and making sure all the stains were out of it. Then she'd laid it over their balcony to let the sun whiten it further. Her efforts were not in vain. Everything was in order.

A knock on the door startled her for a moment, then she remembered their next-door neighbor was coming and smiled. She ushered the elderly man in and showed him the chair she'd set up behind the curtain separating the living area from their bedroom area.

"Will this be comfortable for you, Herr Otto?" she asked, concerned.

"*Ja*, this will be good." He smiled tenderly at her. He placed his violin case on the floor and began unpacking it. Lifting the old violin gently, he raised it to his shoulder and started tuning it.

"You will stay silent until I give the signal, won't you?" Gerdie asked.

The old man winked at her, conspiratorially, "Do not worry, *mein liebling*. I will remain silent, then, at your signal, your hearts will be filled with the music of love."

Gerdie leaned down and kissed his cheek, before returning to her preparations.

Moving into the kitchen, she checked the *kartoffelknödel* and smiled. The potato pancakes were sizzling nicely. Her husband would be pleased. She couldn't afford the *saurbraten* as she'd hoped, but the sauerkraut was fermented to perfection. The apple *strudel* was golden brown and smelled heavenly. The crusty rye bread was fresh from her oven this very day. It was the best she could do.

Her smile broadened as she heard the key in the lock. She removed her apron and fluffed her hair. Rushing to the door, she stopped for an instant to pinch her cheeks and lick her lips. Yes, now she was ready.

May 15, 1914
Nash Mills, Hemel Hempstead, England

"Come on, Tom. It'll be fun," Gerome's voice was nearly a whine. Thomas Bennett hated whiners, so he frowned.

"I don't think so, Gerry," he made his voice as firm as he could. "I hate dances. I don't know how to dance. I don't want to learn. I feel awkward. The girls are pushy. The smoke in the room makes me cough. I have to wash my hair, or do my laundry, or watch my dog scratch his fleas. Pick your excuse. I'm not going."

Gerome shook his head ruefully. "You're missing out, my friend. I hear there are some new girls coming to this one. New girls mean new opportunities. Forgive me for saying so, but you need new opportunities, Tommy-boy."

"Your opinion, my friend. I think I'm doing just fine on my own."

"Right," Gerome's voice was scornful this time. "That's why Beatrice is now seeing Kirk Brown?"

Thomas rolled his eyes. "Her loss, and may they find whatever happiness they deserve."

Gerome looked thoughtful, then grinned. "I'll let you drive my car."

"What? You don't have a car."

"Wrong! My uncle is in town and has promised I can take his Morris out whenever I want while he's here."

"You're lying."

"Am not."

"Prove it."

With Gerome leading the way, the two young recruits ambled the two blocks to a small, tidy home with a shiny, new Morris Oxford parked in front. Shaking his head, Thomas walked around it, admiring the two-seat open-tourer.

"She's a beauty, Gerry," he remarked. "Your uncle really said you can borrow it?"

"He did. He's inside if you want to ask him," Gerome smirked.

Thomas grinned. "I think I do."

Gerome looked shocked, but followed his friend inside.

Margaret, or Maggie as she preferred to be called, was undecided. She held two dresses in her hands. One was dark, emerald green silk with ribbed silk and a blue chiffon overlay. The other was blue satin with cream lace. She preferred the blue satin, but the green one was a better fit.

When Shelly had asked if she wanted to go to the military dance welcoming the new army recruits, she'd hesitated, but had changed her mind when she heard The Giles Bowman Dance Band was playing and her mother offered to buy her a new dress for the occasion. She could never turn down a new band or a new dress! She didn't often have the chance to enjoy either one.

"Which one do you like best, Beth?" she asked her friend who was sitting quietly on a chair nearby.

Cocking her head, Beth examined each dress critically. "I like the blue one. It brings out the color of your eyes."

"I think so, too, but the green one does seem to fit a bit better."

Nodding, Beth agreed. "If you are comfortable in the hobble-skirt styles these days," she laughed.

"Tell me again why you aren't getting a dress?" Maggie asked.

Beth laughed and shook her head. "Michael and I are saving for our honeymoon. I'd rather have a spectacular honeymoon than a dress I'll only wear once or twice."

Maggie started to answer, but was interrupted by her other friend coming out of the dressing room. She was wearing a bold, pink silk shot with gold, a wide gold sash, and a daringly low neckline trimmed with gold braid.

"Which dress do you like, Shelly?" she asked, holding up both dresses.

Barely glancing at Maggie, Shelly waved at the green silk. "That one fits you better," she said dismissively. "I think the sash is too wide on this, don't you think, Mags?"

Smiling indulgently, Maggie agreed that the sash was, indeed, too wide. Beth nodded in agreement, as well.

An hour later, all three girls left the dress shop. Maggie and Shelly had large dress boxes in their hands. Maggie had decided on the one she liked better, and Shelly bought the wide-sashed dress. Maggie was certain that it was the low neckline that was the deciding factor for her friend. She felt a bit sorry for Beth, who didn't have a new dress, but Beth didn't seem to mind at all.

"It's going to be a wonderful time tonight, girls," Shelly proclaimed. "I hear the military dances have all the cutest soldiers attending them. Tonight, there are supposed to be a new batch of recruits, too."

"I don't know about that, but I am looking forward to hearing the band. My cousin said they're great," Maggie answered.

Beth cocked her head. "You wouldn't be hoping to sing with them, would you?"

Laughing, Maggie shrugged. "I wouldn't turn down the chance."

"You're hopeless," Shelly chuckled. "All you think about is music and dresses."

"Is there anything else worth thinking about?" Maggie grinned.

"Yes, men!" Shelly shouted, throwing her arms open wide and twirling a few steps down the street.

"Now who's hopeless?" Maggie called after her.

"Me. I admit it," Shelly waited as Maggie and Beth caught up. The girls laughed as the three of them linked arms and did a little chassé down the street.

Chapter Two

With a sigh of deep satisfaction, Friedrich leaned back and patted his now-full belly.

"That was delicious, Gerdie. The candles, the music, it was a perfect anniversary dinner. *Danke*."

Gerdie ducked her head shyly. Even after five years of marriage, Friedrich's compliments still made her feel self-conscious.

"I'm glad you enjoyed it," she whispered. "Thank you for the rose. Thank you for remembering that it's my favorite."

"How could I forget?" he laughed. "You always stare at them in Frau Schmidt's garden when we walk by."

Gerdie joined his laughter. "I can't help it. They are so beautiful!"

"Yes, they are. But they pale in beauty compared to you, *mein liebling*."

Ducking her head again, Gerdie giggled a little. She felt like a shy schoolgirl on her first date.

Friedrich leaned over the table to clasp her hand in his. "Herr Otto must be getting tired of playing that violin," he whispered. "Shall we tell him he can go home and we'll make some music of our own?"

Looking up, Gerdie's eyes grew wide. "Oh, not just yet. I have something else planned."

She stood abruptly and raced to the curtain. Poking her head inside, she whispered something, then turned to face Friedrich.

From behind the curtain, the soothing strains of Brahm's *"Guten Abend und Gute Nacht"* filled the tiny apartment.

"Shall we dance?" Gerdie asked as she held out her hand.

Friedrich grinned, stood, and pulled her into his arms. As they swayed to the music, he held her close.

"Do you recognize this tune?" she whispered in his ear.

He listened for a moment, then shook his head. "It sounds familiar, but I can't recall what it is."

After a moment, she whispered again. "Listen closely, Papa."

She began to sing the lyrics softly, almost humming them.

"Guten Abend, gut' Nacht
Mit Rosen bedacht
Mit Näglein besteckt
Schlüpf unter die Deck'
Morgen früh, wenn Gott will
Wirst du wieder geweckt
Morgen früh, wenn Gott will
Wirst du wieder geweckt. "

Pulling back to look at her, Friedrich was obviously puzzled. "First you ask me to dance, then you sing me a lullaby?"

Giggling a little, she asked again. "Didn't you hear what I called you?"

Gradually, his expression changed from bewilderment to shock. "You... did you call me Papa?" he stammered.

Nodding happily, she nearly exploded. "Yes! You're going to be a papa!"

Realization dawned and Friedrich whooped as he picked her up and swung her in the air.

"Friedrich, put me down!" she laughed. "I'm sure it's not good for the baby to be swinging me around so."

Gently, he put her down, but the grin on his face told of his joy. "I'm sorry, *mein liebling*. It's just that you have made me so happy. When will..."

"Before Christmas," she smiled.

"What a wonderful Christmas gift!" He bent down to kiss her softly.

Melting into his arms, she wrapped her own around his neck, pulling him into a deeper kiss.

Neither of them noticed as Herr Otto slipped out quietly, turning to smile fondly at the happy couple before he closed the door behind him.

The Giles Bowman Band was every bit as good as Maggie had hoped. She quickly maneuvered her way to the front of the dance floor, but was careful to stay off to one side so she wouldn't get in the way of those dancing.

Beth and Michael were already on the floor. They didn't seem to be aware of anything but each other. They weren't even moving in rhythm to the music. They just sort of swayed together, holding each other, staring into each other's eyes. Maggie shook her head and smiled.

It hadn't taken long for Shelly to find her dance partner for the night, which suited Maggie just fine. She was more interested in the band anyway.

When they took their first break, Maggie made it a point to speak to Mr. Bowman.

"The band sounds great tonight," she commented.

"Thanks," he said dismissively.

Unwilling to lose this opportunity, she stepped up beside him and asked, "Do you boys know 'Daddy has a Sweetheart'?"

Surprised by her request, he looked at her, slowing his gait to match hers. "'...and Mother is Her Name'? Yes. Would you like us to play it?"

"Yes, but..." Maggie hesitated.

"But what, sweetheart?" the songster asked kindly. She had his full attention now.

"But would you allow me to sing it with you?" The words came out rushed and jumbled, but Maggie felt proud she'd finally had nerve enough to ask.

The man stopped and turned to face her. "Can you sing?"

Maggie just nodded.

"Well, come on out here and let's try you out," he smiled, took her elbow, and guided her out into the alley behind the dance hall. "Hey boys, we have a songbird who wants to join us for a song. Come tell me what you think."

Turning back to her, he nodded. "Go ahead. Give us a sample of what you can do."

Swallowing hard, Maggie looked from one face to the other. She wasn't sure what she expected, but they all looked friendly enough. Just expectant, waiting for her to start.

She licked her lips and swallowed. Looking up at the full moon, she started singing "Danny Boy". The song was one her father used to sing to her and it was the one that always calmed her; the one she sang the best.

When she was finished, she looked back at her small audience and saw smiles on all their faces. She smiled back and looked at the leader.

"Well? Can I sing with you? Just one song?" She hated that her voice sounded pleading.

"You've earned yourself a chance, miss," he answered. "We'll do your song first thing after our break."

"Thank you!" Her heart skipped a beat and she could hardly contain her joy. She was really going to sing with The Giles Bowman Band!

She entered the dance hall and moved toward the ladies' room to freshen up. Taking a few minutes to make sure her hair wasn't mussed and her dress laid smoothly, she was ready.

The band was just setting up when she approached.

"There you are. Come on up. We're nearly ready for you." He turned to the band and gave them instructions for her song.

Turning back to her, he asked, "What's your name?"

"Margaret Gilley," she replied.

He faced the audience that had gathered near the bandstand. "Ladies and gentlemen, we have a real treat for you tonight. Your own Margaret Gilley is going to join us for this next number. She'll be singing "Daddy has a Sweetheart". Let's give her a big round of applause!"

The audience clapped politely, then silence filled the hall. The music started and Maggie thought her heart in her throat was going to muffle the words for sure. But she took a deep breath, closed her eyes, and focused on the music. When the introduction ended, her voice flowed into the song without her conscious thought. It was soft at first, then built into the full, rich tone she enjoyed so much.

She heard the audience begin to hum along with her so she opened her eyes and smiled as she sang. Making eye contact with a few in the front, she nodded that they should join in. After a few moments, the entire dance hall rang with voices singing the familiar tune. As the last verse ended, she raised her hands to silence them and lowered her own voice to a throaty whisper. The effect was stunning and she felt the audience's response before the applause even began.

When it erupted, she took another deep breath and smiled, bowed, then smiled at them again. As she scanned the people in the room, she saw smiles, tears, and happy faces all around. This was everything she hoped it would be; an amazing experience that she knew she'd never forget!

She stepped away from the band and greeted a few people who complimented her performance. But most in attendance were interested in dancing, so the crowd around her thinned quickly.

Feeling such a sense of elation, she realized she was thirsty. She wandered around the outside edge of the room, hoping to find the punch bowl. When she finally found it, she chuckled and decided she wasn't that thirsty after all. The line was simply too long to worry about it.

Changing direction, she moved back towards her place by the bandstand. She hadn't gone far, though, when a young recruit caught her eye. He was standing not ten feet away, staring at her with his mouth hanging open like a dead fish. She covered her mouth to stifle a giggle as she angled herself to move away from him.

She couldn't help glancing back, however. Besides the slack-jawed expression on his face, he wasn't bad looking, she decided. His sandy brown hair was a bit tousled, like he'd just run his fingers through it. He had a square jaw and prominent cheekbones. His shoulders were broad and filled out his uniform nicely. Not like some of the scrawny new recruits she'd seen on the street.

He smiled and began walking towards her.

Oh no, she thought. Her breathing quickened as she accelerated her pace to the front of the hall. Please don't let him come over. Please don't let him come over. Please don't let...

"Excuse me," a rich voice interrupted her pseudo-wish.

She looked up and decided that his eyes were most definitely his best feature. She gazed up into the ice-blue pools that drew her in and caused her to forget everything she'd ever told herself about not getting involved with a soldier.

"I said, excuse me," the rich voice had a hint of laughter in it.

Shaking herself mentally, she forced herself to look away. She licked her lips, swallowed, and then looked back, being careful not to look into those mesmerizing eyes. "Yes?" she finally squeaked, then cleared her throat and tried to sound normal again. "Yes?"

"Your performance was incredible." He proffered his hand, smiling the most beguiling smile she'd ever seen.

"Thank you," she responded automatically. Maybe his mouth was his best feature. She watched his lips as they curved into a mischievous grin.

"May I have this dance?" he asked.

Glancing back up to his eyes, she took a deep breath. No. Definitely his eyes.

Private "Eyes" moved his hand a bit forward to regain her attention. Again, she forced herself to look down. Without a word, she put her hand in his and allowed herself to be led to the dance floor, barely registering that the band had started playing again.

The dance was a one-step, which allowed him to hold her close as they moved almost effortlessly around the floor. She studiously looked over his shoulder, but was very aware that he was watching her face intently.

What am I doing? Her thoughts were all jumbled. *I am dancing with a soldier. A recruit who will most certainly be called up when his training is finished. Don't get involved, Maggie,* she scolded herself. *Just stop this right now. Forget his strong shoulders. Forget the way his hands are gently guiding you around the floor. Forget his winning smile. Forget his eyes...*

No. I'll never forget those eyes, she admitted, finally looking up into those beautiful ice-blue pools that promised much without revealing anything. Without thinking any more at all, she allowed herself to be caught up in all of it… the music, his arms around her, his gorgeous eyes…

The song ended and Private "Eyes" led her back to her place by the bandstand. He didn't leave her there, though. He stepped one step back and smiled.

"Thank you for the dance," he nodded his gratitude.

"You're welcome," she managed to say.

"My name is Thomas. Private Thomas Bennett."

"I'm Maggie. Maggie Bennett," she replied, stammering just a bit.

"Really? Maggie Bennett?"

"What? Oh… no! I'm Maggie Gilley." This time she really stammered, her cheeks flushed with embarrassment.

Thomas laughed. "It's nice to meet you Maggie Bennett Gilley. And may I say, the name suits you."

"No, no it doesn't. I didn't mean to say…" Her words were rushed and her breath uneven as she tried to think of a way out of this mess.

Just then, she spotted Shelly and Beth moving towards the ladies' room.

"Excuse me. I need to catch up to my friends." Maggie practically ran, nearly upsetting a chair on the way. She heard Thomas calling after her, but ignored him as she found refuge in the ladies' room.

"What's chasing you? Or should I say who's chasing you?" Shelly grinned at her, then turned back to the mirror to finish repairing her makeup.

"You look scared," Beth commented, concerned.

As Shelly dipped her pinky finger into the little tub she held, she glanced at Maggie again.

"Was he that frightening?" she asked as she dabbed the color onto her lips, smoothing it, then gently patting it with a small piece of blotting paper.

Maggie took a deep breath and tried to calm her racing heart. After a couple of breaths, she felt she could finally speak.

"Yes. No. I mean, he wasn't frightening. I just…" she stopped, realizing with each word she was getting herself deeper into trouble.

"Calm down. Just tell us what happened," Beth admonished.

"Oh, bother," Maggie sighed.

Finishing her makeup repair, Shelly turned and regarded her friend. "What's his name?"

"Private Thomas Bennett."

"Well, Maggie dear, let's go find your Private Thomas Bennett and get to know him better."

"No! I can't go back out there!" Maggie cried.

"Why not? Did you make a fool of yourself or something?" Shelly pressed.

Maggie just looked at the floor and didn't say a word.

"You did, didn't you? You made a fool of yourself," her friend shook her head. "You've got it bad and all you know is his name."

With a pleading look in her eyes, Maggie whispered, "Please, don't make me go out there again."

Beth looked at Shelly. "I think we should cover for her. She looks pretty flustered and that sure won't make a good impression."

After a moment of silence, Shelly agreed. "All right. We'll go out and find this private of yours and keep him occupied while you duck out the nearest exit."

"Oh, would you?" The relief on Maggie's face was evident.

"Sure. What are friends for anyway?"

After Beth and Shelly left, Maggie counted to three hundred. Five minutes should be enough time for her friends to find Private Bennett and engage him in conversation. She opened the door a little, but didn't see them through the small crack. Opening the door further, she slipped out, furtively glancing all around the room.

Finally, she spotted them just off to the left and was alarmed that they were so close. Shelly was obviously trying to get him to dance with her, but he was refusing. Beth was nowhere to be seen. Maggie looked to the right and saw the exit about twenty feet away. Looking back at her friend, she saw that Shelly had maneuvered herself so that Private Bennett had his back to the ladies' room door.

Maggie made a quick dash to the exit and relief washed over her when the door closed behind her. She didn't stop there, though. She ran around the corner of the building and nearly ran into Michael, who seemed to be waiting for her.

"Oh! I didn't see you, Michael."

He laughed. "It's all right. I was expecting you. Beth told me what happened and suggested we walk you home. She's waiting by the big bush nearest the street."

Maggie heaved a great sigh of relief and smiled gratefully at her friend's fiancé.

"Thanks, Michael. I really appreciate this."

He just shrugged and escorted her to where Beth was waiting.

They were nearly halfway home before Maggie realized they'd left Shelly stranded alone at the dance. Turning to Beth, she asked, "Should we go back for Shelly?"

Beth laughed. "No, Shelly's resourceful. She'll find some handsome soldier to escort her home."

Maggie chuckled to herself. Knowing Shelly, she'd have no trouble finding several that would be willing to ensure her safe arrival.

Crisis averted. Taking a deep breath, she slowed to a walk and began to think. Why did this man have such an effect on her? What was it about him that caused her heart to race and her palms to sweat? How was he able to make her mind stop thinking about anything but him? Who was this Private Thomas "Eyes" Bennett anyway?

Thanking her friends for the escort, Maggie quietly entered her apartment. She stepped carefully, unwilling to disturb her mother and sister sleeping in the next room. There would be time for those questions tomorrow.

Tonight, she'd go to sleep and dream about those ice-blue eyes.

Chapter Three

Friedrich glanced up as Gerdie put his breakfast on the table. Trying to be nonchalant, he folded his newspaper and placed it on the floor under his chair.

"Please, don't leave your newspaper on the floor," Gerdie scolded mildly. "I can still bend over to pick it up, but in a few weeks, I'll be too big."

"I'm sorry, *mein liebling*. I'll try to remember." He bent over and picked up the paper, glanced around for a place to put it, then stood. "I'll just put it in the trash so you won't have to do it later."

Smiling disarmingly, he patted her shoulder as he passed her.

"Wait," Gerdie caught his arm. "What's that?" She pointed to the newspaper.

"It's a newspaper," he laughed.

"No. What's that?" She took the paper from his hand and pointed at the headline he'd been trying to hide. He stifled a sigh and let the paper go without an argument. She would probably hear about it from someone today. She may as well read it for herself.

"Headlines: Düsseldorfer Zeitung, August 1, 1914
DECLARATION OF WAR BY GERMANY
AGAINST RUSSIA.
St. Petersburg, Saturday.

The German Ambassador, in the name of his Government, handed to the Foreign Ministry a declaration of war at 7:30 this evening."

As she scanned the article, Friedrich watched her face grow pale. This was what he'd been trying to avoid. He felt helpless so he stood by and waited as she took an unsteady breath and laid the paper on the table. She swallowed hard, then picked up her fork. But her hand shook, so she put it back down and placed her hands in her lap, dropping her chin to her chest. He was certain she was trying to hide tears that were threatening to fall.

Kneeling beside her, he took her hands in his, forcing her to turn and face him.

"It is nothing, Gerdie. I am *Landwehr*, second-line, and am no longer listed in the first reserve. There are many men they will call up before my name is at the top. There is nothing to worry about." Hhis voice was calm and soothing.

Gerdie looked up at him and tried to smile through her tears. "I know, but they have declared war on two fronts, so they will want many men. I don't know how I will manage without you here."

That thought was the final straw and she began to sob.

Friedrich rose onto his knees and pulled her into his arms. He let her cry until her shoulders stopped shaking and her grip on him loosened. Then he leaned back, handing her his handkerchief.

She took it, dabbed at her eyes, and blew her nose. "You must think I'm such a silly woman to worry about such things."

"Not at all, but it has not happened yet. Let's not worry about what might or might not come. Let's enjoy this delicious breakfast and go do something fun today. What would you like to do?"

She sniffled a little, then looked at him hopefully. "Could we take a picnic to the park? I love watching the children play near the water."

"Of course! Whatever you want." Friedrich hugged her, then stood and returned to his seat. Smiling, he waited for her to begin eating before starting on his own.

"Higher, Thomas! Toss me higher!" Katie squealed in delight.

"Any higher and you'll be able to touch the clouds!" Thomas laughed.

"I want to touch the clouds! Higher!"

"All right, but don't say I didn't warn you." Thomas tried to sound concerned, but failed miserably.

He tossed the five-year-old high into the air and caught her deftly as she giggled and laughed.

Sitting on a blanket nearby, Maggie laughed, too. It wasn't often that Katie took to strangers, but Thomas had a way with children. It was good to see her laugh. She hadn't been this happy since their father died four years ago, during the horrible heat wave of 1910.

Maggie remembered what a happy, smiling baby Katie was then. It's amazing how their father's death affected her, even though she was so young. Her bright smiling disposition had turned sad and withdrawn. She rarely spoke, never smiled, and seemed to always want to be alone.

That is until Thomas came into the picture two months ago. Maggie smiled at the memory of his persistence. Apparently, he'd searched for her during and after the dance that night. He even asked to escort Shelly home to quiz her about Maggie's address, but Shelly was a good friend and kept her address secret.

That didn't stop Private "Eyes" Bennett, though. For two weeks, he asked everyone who might know her, searched every street within walking distance of the dance hall, and even hired a cab one afternoon to search further away.

It was sheer luck that he found her in the market one Saturday. He'd walked up behind her and said, "Excuse me."

She remembered how her heart had thumped loudly at the sound of his rich voice. She'd gulped, took a deep breath, and tried to regain some semblance of control over her emotions.

"Excuse me," he'd repeated.

She'd finally turned around and looked up into those ice-blue eyes again and... well, the rest was history, as they say. He had called on her and her mother and sister nearly every day since then.

The first visit, Katie had been her usual shy self, hiding quietly behind the sofa, despite Maggie's coaxing her to come and meet this nice man.

After a couple of attempts, Thomas shook his head and smiled. He'd sat on the sofa and carried on a conversation with Mrs. Gilley and Maggie. After a few minutes, Mrs. Gilley went to fetch some tea and crumpets.

While she was gone, Thomas started telling Maggie an outrageous story about a kitten and a magpie.

There once was a kitten who feared magpies and would hide in a thorn bush whenever one came around. But there was one magpie who was really very nice and wanted to be friends with the kitten. So, she devised a plan.

She found a fish market and flew into the alley behind it every day. She picked out a nice fish head from the refuse pile and brought it to where the kitten was hiding. She dropped it close to the thorn bush and then flew up into a nearby tree to wait and see what would happen.

After a while, the kitten reached out a tentative paw and snagged the fish head with her claw, pulling it in quickly. She licked it a bit first, but it tasted so good that she devoured it in three bites. Then she licked her paws and purred contentedly.

The next day, the magpie repeated her plan. This time dropping the fish head just a bit farther away from the thorn bush.

Again, the kitten snagged the fish, although she had to put her shoulder out to reach the treat. Again, she ate it quickly and then carefully licked her paws, purring contentedly.

This went on for several days, with the magpie dropping fish heads further and further away. Finally, the kitten didn't even bother to take the fish back to her thorn bush hiding place. She ate it right there on the grass.

When she was finished and was cleaning her paws, the magpie spoke up. "I'm glad you are enjoying my gifts," she cawed.

The kitten started to run away, then her curiosity got the better of her. "You are bringing me that delicious fish every day?" she asked.

"Yes," cawed the magpie.

"But why?"

"Because I want to be your friend, but you were too scared to talk to me," the magpie answered. "Are you still scared of me?"

The kitten thought for a moment and then shook her head. "No, I'm not scared of you anymore."

"Can we be friends?"
"Yes, yes we can."
From that day forward, the kitten and the magpie were fast friends.

By the time Mrs. Gilley returned, Thomas had reached the middle of the story, and Katie was peeking around the couch. But Thomas ignored her, focusing his entire attention on Maggie.

When he reached the end, Katie was sitting on the floor next to him, completely engrossed in the story. She'd totally forgotten her fear, as well as the half-eaten crumpet in her hand.

"Were they really friends forever after that?" she'd asked. Both Maggie and her mother were shocked to hear her speak, let alone to a stranger.

But Thomas had taken it all in stride. He'd turned his full attention to Katie and they had a very nice discussion about what good friends really are.

Ever since then, Katie had been as excited to see Thomas as Maggie was. For different reasons, of course.

"Maggie!" Katie shouted, startling her sister out of her reverie. "Thomas is going to show me how to float my boat on the water. Come watch us."

"Your boat?" Maggie asked, confused.

"Yes, my boat. Haven't you been paying attention?" Katie scolded. "Thomas helped me make a boat out of a piece of bark, a stick, and a leaf. See?"

Maggie dutifully looked at the makeshift boat and smiled. "It's wonderful, Katie. Do you think it will sail?"

"Let's find out! Come on, Thomas," she crowed. "Let's sail my boat!"

Off she ran to the little pond without looking back to see if they were following.

"I think we'd better go make sure she doesn't fall in," Thomas grinned, holding out his hand to help her up.

"You're right, of course," Maggie agreed. "She's a totally different girl since you started coming around. I can't imagine why."

She grinned up at him and her heart skipped a beat when he leaned down to give her a quick kiss before pulling her up to her feet.

"Race you to the water," he challenged, then started running before she could reply.

Laughing, she ran after him. "Not fair!" she called. They passed Katie before they reached the water and were waiting, breathless when she ran up to join them.

They spent the rest of the afternoon sailing Katie's boat, walking along the water, and talking about nothing at all.

That evening, while Mrs. Gilley was putting Katie to bed, Thomas sat on the couch with Maggie. He was quiet and almost pensive.

"What's wrong, Thomas?" Maggie asked.

He looked up and smiled. "Nothing you need to worry your pretty little head about," he quipped.

Her eyebrows raised and she pursed her lips. "Now that does worry me! Every time someone says not to worry, I know there's reason to worry. What's wrong?"

He studied her face for a long moment, then reached out to stroke her cheek.

She leaned into his hand, then captured it and kissed his wrist.

"It's not going to work, Private. You can't distract me so easily," she teased, then grew serious. "I really want to know what's bothering you."

"There's a rumor going around the barracks that we're going to war with Germany. Since they declared war on Russia and since France declared war on them, we will have to honor our alliance and join the fighting," he said glumly.

Maggie frowned. "It makes sense, but maybe your unit won't have to go?"

"We're the new recruits, Maggie. We're the ones who will go next," he replied.

Looking at his hand in hers, she stroked each finger thoughtfully. "Then we'll just have to be brave and do the best we can," she said softly.

Thomas tucked a finger under her chin and raised her face to look at him.

"I don't want to leave you, Maggie," he whispered.

"I know," she nodded, "and I don't want you to go, but life

doesn't always give us what we want, does it?"

"No, it doesn't," he agreed, "but maybe…"

"Maybe what?" she asked when he hesitated.

He looked deeply into her eyes, then slid off the sofa to one knee.

"Maybe you'd consent to marry me before I have to go?" he asked hopefully.

Maggie's face transformed from sad disappointment to beaming in a split second.

"Marry you? Of course, I'll marry you!" She threw herself into his arms making him lose his balance. They both ended up lying on the floor laughing and kissing, unable to stop either long enough to stand up.

"Margaret Ann Gilley!" Mrs. Gilley scolded as she entered the room. "What is all this commotion? You are going to wake Katie."

"Mama," Maggie tried to be serious, but failed miserably… or rather, failed happily. "Mama, Thomas has asked me to marry him!"

Mrs. Gilley's face was an exact replica of Maggie's; going from frown to smiles in the time it takes to blink.

"Well, I'll be," she exclaimed. "Congratulations to you both!"

There were hugs all around, then they sat for the next couple of hours making wedding plans.

Chapter Four

"Headlines: Düsseldorfer Zeitung, August 4, 1914
DECLARATION OF WAR BY GREAT BRITAIN
AGAINST GERMANY.
St. Petersburg, Tuesday.

Great Britain declared war on Germany at eleven o'clock last night. British Parliament sent ultimatum to the German Ambassador during the day, requiring assurances that the neutrality of Belgium would be respected, a reply being requested by midnight. The German Government rejected the British demand, whereupon war was declared."

"Please don't cry, Gerdie!" Friedrich was beside himself. He didn't know how to comfort his pregnant wife. She was quite emotional and not very rational, so logic wasn't going to work.

"I can't help it," Gerdie cried, fresh tears streaming down her face. "I know we still have two weeks before you have to go. I know we have no choice. But how am I going to have this baby without you? How am I supposed to go on with you so far away to a battlefield where you could be killed at any moment?"

Her hysterics were becoming worse, and Friedrich knew he had to do something and fast, but he couldn't think of anything that wouldn't make matters worse. So, he did the only thing he could do. He held her close and let her cry. He didn't try to calm her. He didn't try to make sense of what she was crying about. He didn't try to distract her with jokes or stories or any of the other tactics that usually worked when she was upset. He just held her close and let her cry.

After what seemed like forever, her sobs began to soften and her breathing began to return to normal with only a few hiccuppy sobs, punctuated by a few sniffles into his handkerchief.

Finally, she took a deep breath, hugged him, then pulled back.

"Thank you," she whispered. "Thank you for letting me cry it out."

He smiled and kissed her forehead. "Something cleansing about a good cry, isn't there? That's what my mother used to say."

Gerdie chuckled a sad little chuckle. "She was right."

"So, what can we do to make it easier for you?" he asked.

She thought for a moment, then ventured, "Can we get the nursery ready before you leave?"

"Of course!" Friedrich was relieved to finally have something constructive to do to help his wife.

The space they'd allocated for the "nursery" was simply a corner of their sleeping space. He moved their little dresser into the corner to make room for the cradle next to the bed while Gerdie washed the cradle linens. The cradle and linens had been given to them by a neighbor whose baby had outgrown the little cradle, so she took extra care to make certain there were no holes that needed mending. Meanwhile, Friedrich whitewashed the cradle and let it dry in the sun.

Gerdie crocheted little baby blankets, booties, bonnets, and sweaters. She was skillful with a crochet hook and didn't seem to mind unravelling a couple of her sweaters to recreate them into things for the baby.

While he repaired his mother's old rocking chair for her, she took her wedding dress, cut it, pinned it, and sewed it into a delicate, lacy christening gown, complete with booties and a fine bonnet.

As she laid it carefully in the chest at the end of their bed, she looked up at the nursery corner and smiled.

"It's perfect, Friedrich." Her voice was soft. "I know our little *kleiner* will be content here."

Smiling, he took her in his arms. "How could he not be content with you for his mother?"

Her eyes twinkled as she playfully nudged him. "How do you

know our baby is a boy? Maybe we'll have a girl. Then how will you feel?"

The twinkle in his eyes matched hers. "I will feel like the proudest papa in all of Germany! I will show her off to everyone, and when she grows into a young beauty, I will buy a gun and fend off all unsuitable suitors."

He feigned a fierce look and Gerdie laughed. "She will have you wrapped around her little finger, my love. You will be helpless against her winning smile and soft brown eyes!"

Looking thoughtful, Friedrich nodded. "You are probably right. So, you will have to be the tough parent. I'll give her everything she wants and you can teach her how to behave properly."

Gerdie's shocked expression broke his concentration and he laughed again. "I am teasing you. We will raise our child together, both of us will discipline and both of us will spoil. That's only fair, right?"

"Right." She smiled and laid her head on his shoulder. After a moment, he felt her sigh and held her closer.

A few more moments of silence, then he heard her whisper. "But it's going to be harder to raise our baby together when you are so far away."

"I know, *mein liebling*," he crooned, "but it won't be forever. I'll be back as soon as I am able."

Gerdie looked up into his eyes. "Promise you will stay out of harm's way… as much as you can."

Tucking his finger under her chin, his face sober, he nodded. "I promise. I will stay as safe as I possibly can."

He leaned down and kissed her gently, then pulled her closer and deepened the kiss. She melted into his embrace and returned his kiss fervently.

Their kiss ended abruptly when Friedrich suddenly jumped back, holding his belly. "What was that?"

Laughing, Gerdie pulled his hand over to touch her swollen abdomen. "Apparently, our little *kleiner* likes it when we kiss. He was kicking to let you know he's there."

With a look of serious concentration, Friedrich held his hand on his wife's pregnant belly and waited, willing his child to kick again.

Finally, he felt a gentle pushing out right under his palm. It lasted only an instant and he started to pull his hand away, but Gerdie held it in place.

"Just wait," she admonished him.

Sure enough, a minute later, he felt a solid thump just under his thumb, then another under his pinky finger.

"*Tolle!*" he exclaimed. "Amazing! He certainly is strong."

"Just like his papa," she smiled softly.

On an impulse, Friedrich leaned over and kissed her belly, then whispered, "Keep growing, *mein kleiner*. I have to go away for a little while, but I'll be back soon and we will enjoy the rest of our lives together. Just you, your mama, and me."

Two days after the nursery was finished, Friedrich stood by his front door holding his crying wife. He stroked her hair and kissed the top of her head.

"I know you are sad, my love. I wish I didn't have to go."

He felt her take a deep breath and try to regain control of herself.

"I know," she said softly. "But we will make the best of it and you will be home soon, unharmed. We will have a happy, healthy baby, and will live a wonderful life."

Her smile was brave and he admired her strength of will.

"That's right," he replied. "*Gott segne dich bis wir uns wieder treffen.* Blessings upon you until we meet again, *mein liebling*."

As he picked up his duffle and put his hat on his head, he looked out to the sidewalk where Herr Otto was standing.

"Watch after my wife, Herr Otto," he called. "Keep her safe for me."

"*Ich werde*," Herr Otto replied, nodding. "I will."

With that assurance, Friedrich Krause kissed his wife once more, then marched down the street to whatever destiny this war had in store for him.

Gerdie watched him for as long as she could see him, then quietly opened the door and let herself in. The apartment felt lonely already. Reaching into her pocket, she pulled out her husband's handkerchief, moved to sit in his mother's rocking chair, and allowed herself to have a good, long cry.

Thomas sat in the park, idly watching Katie chase a butterfly. But his thoughts weren't on the butterfly, Katie, or even sweet Maggie who sat beside him looking concerned.

"Ha'penny for your thoughts," she said as she touched his arm.

"What?" he asked, startled. "Wait... did you say ha'penny for my thoughts? I thought they were worth at least a full penny."

"Oh," she waved dismissively, "thoughts these days aren't worth what they used to be."

Chuckling, he took her hand and kissed her palm. "Well, these thoughts aren't even worth a ha'penny."

"Perhaps, but I'd like to hear them just the same." She cocked her head and waited.

Taking a deep breath, he looked out over the grass, uncertain how to soften the blow, finally deciding to just blurt it out.

"I received my orders this morning." His voice was matter-of-fact, but his heart was pounding.

Maggie watched his face, her own a perfect mask for what was churning in her heart.

"How soon do you leave?" she asked.

"Thursday."

Her eyes grew wide at the implication. "But we were going to be married next month!" she cried.

"I know."

She sat back and pursed her lips, her eyes narrowing in thought.

After a moment, he dared look at her and was surprised to see such a determined look on her face.

"What? What are you thinking, Maggie?" he asked.

"I'm thinking we need to call the vicar," she replied resolutely.

"The vicar? Why?" he was truly puzzled.

"To change the wedding date, silly." Her face broke out into a huge grin.

"Change the date?" Thomas was in shock. "You'd really be willing to change the date?"

"Of course!" she laughed. "You don't think I'd let you go off to war without putting a wedding ring on your finger, do you?"

He shook his head. "But I thought the wedding finery and pageantry were all important to the bride. At least, they have been to every bride I've known."

"And how many brides have you known?" she chuckled.

"Well, my cousin, my neighbor... just two, I suppose. But everything about the wedding was of utmost importance to them. Their gowns had to be just so, the flowers had to be absolutely fresh, the chapel had to be decorated perfectly, all the right people must be invited..." his voice faded as she put her finger on his lips and smiled tenderly.

"This bride cares only about her groom." She leaned in and kissed him.

"Truly?" he asked, still not believing.

"Truly." She jumped up. "But if we are to be married tomorrow, I have work to do!"

"Tomorrow?" His head still swam with the swiftness of her decision.

"Of course, tomorrow. Otherwise we won't even have one night for a honeymoon," she laughed.

"Oh, the honeymoon. Right." His mind seemed to be working in slow motion. It didn't seem real that by this time tomorrow, he would be married.

He helped her gather their picnic supplies. She called Katie and told her it was time to go. Katie, of course, protested until Maggie told her they were getting married tomorrow so they had to go and get everything ready.

Katie whooped and hollered and hugged Thomas tightly before being whisked away to help with the wedding preparations. Thomas brought up the rear, carrying the supplies.

Once they arrived at Maggie's apartment, she took the picnic supplies from him and gave him two directives. First, make sure his dress uniform was clean and pressed, and second, make sure he was at the church at ten a.m. tomorrow morning. Until then, leave her to her preparations. She kissed him full on the mouth, then gently pushed him out the door, closing it behind him.

He stood for a moment, staring at the closed door. Then it hit him. He was getting married tomorrow morning to the most beautiful, most understanding woman in the entire world!

"Wahoo!" he shouted, shoving his fist in the air. "Wahoo!"

Chapter Five

August 6, 1914

Gerdie looked up when she heard a knock at the door. She hurriedly dabbed at her eyes, blew her nose, and called, "*Komm herein,* come in."

Frau Schmidt opened the door and peeked inside. "Is this a bad time, Frau Krause?"

"Not at all, Frau Schmidt. Please come in," she smiled, hoping her eyes weren't puffy from crying.

"I thought I would bring some edelweiss to brighten your day," the older woman said as she looked around the small apartment. "Do you have something I can put them in? They will need water right away."

"They are beautiful! The blue pitcher on the dresser would be lovely," Gerdie suggested.

"*Ach,* that is perfect. How are you feeling?" she asked as she fetched the pitcher and filled it with water.

"I'm feeling well," Gerdie replied. "Missing my Friedrich already, though."

Frau Schmidt nodded. "I know what that is like. When my husband went to war, it was difficult. But he came home to me safe, and so will your Friedrich."

She patted Gerdie's hand as she took a seat on a stool near her. Reaching her hand over the arm of the rocking chair, she patted Gerdie's belly. "And how is our *kleiner* this morning? Is she kicking and moving well?"

"Oh yes," Gerdie laughed. "This baby is very active, especially at night."

Frau Schmidt laughed. "Oh, *mein mädchen,* it has only begun for you! You have several months before you'll be relieved of the inner kicking of this baby. Then comes the crying… and feedings… and *windelwechsel,* diaper changes… oh, so many *windeln!* And it goes on and on!"

They laughed merrily together, and Gerdie was glad for the distraction.

"Come," Frau Schmidt invited. "Let us take a walk in the cool morning air. It will be too hot to go out later, so let's take advantage of the morning."

"That sounds lovely," Gerdie agreed. "Let me get my shawl."

They walked for an hour in the park beside the river. It was a beautiful morning and Gerdie felt much better because of the exercise and the company.

They'd been walking for about thirty minutes when Gerdie spotted Herr Otto coming towards them. He waved as he drew closer.

"Frau Krause, it's good to see you out in the fresh air." He smiled.

"*Guten morgen.*" She smiled in return.

"You are looking well. The fresh morning air has put color in your cheeks."

The older gentleman's compliment was welcome, and Gerdie's smile broadened. "*Danke,* Herr Otto." Then she remembered her friend. "May I introduce my friend, Frau Schmidt? Frau Schmidt, Herr Otto, our neighbor."

"*Schön dich zu treffen,* Frau Schmidt," he said with a little bow.

Frau Schmidt smiled pleasantly. "My pleasure to meet you, as well, Herr Otto."

"What brings you out this beautiful morning?" Gerdie asked politely.

"I'm off to the baker for a loaf of bread," he answered. "There is something about a fresh-baked loaf that starts a morning out right, don't you think?"

"I agree," both ladies answered in unison, then looked at each other and laughed.

Herr Otto joined their laughter, then tipped his hat. "I'd best be off before the best loaves are gone. I wish you ladies a pleasant morning."

They bid him *auf weidersehen* and continued their walk.

"He seems a pleasant man," Frau Schmidt observed, chancing a glance back.

Gerdie grinned. "He is. He has been a good friend to us since we moved into the building next to his. In fact, he's the one who arranged for us to borrow Frau Gunter's cradle. Her baby has outgrown it."

The rest of their walk was spent chatting about baby necessities and raising children. Gerdie was coming to cherish the older woman's friendship and wisdom.

As they reached her apartment, Frau Schmidt hugged Gerdie, and patted her shoulder. "I enjoyed our little walk and talk. If you'd like, I will return in the morning and we can do it again. I'm also thinking we might enjoy a *schnitzel* tomorrow. What do you think?"

"A walk, talk, and *schnitzel* sounds wonderful," the expectant mother smiled. "I have been wanting a *schnitzel* for several days now."

"*Ach*, the dreaded *heißhunger*, the cravings! I remember them well. For me it was *kasespatzle*. I could not get enough of those noodles, and I think they must still be with me." She laughed and patted her own robust belly.

Gerdie laughed as she hugged her friend. "Now you make me crave those, as well," she joked.

"Then, tomorrow is *schnitzel*, and Friday will be *kasespatzle*. Until then, *mein mädchen*, rest and think only of your little one. The rest will work out as God intends. *Auf wiedersehen.*"

Gerdie sighed as she closed the door. *Frau Schmidt is a dear*, she thought.

"Oh, Maggie! You look like a princess!" Katie cooed.

Her sister laughed. "What makes you think I look like a princess, poppet?"

"Mama's gown is so pretty on you and the flowers in your hair look just like a crown," was her reply.

Smiling, Maggie leaned down and hugged her. "Well, you look like a little princess yourself. That pink dress is beautiful, and with your hair up and the flowers in it, I'd believe you were a princess from any story book!"

Katie giggled.

"Now, why don't you run and see if Mama is ready to go."

"All right, Maggie." The little girl dashed off to her mother's room.

Maggie took a minute to look in the mirror. Her mother's wedding gown did fit her well, and Katie had arranged the flowers in her hair so they did look like a crown. She smiled. Thomas would be pleased.

It had been easy to rearrange the wedding. The vicar had been quite accommodating, and the church was available. She had arranged for a cab to pick them up and take them to the church. It was an extravagance, but you only marry once, she rationalized.

Mrs. Gilley came in wearing a lovely pink satin gown, with Princess Katie in tow. "I'm glad Mr. Gant had these dresses on sale last week. Who would have guessed we'd need them so soon?" she commented as she handed Maggie her bouquet.

"And how fortunate that Mrs. Harris was willing to reopen the flower shop last night so we could have flowers for this last-minute wedding," she countered.

Taking a small box from her beaded bag, Mrs. Gilley handed it to Maggie. "I thought you might like to have this today," she said simply.

Curious, Maggie opened it and gasped. "Mama! I can't take this!"

"Yes, you can. Your father has no need for it in heaven, and your Thomas does have need for it where he's going," she insisted.

Maggie looked at the simple wedding band and tears filled her eyes. "Thank you, Mama. Thank you."

She put the box in her silk drawstring bag and dabbed at her eyes with her handkerchief. With one final sniffle, she smiled. "Shall we go?"

The cab ride was uneventful and they arrived in plenty of time, but Maggie found she was feeling more anxious by the minute. As they pulled up to the church, she took a deep breath.

Her mother reached over and patted her hand. "It's just bridal nerves, dear. You'll be fine."

Maggie tried to smile, then she paid the cabby and they walked up the short walk to the church.

Mrs. Gilley went in first, to see that all was in order while Maggie and Katie waited in the antechamber. After a few moments, their mother poked her head in and nodded.

Maggie brushed her gown, took a deep breath, and smiled at Katie.

"It's time, poppet. Let's get married!"

Katie grinned and started through the huge wooden doors, studiously marking time to the organ music.

Maggie stepped up to the doorway and waited. When Katie was halfway down the aisle, she started. The only people in the chapel were her mother, Shelly, Beth and Michael, and one of Thomas's friends. Thomas stood at the front by the vicar. He looked so handsome in his dress uniform. Once Maggie saw him, her anxiety began to vanish and all she could think about was becoming Mrs. Thomas Bennett.

She smiled at her mother as she passed, then handed her bouquet to Katie who was standing very still on the other side of the vicar. She was trying hard to be so grown up that Maggie had to lean down and kiss her cheek. Of course, Katie giggled, which relieved the last bit of tension that Maggie had been feeling.

She turned and faced Thomas, who was grinning like he'd just been crowned king. He took her hand and they turned to face the vicar.

The ceremony was short and simple, just as Maggie had hoped. When Thomas kissed her as her husband, she melted into his arms and never wanted to leave them. After a moment, the vicar cleared his throat and they pulled apart, feeling only a little guilty.

There were hugs and congratulations all around, then they made their way to Mr. Clancy's pub for a simple wedding breakfast. Maggie didn't feel much like eating, though. Her emotions were flying high. She was Mrs. Thomas Bennett, and no one could take that away from her, ever!

Chapter Six

August 7, 1914

"*Stehe in die Arme!*" the corporal commanded. "Stand to arms!"

Friedrich rolled out of bed and was on his feet before his eyes even opened. He blinked twice, then following the lead of the soldier next to him, pulled on his boots and grabbed his rifle. He checked that the bayonet was affixed, then stood at attention until the corporal gave the order to move out.

The soldiers filed out of the tent and quick-marched the short distance to the trenches. Friedrich was impressed with their construction. They were wide and deep with strong parapets, embrasures and loopholed steel behind which a rifleman could find cover.

He surmised that in daylight these loopholes would afford a safe and excellent view across the terrain in front of the trench. However, at night the small holes would be quite useless. A soldier would have to place something on the firing-step to stand on, if he wanted to see over the sandbags.

Falling into the trenches like so many lemmings falling off a cliff, he and the rest of the men quickly stepped up onto the firing-step and aimed their rifles over the far edge.

The mist was dense, so they couldn't see much, but each one peered into the fog, hoping they wouldn't see anything moving on the other side.

He'd been told that the other side would be "standing-to" an hour before dawn, just as they were. The theory was that most attacks are launched just before dawn and just after dusk, when it was dark and supposedly the enemy was the most vulnerable. It didn't make much sense to Friedrich. If both sides were standing-to, then neither side was vulnerable. But he followed orders, nonetheless.

As he stood there, he tried to keep his mind on his task, which was to watch for enemy movement. But his thoughts kept wandering back to Gerdie, wondering what she was doing, if she was well, if she needed anything. Each time he'd catch himself, he'd swallow hard and bring his mind back to the task at hand.

Down the line, someone fired a machine gun blast and Friedrich jumped.

"Settle down, *soldat*," the soldier next to him cautioned. "Someone's just letting off a little steam."

"How do you know?" Friedrich asked, still feeling anxious.

"The other side isn't firing back," was the frank reply.

After an hour, they were ordered to stand down.

"Time for breakfast," his trench comrade commented. "Come on. I'm hungry."

Friedrich followed him into the mess tent and grabbed a tray. Once their trays were filled, they looked around for a place to sit. Spotting a place halfway down, they wove their way between the benches, dodging soldiers with empty trays who were finished and making their way outside.

As they sat down, his comrade introduced himself. "My name's Fritz Wagner."

"I'm Friedrich Krause," he answered smiling. "Thanks for your help out there."

"No problem. It's a bit unnerving the first few times. But you get used to it." Fritz shrugged.

"How long have you been here?" Friedrich asked.

"Hm, let's see. I arrived in France last month, but only got here a week ago."

"And you're already used to it?" Friedrich was surprised.

Fritz laughed. "My father's a Colonel, so I grew up around military bases. Lots of guns firing, lots of soldiers running around.

Papa used to call us kids to stand-to each morning, just to get us used to it."

"How many kids?" Friedrich asked around a mouthful of potatoes.

"Five. My older brother, myself, and three younger sisters. I think Papa was hoping for another boy, but Mama decided five was enough little mouths to feed," he laughed. "What about you?"

"Just me, but I have enough cousins that I never felt like an only child. Do you have any children of your own?"

"Two. A boy and a girl." Fritz grinned proudly. "My boy looks just like me and my girl looks just like her Mama."

"I'm going to be a papa by Christmas." Friedrich's grin matched Fritz's for pride.

"Well, congratulations, *kumpel!* We're going to be great friends, you and I," he promised.

Later that afternoon, they were back in the trenches, but all was quiet. No shooting from either side broke the hot silence of the afternoon.

Some of the soldiers who had been there awhile took off their shirts and began picking at them studiously.

"Hey, Fritz, what're they doing?" Friedrich leaned over and whispered.

Fritz looked over and whispered back. "They're picking fleas. See that guy? The one with the red blotchy marks on his back? Those are fleabites. They itch like crazy and can get infected if you scratch them."

Friedrich frowned. "Seems like there'd be a better way to get rid of them than picking them off one by one."

"Yeah, it's not the most effective way," Fritz agreed. "Some guys used to use a candle to burn them off, but too many of them burned their clothes, so the Colonel forbade them from doing that anymore."

"Makes sense," Friedrich nodded, making a mental note to check his own shirt for fleas before he went into the dugout to sleep.

The dugouts were on the backside of the trench. Some were cut so deep into the ground that he was sure they'd be proof against artillery shells. Some were large, sheltering eight to ten men and were roofed with massive wooden planks supported by iron beams. Those wouldn't resist a direct hit, he knew, but would afford protection against shell splinters and shrapnel balls.

His dugout was smaller, only housing four soldiers, but the ground was covered with straw for sleeping on, and they had a small table and two benches. There was a window opening on the back side which he was told would be blocked off with a straw bale when it turned cold outside. Friedrich hoped he wouldn't be here that long.

He yawned and stretched before lowering himself onto the straw. He was looking forward to a few hours of rest before his shift on guard duty.

Fritz was reading a letter by candlelight on the other side of the dugout.

"Watch out for the rats tonight, *kumpel*. I thought I heard a big one a while ago," he commented, glancing up.

Friedrich snorted. "I'm so tired, I think rats could nibble on my ears and I wouldn't notice."

Chuckling, Fritz went back to his letter and Friedrich climbed under the blankets. After a few minutes of tossing and turning, he threw the blanket off. It was too hot to cover up.

"You don't want to do that," Fritz warned.

"Too hot," mumbled Friedrich before he finally drifted off.

What seemed to be only moments later, he was disturbed by what felt like a cat climbing over his legs. He kicked out a couple of times, then turned on his side and tucked his legs in.

Again, he dozed off, but woke up when he felt something land on his hip and run down his leg. He swatted and kicked, then waited. When no other "attacks" happened, he took a deep breath and willed himself back to sleep.

An hour later, Friedrich jumped up yelling, nearly hitting his head on the low ceiling of the dugout.

"Quiet!" Fritz hissed. "Do you want to give away our position to the Tommies?"

Shuddering, Friedrich tried to regain control of himself. "Sorry. It's the rats."

Fritz chuckled. "Weren't you the one who boasted that you were so tired it would take more than rats to disturb your sleep?"

"I was badly mistaken," Friedrich groused. "The *verdammt* things ran over my legs, body, chest and feet. I handled that, and was even starting to relax. But when they started on my face, I knew I must surrender. I'm going to step out for a breath of air."

"Don't get lost," Fritz cautioned. "I've heard the Tommies' rats are bigger than these."

"Very funny," Friedrich grumbled as his friend laughed.

He stepped out into the trench and looked up at the sky. The stars twinkled brightly, as if they had no concern for the war and deprivations going on beneath their soft glow. He thought of Gerdie and wondered if they might be looking at the same stars.

Walking quietly, he tapped the railing along the wall, tap tap tap pause tap tap, then repeat. That was the signal they'd devised so those on watch wouldn't shoot them, thinking they were the enemy.

"*Halt!*" The order was firm, but only the volume of a whisper. "Who goes there?"

"Private Krause," Friedrich replied. "The Kaiser likes only butter on his biscuit." The code was silly, but effective.

"Come on up, Krause," the guard invited.

Friedrich climbed the ladder to the watchtower, grateful that the moon was not yet risen. They'd lost two guards to enemy fire as they climbed the ladder under the bright moonlight. From the top of the tower, he could see the enemy trenches not two hundred meters away. He shuddered a little, thinking of how close they were and how easily a man could be killed at any moment.

"Everything quiet?" he asked.

"*Ja.* It seems the Tommies are sleeping tonight." The guard surveyed No Man's Land as he talked. It wasn't smart to become lax while on guard duty. "What brings you up here? You're not on duty for three more hours."

"Rats," was all Friedrich had to say.

"Ah, next time try covering your face with the blanket. It's hot and not too comfortable, but better than having a rat chewing on your nose."

Friedrich chuckled. "I'll try that. I'm going to get a drink. Do you want anything?"

"*Nein.* I'm good, thanks."

Climbing down, Friedrich shivered a little. The night air was turning colder. He wondered how cold it would get here in Belgium, then decided that dwelling on negative possibilities was not conducive to getting back to sleep, so he thought about Gerdie instead.

Drinking the tepid water, he tried not to choke on the taste. It was not a good idea to question where the water came from. Just drink and hope you didn't become ill after.

As he made his way back to his dugout, he deliberately thought about Gerdie. He wondered how big her belly was now. He smiled when he remembered her scolding him for putting his newspaper on the floor. He nearly chuckled when he thought about how she must look trying to bend over to pick something up now.

Fritz was snoring softly when he came in, so he slid under his blanket and carefully pulled it over his head, tucking it in so he'd not be such a tempting treat for any hungry rats. His last thoughts of the night were of Gerdie. Her hair... her eyes... yawn... her smile... yawn... her...

Herr Gustav Otto stared at the moving water of the Rhine, but he wasn't really seeing it. His thoughts were a jumble of wishes and doubts like he hadn't felt since he was a teenager falling in love for the first time.

Sophie had been gay and carefree, with a laugh that would cheer the grumpiest fellow. How happy he'd been when she agreed to go to the dance with him. He was even happier when she'd agreed to marry him a year later. They'd enjoyed forty-seven years together before the pneumonia took her.

He'd been alone for the past four years, and at no time had he even thought about looking for another wife. Then Frau Klara Schmidt entered his life. She wasn't gay or carefree. Life had been too hard on her for those qualities to be sustained. But she was kind and generous, as he tried to be. She loved flowers and children, just as he did. She was alone, as he was. She always seemed happy to see him when they "accidentally" met in the park on their morning walks. Her smile was infectious, and he always felt better after having chatted with her.

So why was he so nervous now? Gerdie had suggested he invite her to dinner some evening. She had even offered to cook for them, in payment for the music he'd provided for their anniversary dinner so many months ago. He wanted to ask her. He felt she would say yes. But what if she said no? What if that invitation ruined the casual friendship they enjoyed now? What if...?

Hör auf, Gustav, he told himself. *Stop thinking in circles.*

The birds on the grass pecking at worms suddenly took flight. He looked and saw Gerdie and Frau Schmidt walking towards him.

Right on time, he thought. *It's now or never.*

Standing as they approached, he tipped his hat to each lady in turn.

"Frau Schmidt, Frau Krause, *guten morgen.*"

"*Guten morgen,* Herr Otto," they replied in unison.

"It's a lovely day," Frau Schmidt added.

"*Ja,* it is," he looked at the sky and nodded.

"The bread looks good in the bakery this morning," Gerdie commented. "The pumpernickel smells especially appetizing."

He smiled. "Does it? I shall have to take a sniff when I go in."

Gerdie raised an eyebrow and tilted her head toward Frau Schmidt. Her meaning was clear, *ask her!*

Clearing his throat, he took a step closer to the women. "Uh... er..." he swallowed hard.

"Yes, Herr Otto?" Frau Schmidt asked. "Was there something you wanted to say?"

Taking a deep breath, he plunged in. "*Ja,* Frau Schmidt. Would you do me the honor of having dinner with me tonight?"

Frau Schmidt's face lit up. "I would enjoy that, Herr Otto. Thank you for the invitation."

Shocked, his mouth dropped open for a moment. "Does that mean yes?" he asked, not daring to believe.

She laughed. "Yes, it means yes."

"Fine. *Wunderbar,*" he stammered. "Shall I call for you around six?"

"Perfect," she smiled. "I'll see you then."

With a wave and a nod, the women continued their walk. Gustav watched them for a moment, then turned and walked the opposite direction towards the bakery. He took five measured steps, then did a little shuffle dance of joy. She said yes!

As their cab pulled up in front of the Olde Kings Arms hotel, Thomas paid the cabby and jumped out to open the door for his new wife. She must have looked nervous, because he leaned in and kissed her before offering her his hand.

She smiled and kissed him back, then allowed him to help her from the cab. They greeted the desk clerk, who nodded politely and proceeded to check them in, but he never cracked a smile.

While Thomas took care of the check-in, Maggie looked around. She'd never been inside the hotel before. It was more elegant than she imagined. The walls were dark wood with heavy draperies at the windows. There were several chairs near the fireplace on one side of the room, with a large, thick rug in the center. The lighting was dim, but didn't seem somber to her.

"Are you ready, wife?" a familiar, deep voice interrupted her reverie.

She smiled. "I am, husband."

The bellboy carrying their bags led the way up two flights of stairs and down a long hallway to their room. He unlocked the door and motioned for them to enter.

Thomas grinned, and Maggie's eyes opened wide as he bent and swept her off her feet, carrying her effortlessly into the room. He placed her gently on the bed then turned to tip the bellboy.

Again, the elegance of the room awed Maggie every bit as much as the lobby had. The same heavy draperies covered the windows, and another thick rug lay at the side of the bed, which had a warm comforter covering it. It all felt like a wonderful dream. She heard the door lock and was suddenly nervous again.

She must have looked anxious, because Thomas moved slowly to sit beside her. He kissed her gently, then said, "Would you like help getting out of that gown or would you rather do that yourself?"

"I... I..." she swallowed and tried again. "I think I can manage," she replied. Picking up her bag, she placed it on a table by the window and opened it.

Suddenly shy, she sat down in the stiff-backed chair and closed her eyes, and willed her heart to calm its frantic beating. Taking a few deep breaths, she opened her eyes to see her husband staring at her.

Oh dear, she thought. *I must look like a frightened rabbit. This will never do.* She began removing her gown, struggling with the two buttons between her shoulder blades.

Smiling, Thomas again offered to help. She turned and shivered a little as his fingers brushed her back. Once they were open, she let the gown slide to the floor. Stepping out of it, she picked it up and laid it on the chair.

She hadn't had time to buy any wedding night attire, so she hoped her slip would serve as a nightgown. She smiled at her husband and hoped her nervousness didn't show too much.

"It's time, Mrs. Bennett," she told herself. "It's time to show Thomas just how much you love him."

Then she noticed something strange. Her husband looked as nervous as she felt. He smiled tentatively, then whistled, taking her in his arms. Holding her close, he kissed her nose.

"You look ravishing, Mrs. Bennett," he whispered, then kissed her lips gently at first, then with all the fervor of a man in love.

Maggie's nerves disappeared as his kisses engulfed her. All thoughts were gone as she surrendered herself to the love of her life.

The next morning, as the sun peeked in through the draperies, Thomas stretched and took in a deep breath. Then he remembered.

He looked over to see that it wasn't a dream, after all. He really was married to Miss Margaret Gilley... rather, Mrs. Thomas Bennett, now. Glancing at his watch on the nightstand, he realized he must wake her, but she looked so peaceful lying there, he hated to disturb her. Softly brushing a strand of hair from her cheek, he gazed at her lovingly, still not quite believing that she was his wife.

She stirred, opened her eyes, and smiled. "Good morning, Mr. Bennett," she said sleepily.

"Good morning, Mrs. Bennett," he replied, leaning down to kiss her.

She made a happy little sound and pulled him closer for a deeper kiss. He accommodated her, then pulled back a bit.

"We really should get up. I have a train to catch," he said half-heartedly.

"Mmm," she murmured, pulling him to her again. "We'll run."

He closed his eyes and whispered. "Just another minute."

An hour later, they were rushing around, frantically trying to get everything together. They kept running into each other and laughing. Occasionally, they'd stop for a quick kiss, then remind each other that Thomas had a train to catch, and resume their rushing.

Finally, they were out the door and running down the street. Unfortunately, the Boxmoor and Hemel Hemstead train station was nearly two miles away, so running was required.

As they ran into the station, they heard last call for Thomas's train. No time for long goodbyes. Running onto the platform, he threw his duffel onto the train, then turned to his new wife. There were tears in her eyes, but she was obviously trying to be brave. He pulled her into a hard hug, followed by a short, but fervent kiss.

"Stay safe," she whispered.

"I will," he vowed as he stepped away.

The train started to pull out, and he took one step back for another stolen kiss, then ran to catch the vertical grab bar, pulling himself up onto the retreating train. He leaned far out, to wave at her, watching as her form grew smaller until he couldn't even see the white handkerchief she was waving. Only then did he pull himself fully into the train, pick up his duffel and make his way into the car to find a seat.

On the platform, Maggie watched with the mothers and wives as the train grew smaller and smaller in the distance, tears streaming silently down her cheeks. Long after it was gone, she stood and stared at the horizon where it had disappeared. She was Mrs. Thomas Bennett, army wife. She said a silent prayer that her husband would return to her safely and soon.

Chapter Seven

September 30, 1914

Friedrich lay as quietly as he could, every one of his senses on high alert. He was on *horchposten* duty. Listening post was perhaps one of the most dangerous duties he'd been assigned. He lay under the barbed wire, about thirty or forty meters in front of the German trench, which put him almost one hundred and fifty meters away from the enemy. He wondered if there were any British soldiers lying similarly on the other side. If so, he was only one hundred meters from the enemy. That thought gave him chills.

Working to buoy up his courage, he thought about everything they had in their favor, including the machine guns, a Belgian and an English one, a revolving cannon, and lots of hand grenades. There were artillery trenches leading towards the rear, which afforded the men with plenty of cover.

When he first arrived, he had imagined there would be lively exchanges of fire here in the foremost positions, but it proved not to be the case. It seemed the only time the enemy fired was when there was something happening on the German side, for example, when the listening post made his way towards the position. Then some enemy rifle bullets whistled towards them.

Sometimes a "Franzman" or "Tommy" would shoot partridges or rabbits that ran between the lines, but apart from that, it was surprisingly quiet.

During the first nights after he'd arrived, there had been a full moon and they had excellent visibility. Now it was the new moon, so they used flares to illuminate the dark terrain.

It had been a quiet day. In the evening, some artillery shells were fired over their heads. It seemed the enemy was targeting an old windmill a couple of hundred meters behind them. Now and then, a smoky fire was lit there to draw enemy fire away from other sectors of the front.

Friedrich heard a noise just ahead of him and froze, eyes scanning as far as he could see. He did not hear it again, but he continued listening anyway.

He was very focused on his task, so when his stomach growled, he frowned. It sounded too loud out here in the silent night. He took a deep breath to try and calm his nerves.

Since the last enemy attack had taken out their food stores, they'd had to rely on whatever they could scrounge. Three times a day, some men would be sent back to the village to fetch coffee and food. A communication trench led to the village, and without it, there would be no way to retrieve more supplies.

Sadly, the food they brought back was generally terrible. Sometimes, it contained sauerkraut or green beans. Then it was a little better. There was always a bit of bread and sometimes cheese, sausages, and butter, but there was never enough to feed so many men. They'd portion out the rations and try to convince themselves that it was sufficient.

The weather had been good so far, chilly at night and warm in the day. Still, they spent most of their time inside the dugout as the trench afforded little room for a walk, and there was a constant danger of falling victim to a stray piece of shrapnel or an aerial bomb.

Each day, Friedrich saw enemy aircraft circling above their position. He'd watched the anti-aircraft boys target them with anti-balloon guns. Their shells detonated close to the aircraft without ever bringing one of them down. Most of the time, he knew, the enemy planes don't drop any bombs. *That must mean they are reconnaissance planes, mapping and photographing our positions and trenches,* he thought.

Overall, it was a monotonous life. There wasn't much to see in the trenches. Looking over the parapet in daylight is extremely dangerous, so there is not much to see there either. The only diversion was the mail, which was delivered every morning. Most of the time everyone received something, even if it was only a newspaper from home. The day before, Fritz had received a letter from Gerdie, a photographic card, and a box of cigarettes.

Friedrich had only been there a couple of weeks when a heavy rain made the trenches unbearable. The rain turned the hard chalk into a sticky and slippery surface, which forced everyone to cling to the parapet when walking the trench to avoid falling down.

Friedrich was looking forward to rotating back to the second line. Normally the battalion spent six days in the foremost trench, six days in the second line around the village, and six days in the third line, twelve kilometers behind the front.

The last time he'd been on the second line, Sergeant Haas had allowed him, along with Fritz and several others, to go into the village when they weren't on duty.

Most of its inhabitants had left, and most of the houses were shot to pieces, but there were some undamaged houses left which could be used for quarters.

This allowed them to sleep in a proper bed for a change. Still, they slept with one eye open, as one never knew when the enemy might break through the front line and attack the second.

"Krause," came a whisper from behind him.

"Who goes there?" he whispered back.

"It's Fritz," came the reply.

"What's the code?"

"Come on, *kumpel,*" the voice groused. "You know my voice."

"What's the code?" Friedrich insisted. He'd heard stories of the enemy impersonating a German soldier so he could infiltrate their lines and learn their positions.

"The Kaiser's cat had kittens," Fritz recited with a sigh.

Friedrich could almost hear him rolling his eyes. He smiled. "Was that so hard?"

"No, but it's stupid."

"Would you rather be shot?" Friedrich asked. "What if I'd been spooked up here and thought you were the enemy?"

"You wouldn't do that, would you?" Fritz asked.

"I would if I thought you were the enemy!" Friedrich insisted.

"Well, I'm not. I'm here to relieve you."

"Good, my eyes and ears are tired from watching and listening so hard."

"Go rest them, then," his friend ordered as he slid into position, allowing Friedrich to slide down into the access trench.

As Friedrich made his way back to his dugout, he remembered the first night he'd spent in the village. He was luxuriating in the nice, soft bed when a loud crash woke everyone out of their sleep. He remembered watching everyone dive for cover as they thought that they were being targeted by artillery. They had all slid to the ground and waited for the real attack to begin. When nothing happened, he lit a candle and they saw a large oil painting that had fallen from the wall to the floor, causing the crash.

When they were in the village, they spent days drawing, reading, and writing. The newspapers they had were already three days old, but for most of them, any news was new news.

As Friedrich dropped off to sleep, he dreamed of Gerdie and wondered how she was doing. Her last letter had been short, but at least she was still writing to him.

The next day, about four o'clock, he was about to go on guard duty when the enemy started shelling, forcing them to take cover in the dugouts. One man was killed and two wounded. The German artillery retaliated in kind, but there was no way to know if it had any effect.

When the barrage was over, he took his position along the parapet, watching for enemy movement. He was one hour into his shift when an enemy barrage hit a trench section close by. The alarm was sounded and all available men armed themselves and prepared to repel an attack.

Fritz joined him at the parapet and asked, "Seen any movement?"

Friedrich shook his head no, but didn't say anything. The thunder of the guns and cracking of the rifles was getting more intense every minute.

The German artillery continued firing, sending its shells in a low trajectory over their heads. The firing continued until long after sunset. It was unusual behavior, since most firing stopped when it got dark. The night was pitch black, making it impossible to see anything.

"Everyone have a full supply of ammunition?" Sergeant Haas asked as he walked behind them. Someone down the line whispered no. The sergeant tapped Fritz and Friedrich on the shoulder and they followed him to the ammunition storage. They handed out all the bullets they could find and returned to their posts on the parapet.

Meanwhile, the firing continued. Every minute, an illumination flare was fired which provided enough light to check the terrain in No Man's Land. Neither side left their trenches, but both continued firing.

Suddenly, as quickly as it started, the shooting died down. A few more rifle shots rang out through the night, then it was quiet.

Friedrich finished his shift, then slipped back into the dugout for some much-needed sleep. He slept soundly for a change.

The next morning, he met Fritz for breakfast. When they sat down, Fritz asked, "You hear about what happened last night after the firing stopped?"

Friedrich shook his head. "I slept like a rock and didn't hear anything. What happened?"

"A platoon of pioneers, front-line men, were sent to repair the damage to the barbed wire entanglements caused by last night's attack. The men who were manning the listening post fired on them. They hadn't been informed about the repairs and were under strict orders to shoot as soon as they noticed anything suspicious. They'd been expecting an enemy patrol because of the barrage, so they opened fire and killed one pioneer. Another one was shot through the head. He was still alive when he was recovered but he will be dying soon, I'm sure. How terrible it is to be killed by your own side!"

Friedrich agreed and found he'd suddenly lost his appetite.

"Are you all right?" Frau Schmidt asked, worry in her voice.

Gasping a little for breath, Gerdie nodded. "I'm all right. It will pass."

"What will pass?" her friend asked suspiciously.

"It's just a little twinge," Gerdie tried to reassure her.

Frau Schmidt was relentless. "How often are these twinges happening?"

"Not often. A couple of times a day. I'm fine," Gerdie tried to sound nonchalant.

Frau Schmidt frowned. "Just the same, I think we'll forgo our walk today and let you rest."

"Oh, we can't do that!" Gerdie protested. "I enjoy our walks so much. Besides, you'll miss seeing Herr Otto," she teased.

Frau Schmidt smiled. "Do not worry. I will be seeing him tonight."

"Tonight?" Gerdie's curiosity was piqued.

"Yes, he's taking me to the concert in the park just after sunset. It's the last one of the season and we've enjoyed every one of them."

"You have? You didn't tell me you'd been seeing him so regularly!" Gerdie grinned as she settled into the rocking chair with her feet up on the stool.

"Several times a week since that beautiful dinner you cooked for us," Frau Schmidt winked at Gerdie. "Didn't think I knew, did you?"

Gerdie laughed. "How did you know? Did he tell you?"

"Only after I threatened to leave," Frau Schmidt admitted. "I didn't think he was the cooking type, and I recognized your *kartoffelknödel*. You are the only one I know who puts nutmeg in them. They are delicious that way and you must give me your recipe," she smiled.

Laughing, Gerdie agreed. "I'll happily give you my recipe if you'll give me yours for apple *strudel!* I can't figure out why yours taste so much better than mine."

Frau Schmidt pursed her lips. "I don't think I do anything differently than anyone else. But we can compare recipes some afternoon and see. For now, I want you to rest. Sleep, if you can. I'll bring some dinner over later."

"You don't have to do that," Gerdie said with a yawn, "but I think I will take a little nap."

"Good. Rest well, *mein mädchen.*" Frau Schmidt covered Gerdie's legs with a blanket, kissed her on the forehead, then quietly let herself out.

Private Thomas Bennett stepped off the train and fell in with his troop. Standing at attention, he couldn't help but feel nervous as he wondered what awaited him here in Belgium. He'd heard stories, and if only half of them were true, he was in for a rough time. But, this is what he'd signed up for, so this is what he would endure. At least, until he could return to England and his sweet Maggie.

His training had been rushed, but he hoped he had all he needed to survive the war at the front. He had practiced movement from cover to cover, the advance under fire, a combination of fire and movement, the use of the Lewis machine gun, rifle, bayonet, and the frontal assault. His training had culminated with the occupation of captured ground for defense. It had seemed like thorough training at the time. But now, faced with the idea of actually firing on another human being, Thomas wasn't sure he was ready.

When everyone disembarked the train, they assembled quickly and the order came to march. Row by row, the platoon moved out. After what seemed like an eternity, Thomas finally saw the tents as they marched over the little hill near Ypres.

They were assigned to their places and given fifteen minutes to stow their gear and report to the mess tent to eat. Apparently, after they ate, there would be drilling, rifle practice, bayonet practice, and other duties as assigned.

His first assignment was to work with a detail to dig more dugouts in the trenches for the new recruits. The work was hard, as the soil was more clay than dirt. But with a little water added to the trench side, the clay softened so they could scrape it out.

At one point, Thomas hit a vein of rock. He was chipping away at it with a pick when his sergeant came up behind.

"Don't waste too much time on that, Private," he cautioned. "It's high enough that the men can duck beneath it, so just dig out the dirt under it."

"Yes, sir," Thomas replied and switched to a shovel.

The private digging next to him shook his head. "If I'm assigned to that dugout, I know I'm going to hit my head every time I go through there."

Thomas laughed. "I'll be lying on the ground with you, then."

"The name's George Ellis, but my friends call me Budgy." the private stuck out his hand in greeting.

"I'm Thomas. It's nice to meet you Budgy. Where'd you get a nickname like that?"

"When I was a kid, I was as wide as I was tall. My brother called me Pudgy, but my kid sister couldn't say her p's so she called me Budgy. That one stuck," he laughed.

"Well, you're certainly not pudgy now," Thomas observed.

Budgy patted his flat belly. "Nope. Nothing like army rations to trim a fellow down."

"That bad, huh?"

"Nah. It's not bad at all if you don't have taste buds." Budgy laughed at his own joke, and Thomas joined in.

The work went slowly, but they managed to dig out several new sleeping holes that afternoon.

When the order came to assemble for the evening's stand-to-arms, Thomas was only too glad to exchange his shovel for a rifle. He'd been told that although everyone was on heightened alert both morning and evening, the enemy was also observing stand-to, so nothing usually happened, except an occasional spat of rifle fire as someone got nervous and pulled a trigger without thinking.

After stand-to was dinner. Thomas couldn't have told you what he ate, he was too tired to even notice. Unfortunately, he didn't get to sleep right away, as he pulled guard duty. He was grateful that Budgy was on guard, too.

A couple of hours into their shift, Thomas's eyes started drooping. Budgy nudged him.

"Stand alert, Tommy-boy," he whispered. "If the sergeant

catches you napping, you'll be court-martialed, for sure."

"Mm," Thomas mumbled sleepily. "I have another friend who calls me Tommy-boy. Talk to me, Budgy. I can't stay awake if all I have to keep my mind occupied is staring into this fog for movements that I don't see."

Budgy chuckled. "Guard duty can be pretty dull, but when it's not, it's really not and you'd better be ready."

"I'm serious, Budgy. I need some stimulation to my brain. Talk to me."

"Okay. What do you want to know?"

"Tell me about what it's like up here. Tell me some stories."

Budgy thought for a moment. "All right. Here's one for you. There's a certain officer, who shall remain nameless, who was in the middle of a battle. He became quite irritated when he had to put his pipe in his pocket because the smoke was drifting into his line of fire."

"Really? He was irritated?" Thomas asked, not quite believing his new friend's story.

"I swear on the grave of my mother that's how I heard it," Budgy put up one hand to swear.

Thomas chuckled.

"Word has it that after his third or fourth shot, he found that the bowl of his pipe and the smoke from it was obscuring his line of vision and he was firing slightly downwards with each shot. They say that just as he got his rifle working, he saw a German calmly kneeling down and taking an aim at him. The moment he saw him, the kraut fired. But somehow, he missed and the officer is around to tell the tale himself, if you could get him to admit it in the first place."

"That's a whale of a tale, Budgy," Thomas laughed. "Tell me another."

"How about one by way of warning," Budgy obliged. "The dugouts in this part of the line are infested with rats. They will frequently walk over you when you're sleeping. I, myself, have been much troubled by them coming and licking the brilliantine off my hair. That's why I gave up using grease on my head." He took off his hat and ruffled his curly hair.

Thomas groaned and laughed. "Is that true? Are there really rats in the dugouts?"

"Sad, but true, my friend. I suggest sleeping with one hand on a stick to fight them off."

Frowning, Thomas shook his head. "Doesn't sound like we get much sleep between the rats and the drills and the assignments."

"After a while, you'll learn how to catch a few winks wherever you are. You'll see chaps dozing in line for meal or while squatting against a trench wall. In fact, even the rats won't keep you awake once you get used to them. I haven't heard of anyone being bitten by them. They're just annoying."

"Good to know," Thomas nodded. "Tell me another one."

Budgy thought for a moment, then began. "There was another officer I heard of who became very much annoyed by all the memos sent round from headquarters. They came in at all hours of the day and night and stopped him from getting a full night's rest. Some of them, he felt, were very silly and quite unnecessary. The story goes that one night when he was very tired and just getting off to sleep with cold feet, in comes an orderly with a chit asking how many pairs of socks his company had a week ago. He replied 'one-hundred forty-one and a half'. Then he goes back to sleep. He'd just dozed off when back comes a memo. 'Please explain at once how you come to be deficient of one sock.' He replies, 'man lost his leg'."

Thomas clapped his hand over his mouth to keep from laughing aloud. When he regained control, he slapped Budgy on the back. "That was a good one!"

"Sounds like you two are having way too much fun up here," commented a voice from the darkness. "I could have been a kraut sneaking up to kill you and you'd never have heard me."

Thomas's eyes grew wide, but Budgy didn't seem phased. "I knew it was you all along, Bernard."

A tall soldier poked his head up over the ledge of the guard tower. "Sure you did," he said sarcastically. "I'm here to relieve you. Go get some sleep."

"Yes, sir!" Budgy performed a snappy salute, then scampered down the ladder.

Thomas followed a little less enthusiastically. He wasn't looking forward to sharing his bed with rats.

Chapter Eight

October 1, 1914

Friedrich stared at the letter long after he finished reading it. He shook his head, closed his eyes, and said a silent prayer for his Gerdie's health and safety. He'd just finished when Fritz came up and slapped him on the shoulder.

"What's wrong, *kumpel?*" he asked. "You look like someone just died."

Friedrich glared at him. "Don't ever say that!" he growled, then stood and stormed outside.

He blinked as the bright sunlight hurt his eyes for a moment, then he started walking. He didn't think, he just walked.

Fritz stood in the doorway of the tent and watched him for a few moments, then ran to catch up.

"Where're you going?" he asked.

Friedrich didn't answer and didn't slow down, but kept walking, his eyes straight ahead.

Fritz tried to keep pace, but Friedrich's longer legs made him need to jog every few steps to keep up.

"Hey, Friedrich! Slow down and talk to me!" he tried again. "What's wrong?"

Still, the distraught soldier kept walking, staring straight ahead, not speaking.

Finally, Fritz had enough. He ran to place himself in front of his comrade holding his arms out to stop him.

Friedrich tried to keep walking, but his wiry friend was stronger than he looked.

"Get out of my way, Fritz," Friedrich demanded.

"No, not until you tell me what's wrong," his friend replied, standing firm.

Friedrich tried to go around, but Fritz simply moved in front of him again.

"I swear, I'm going to flatten you! Get out of my way!"

"No. You do what you have to do, *kumpel,* but I'm not budging."

Friedrich finally looked at Fritz and saw nothing but determination on his face and caring in his eyes. He balled up his fists, but kept them at his sides. Trying to hide his pain behind a mask of fury, he narrowed his eyes and set his jaw.

"I said move, Fritz." Friedrich's voice was low and sinister.

Fritz folded his arms in front of his chest, but didn't budge. He lifted his chin, daring his friend to make his move.

The two soldiers stood and glared at each other for a few long moments. Finally, Friedrich took a deep breath and let it out slowly. Reaching into his pocket, he pulled out the letter and shoved it toward his friend.

Fritz took it and started reading as Friedrich moved to sit on a fallen log on the side of the road.

"Dear Friedrich,

I write to you not so you will worry, but so you will pray for your dear Gerdie. The doctor has put her to bed until the baby is born. It is for her safety, as well as that of your child. She will be fine if she stays in bed and follows the doctor's instructions.

Herr Otto and I are caring for her. He stays with her during the day and I am with her at night.

Your Gerdie is handling her confinement well, and is a courageous lady. She is looking forward to having a healthy baby in a couple of months.

She says to tell you not to worry, but to keep your head down. We all pray for a swift end to this war so you can come home to her.

Herr Otto says hello and be safe. My wishes for you are the same as Gerdie's, for your safe and swift return.

Sincerely,
Frau Klara Schmidt"

When he'd read the letter, Fritz whistled a long, low whistle. "No wonder you're upset." He looked up. "Were you thinking of going *underlaubt abwesend*?"

Friedrich put his head in his hands. "I wasn't thinking, Fritz. All I felt was that Gerdie needed me and I was going to her."

Moving to join his friend on the log, Fritz shook his head. "Um, *kumpel*... friend... that's called leaving without permission. They'll put you in front of a firing squad and shoot you for that. Then where would your Gerdie be?"

Looking up, Friedrich nodded. "You're right," he admitted, "but I can't just stay here when she needs me there!"

Fritz folded the letter and handed it back. "Sounds to me like Frau Schmidt and Herr Otto are taking diligent care of her."

"That's not the same as me being there!" Friedrich's voice was husky with unshed tears.

"I know." Fritz looked out at the war-torn land and was quiet for a few moments.

"Why don't you put in for a hardship discharge? If they grant it, you could be on your way back to her in just a few days."

Friedrich looked up. "Do you think they'd grant it?"

Fritz shrugged. "I don't know, but if it were me, I would try."

A little snort escaped Friedrich's nose. "If it were up to you, we'd all go home!"

Laughing, Fritz stood up. "That's true enough. I don't know why we're here in the first place."

"Because the Kaiser wills it," Friedrich grumbled.

"I suppose. Let's go see about that discharge."

Friedrich had cooled off, and was ready to face the colonel and ask for a discharge. But before he could make his way to the colonel's tent, two things happened. It began to rain, and an alarm sounded. He raced back to his place in the trench, nearly tripping in the already-forming mud. He'd barely settled into his assigned place in the trench and prepared to fire when the sergeant raced down the line and ordered them forward.

"But Sergeant…" Fritz started to protest.

"Orders from the major," the sergeant called over his shoulder as he continued to spread the word.

Fritz swore and prepared to move out.

"This makes no sense, Fritz," Friedrich said.

"No, it doesn't, but that doesn't matter," Fritz growled. "Major Müller is famous for remaining far behind the lines, safely under cover, while he orders his men to advance into danger."

The men moved out and were met with a storm of bullets. Friedrich was so focused on staying upright in the slippery mud, dodging bullets, and firing randomly where he thought the enemy trench was, that he barely registered when their captain fell. He didn't even notice when his section leader fell, and the men who fell all around him were merely another obstacle to stumble over in his fear-filled advance toward the enemy lines.

They managed to force the enemy to retreat out of one trench, but no one ordered them to occupy it. Reaching a small hedge near it, they hunkered down and remained there under cover. Bullets were flying in both directions, so they were unable to go forward or back. There wasn't even room to shoot from that angle.

They heard an adjutant shout at them to cut down the hedge, but they had nothing but their bayonets to cut with. Each time they tried to follow his orders, bullets whistled all around from in front and from behind, forcing them to take cover again. The officer himself, of course, remained behind.

Near dawn, the firing ceased. Friedrich, Fritz, and two other men were all that were left hiding under the hedge. As the sun rose, Friedrich noticed that the English had taken back the trench they'd abandoned the night before.

He shook his head in wonder at the stupidity of the entire exercise. No purpose was served by the advance, and it had cost many lives.

Fritz used his mirror to signal the guard tower, asking for orders. After what seemed like an eternity, the answer came; stay put.

"How can they strand us out here?" Fritz asked no one in particular. "If we don't get reinforcements, we shall have a poor time of it. The English fight like mad dogs and we have fools for leaders."

"Hush!" a frightened private hissed. "Do you want to be court-martialed for insubordination?"

"At this point, I don't care," Fritz said stubbornly. "At least in prison I'd get real food and clean water, not to mention the fact that I wouldn't be shot at!"

"Unless they sentence you to the firing squad," the other private muttered.

Fritz looked at him and frowned. "I suppose that's true. I'm hungry. Anyone have anything to eat?"

Friedrich had an apple in his pack, so they divided it between them. As they munched, Friedrich hoped that peace would come soon. *War is too awful,* he thought.

Sirens and gunfire awakened Thomas abruptly. He rolled out of his blanket and grabbed his rifle before his mind fully registered what was happening. He stumbled into the trench and was soon drenched with rain. He stopped to wipe his wet hair from his eyes and was slammed against the far wall as soldiers rushed past him, shoving him out of the way.

He turned to face the wall of the trench and fumbled with his rifle.

"Set your rifle up this way, Tommy-boy," Budgy nudged him, then showed him how to brace his rifle against his shoulder and rest it on the top of the trench.

Thomas followed his lead, but felt dazed and confused by the noise and chaos that surrounded him. "What am I shooting at? I can't see anything in this rain!"

"Shoot at anything out there that moves. All our men should be in the trenches, so anything out there must be the enemy."

With a single nod, Thomas stared into the rain, waiting for something to move, willing it not to be there. He didn't have to wait long. A faint shadow crossed his vision. He fired. Then fired again, and again, until his clip was empty.

Ducking down, he loaded a fresh clip into the rifle, his hands trembling so hard, he could hardly hold the bullets.

"Take a deep breath, Tommy-boy," Budgy yelled near him. "Don't give in to the fear."

Thomas took a couple of deep, shaky breaths, finished loading his gun, then stood up and began firing again. His breathing was hard and fast. He was certain his aim was no good. He was shaking too badly.

Suddenly, everything went quiet. Then the order came to go over the top.

"Over the top? What top?" Thomas's fear escalated.

"Over the parapet and across No Man's Land, Tommy-boy. You have to do your duty and fight. Stay close. You'll be fine," Budgy tried to reassure him.

A soldier on his other side moaned, "This is the end of us."

Soldiers all down the line scrambled over the edge of the trenches into the barren No Man's Land. Instantly, the firing began again and British soldiers dropped like flies. The young soldier who'd bemoaned his fate was one of the first to fall. Another was blown to pieces by a shell, while still others found themselves with limbs severed by flying shell fragments.

A few eternal minutes later, they heard the call to retreat and retreat they did. Scrambling even faster than they'd moved out, the soldiers that were left ran, crawled, and inched their way back to the safety of the trenches, stumbling in the mud, and some falling into the new shell holes that had just been formed.

Hearing a sound to his left, Thomas stopped for an instant to identify it. Even through the horrific noise of the battle, he registered that it was the sound of a man crying for help. Without thinking, he dropped to his belly and crawled in the direction of the sound. What he saw made him retch.

His friend, Gerald, was lying at the bottom of a newly made shell-hole. He seemed unable to pull himself out of the rising water to safety.

Thomas leaned over the edge and tried to grab his hand.

"Reach up, Gerry! Lift your arm so I can reach you!"

But Gerald just lay there, calling weakly for help. No matter what Thomas said, it seemed he couldn't hear him. Finally, in desperation, Thomas jumped down into the hole. The rainwater was up to his thighs and rising fast.

He tried to put his arms under Gerald's shoulders to lift him out, but he was limp and seemed unable to help himself.

"Gerry! You've got to help me save you!" Thomas cried. He kept lifting and tugging. After a few minutes, he'd managed to lift his friend out of the water.

Adjusting his grip to pull his friend over his shoulder, he looked down and realized that his arms were hanging off by a thread of skin, and his legs were nowhere to be seen. He swallowed hard and tried not to retch. The action caused him to lose his footing and they both splashed back into the water.

Thomas sputtered and coughed as his mouth filled. Once he had his footing, he slid over to put his arm around him.

"It's okay, pal," he said weakly. "I'm here with you."

It was only a few minutes before he felt Gerry's last breath. Not wanting to believe his friend was dead, Thomas looked at his face. His head was leaning at an unnatural angle and his mouth was gaping open, allowing the water to flow in. There was no coughing, no sputtering, and he knew it was over. Thomas laid him gently against the wall of the hole.

"Tommy, what are you doing down there?" Budgy peered over the edge of the hole. "Grab my hand. Let's get out of here!"

He grabbed Budgy's hand, pulled himself up, and the two scrambled for the trenches. Falling over the edge headfirst, Thomas pressed himself against the wall, willing his stomach to maintain its contents.

After a few moments, he looked around and saw their numbers had greatly diminished. He felt nauseous and weak, unable to comprehend what had just happened.

But rest wasn't his to enjoy just yet. Budgy nudged him. "They're calling retreat. Move out."

Not knowing how he managed to move, Thomas stumbled after Budgy. Over the back of the trench wall, running for the second line defense, bullets whizzing overhead, shells going off near and far.

Establishing themselves in the second-line trench, Thomas turned and faced the enemy once again. The rain had let up some and he could see them advancing, but they were falling hard and fast as the British line fired again and again.

Thomas fired almost blindly, not noticing whether his bullets hit their marks. He saw a small group of Germans take shelter behind a hedge just on the other side of the trench they'd just abandoned. A small part of his mind wondered why they stopped there and didn't take the trench. The thought didn't last long, though. The battle numbness was setting in and he stopped thinking altogether.

He had no idea how long they continued to fire, but when the order came to cease fire, he slumped down in the trench and laid his rifle down in the mud. Curling up with his head on his knees, he just sat, not thinking, not feeling, not moving... and barely breathing.

"You okay, Tommy-boy?" came a voice that faintly registered in his mind. He didn't have the energy to reply.

"Hey, Thomas," came the voice again, more urgently. "Snap out of it!"

Thomas managed to swallow, lick his lips, then lift his head for a moment. He saw Budgy's muddy face looking worried. Thomas tilted his head, noticing a smudge of mud on his new friend's forehead that looked a bit like a rabbit with long ears sticking straight up from its head.

"Budgy," he said, and the voice that came from his mouth didn't sound like his own. He didn't recognize it at all. So, he cleared his throat and started again. "Budgy, you have a rabbit on your forehead."

Budgy leaned back and frowned. "What? Did you get hit in the head? You're not making any sense."

Suddenly, Thomas was struck by the absurdity of it all. The wry laugh that erupted from his throat wouldn't be denied. He couldn't stop it. He pointed at Budgy's head.

"The mud..." he choked out, "looks... like... a rabbit."

Budgy rubbed at his forehead and looked at his hand, which was also covered with mud. Shaking his head, he looked at his friend. He wiped his muddy hand on even muddier pants, then offered it to help

Thomas up.

"Come on, Tommy-boy. We're being rotated to the rear."

Together, they stood and followed other muddy, bloody, tired soldiers out of the trench and towards what they hoped was a hot meal and well-deserved rest.

Later that night, Thomas found himself lying on a cot, still soaked with mud and blood from head to foot. After assessing himself and finding that his only souvenir of the horrific battle was a bullet hole in his cap, he realized how close he'd come to joining Gerry in heaven that night.

He lay on the cot and said a prayer, grateful to be alive. He prayed for all those that had fallen on both sides. He was grateful that his friend hadn't died on his own. That he'd been in the arms of someone who cared for him in his last moments. He prayed for Maggie, Katie, and Mrs. Gilley. Most of all, he prayed for a quick end to this bloody war.

He wanted to sleep, but sleep wouldn't come. So, he got up and looked over at Budgy, sleeping the sleep of the drunken. He had a half empty bottle of whiskey that he'd scrounged from who knows where still clutched in his hand. Thomas felt no remorse as he took the bottle and drank a long swallow from it. He stepped back to his cot and slugged back swallow after swallow until it was as empty as the black and empty future he envisioned for all of them.

As he fell into his own drunken sleep, he had an absurd thought. *I wonder what happened to the krauts that were hiding behind that hedge. I hope they made it home okay.*

Chapter Nine

November 3, 1914

Gerdie's eyes twinkled. "You do like her, then?" she asked.

Herr Otto ducked his head. "Well…" he hesitated, then continued. "Actually, I love her," he admitted.

"Love? That's wonderful! I'm so happy for you," Gerdie crowed, then looked closer at his face. "Wait. You haven't told her, have you?"

The old man shook his head.

"Why not?"

He sighed. "I don't think she loves me."

Puzzled, Gerdie frowned. "That doesn't make sense. She talks about you all the time. She enjoys the adventures you've shared with her. She admires your heart and your generosity. If I had to guess, I'd say she loves you, too. What makes you think she doesn't?"

Herr Otto ran his fingers through his thinning grey hair and frowned. "We had a little… discussion last night."

"A discussion? What kind of discussion?" Gerdie asked suspiciously.

"Well…" he grimaced.

Gerdie's eyebrows raised. "Well? Did you argue?"

"It wasn't really an argument. It was more of a…" Again, he hesitated.

"A discussion." Gerdie's voice was flat. "What did you say to her?"

Herr Otto ducked his head again, this time in shame. "I may have called her a silly, emotional woman."

Pressing her lips together, Gerdie fought hard not to laugh. When she felt she had a little control, she asked, "And why did you call her that?"

"Because she said she didn't want to see me again!" he finally exploded, stood abruptly, and paced the floor. "Out of nowhere, she says she doesn't want to see me again. Why would she do that if she's not being a silly, emotional woman?"

Puzzled, Gerdie asked, "What happened before she said she didn't want to see you again? Why don't you start at the beginning?"

"When she came to sit with you, you told us to go for a walk. You were going to take a nap and wouldn't need either of us for a little while. Remember?"

Gerdie nodded.

"We went to the park. The leaves have turned and she wanted to enjoy their colors. At one point, she kicked a pile of leaves and giggled like a school-girl."

Gerdie smiled.

"I laughed and told her she was adorable. She got the strangest expression on her face. Kind of sad-like. When I asked what was wrong, she just shook her head, turned, and walked away. I saw her dig her handkerchief out of her pocket and wipe her eyes. That worried me, so I ran to catch up to her." He frowned, remembering.

"Then?" Gerdie prodded.

"When I saw her face, she was crying. I tried to hold her, but she pulled away and asked me to leave her alone. I asked what I'd done wrong and she just shook her head. It seemed that no matter what I did to try and comfort her, I just made it worse."

Frowning, Gerdie nodded. "Go on."

"Finally, she just yelled at me to leave her alone. She started to run away and when I tried to stop her..." he stopped, overcome with emotion.

Gerdie waited a moment, then gently prodded, "When you tried to stop her...?"

Herr Otto's eyes filled with tears as he replied gruffly, "She told me she never wanted to see me again."

"What?" Gerdie was shocked. "I can't believe that!"

"It's true. I was so shocked I told her to stop being a silly, emotional woman. She stared at me for just a moment. I thought she was going to slap me! When she didn't, I tried to apologize, but she backed away from me, then turned and practically ran down the street. I didn't dare follow her. I don't know what I did wrong, Gerdie. I don't know how to make it right. I don't know. I just don't know." He turned away and walked into the other room, his shoulders shaking as he tried to stifle the sobs.

Gerdie didn't know what to think. She had still been asleep when Frau Schmidt came back from their walk, so hadn't seen the teary face that Herr Otto described.

When she woke up, Frau Schmidt was busy scrubbing the kitchen floor. She had been quiet, but Gerdie hadn't thought much about it. When she brought in her dinner, she had let Gerdie do most of the talking, which was a little unusual, but not completely out of character. She had left early this morning, before Herr Otto came, but had explained it by saying she wanted to go to the bakery while the bread was still fresh from the ovens.

Trying to think of any other clues, Gerdie was stymied. It just didn't seem like her to behave that way. What could have happened to create such a strong reaction?

After a few moments, Herr Otto came back in and asked if she needed anything. When she said no, he asked if it would be all right if he left early. He didn't think Frau Schmidt wanted to cross paths with him, even here.

Gerdie nodded and promised to see if she could find out what was wrong. The old gentleman thanked her and quietly left.

An hour or so later, Frau Schmidt knocked, then came in. She had some groceries in her arms, but poked her head into the sleeping area to check on Gerdie.

"I'm here, *mein mädchen*. Do you need anything before I start *abendbrot*? It's dinner time and you must be hungry." she asked.

"No, thank you, Frau Schmidt. But I would like to talk when you have a few minutes," she replied.

The older woman nodded. "I'll come in and eat with you. We can talk then."

Listening to the hustle and bustle in the kitchen, Gerdie couldn't tell if Frau Schmidt was upset or not. It didn't seem that way. There was no banging or clanging of dishes. No slamming of cupboard doors. She had seemed normal when she came in. The puzzle grew more puzzling by the minute.

Gerdie sighed. Patience was not one of her best virtues. Perhaps this was a good time to practice it. That thought made her smile a little and she relaxed into the pillow to wait.

When Frau Schmidt brought in the dinner tray, she smiled as she sat it on the little table by the bed. She gave one plate and fork to Gerdie, then took one for herself.

"Do you need more water?" she asked.

Gerdie glanced at her cup. "Not right now. I have enough."

She took a bite of bread and smiled. "This is delicious, Frau Schmidt. Your cooking always tastes so good to me."

Her friend returned her smile. "That's because you are eating for two. Besides, food always tastes better when someone else cooks it."

Gerdie laughed. "That's true."

She took another bite and closed her eyes, savoring the flavors.

Frau Schmidt smiled and took a bite herself. When she'd swallowed, she asked, "What did you want to talk about?"

Now that the opportunity was here, Gerdie didn't quite know how to start. After chewing slowly to give herself time to think, inspiration struck.

"How was your walk last night? I can imagine the leaves are beautiful right now. Maybe even some crunchy ones on the ground?" she grinned. Then her grin faded when Frau Schmidt's face fell.

She was silent for a few moments, seeming to chew her food extra slowly, too. Finally, she answered, "The walk was fine. The leaves are beautiful, although many have fallen already. There were some fine crunchy ones near the *Volksgarten* in *Südpark*."

Gerdie waited, hoping the frau would go on. She didn't. Thinking quickly, she commented, "I'm so grateful to you and Herr Otto for taking such *gut* care of me. I don't know what I'd do without you!"

Frau Schmidt smiled a little and nodded. "It's our pleasure. You are a joy to serve. Besides, I'm hoping your little one will call me *Oma*. All my grandchildren have moved away and I have no one to spoil."

"We would be honored to have you as our little one's *oma*," she said sincerely. "It will be lovely to have an adopted *oma* and *opa* so near. Maybe we should plan to have our Sunday dinners together? Wouldn't that be grand?"

Looking at her plate, Frau Schmidt didn't answer for a moment, then said, "Perhaps."

That was the opening Gerdie was hoping for.

"What's wrong? Suddenly you seem sad."

"It's nothing, *mein mädchen*," she answered shortly. "Are you finished? I'll wash up the dishes."

She started to take Gerdie's plate, but Gerdie reached out and held her arm. "Wait. I see my friend is sad. I'm not much good in this bed, but I can listen and maybe offer a bit of insight?" she offered.

Looking at Gerdie's hand on her arm, Frau Schmidt swallowed hard, sighed, then sat down again.

"I... I don't know if Sunday dinners together would be a good idea," she began. "I am happy to come and I'm sure Herr Otto would be, too. But perhaps you could invite us on different Sundays?" she ventured.

"Why?" Gerdie feigned surprise. "Has something happened between you?"

Frau Schmidt looked at the ceiling, then at the floor, biting her bottom lip. Finally, she sighed. "No... not really... maybe..."

Gerdie couldn't help but laugh. "That's a lot of answers to one question."

Chuckling, Frau Schmidt agreed. "You're right. I'm having difficulty talking about it."

Gerdie sobered. "Take your time, then. We have all night."

After a few moments, Frau Schmidt continued. "We were having a wonderful walk. The leaves were so pretty and the ones on the ground so crunchy. I don't know what got into me, but I kicked one pile of leaves and giggled. Can you imagine an old lady like me giggling?"

Smiling, Gerdie nodded. "Yes, I can."

Frau Schmidt returned her smile, then looked down, sad again. "Herr Otto said I was adorable."

"That sounds like a compliment to me," Gerdie offered.

"That's what Herr Schmidt used to say to me."

"Oh," Gerdie replied, comprehension dawning. "So, the compliment reminded you of your husband?"

Frau Schmidt nodded. "Yes. And I started to feel guilty."

Gerdie was puzzled again. "Guilty? For what?"

"Can you keep a secret?" the older woman asked.

Gerdie nodded.

"I think I'm falling in love with Herr Otto."

Smiling, Gerdie replied, "I was hoping that was the case. You make a handsome couple."

Frau Schmidt shook her head. "You don't understand. It feels like I am betraying my love for Herr Schmidt. He's the only man I ever felt this way about... until now."

Gerdie pursed her lips. "Did Herr Schmidt love you?"

"Of course! We were married for thirty-seven years."

"Did you try to make each other happy while you were married?" Gerdie pressed.

"Yes. I tried my best to please him and he always did little things for me that made me smile."

Gerdie nodded. "Do you think he would want you to be happy now?"

Frau Schmidt hesitated, then nodded. "Yes."

"Are you happy living alone?" Gerdie continued.

Shaking her head, Frau Schmidt admitted, "Not really. Oh, I'm fine living alone, but I do get lonely sometimes. That's one of the benefits to helping you, *mein mädchen*. You keep an old woman from feeling so lonely."

Unwilling to be deterred, Gerdie asked one more question, "Would Herr Schmidt want you to be lonely or would he want you to be happy?"

Frau Schmidt dropped her head. She reached into her apron pocket, pulled out a handkerchief, and dabbed at her eyes.

Gerdie smiled when she saw the initials on the handkerchief. She tugged a little at the corner to get Frau Schmidt's attention.

Looking up, she saw Gerdie pointing to the initials G.O. and smiled.

"I understand. I think Herr Schmidt would want me to be

happy."

"I agree," Gerdie nodded happily.

"I will clean up the kitchen and think about what you've said," Frau Schmidt promised. "Thank you. You have a lot of wisdom for one so young," she grinned.

"I gleaned it from those old wise ones around me," Gerdie quipped.

Frau Schmidt laughed and took the dishes into the kitchen. *I certainly have much to consider,* she thought, *such as how to apologize to Herr Gustav Otto.*

"Mama, you'll never guess what I just did!" Maggie rushed into the apartment, breathless and obviously excited.

Mrs. Gilley laughed. "You're probably right. Why don't you tell me?"

"I just accepted a position at the John Dickinson factory," she announced. "I'm going to be a munitionette!"

Instantly, Mrs. Gilley's face fell. "The munitions factory? Oh, Maggie. That sounds too dangerous. I'm not..."

"No, no, Mama," Maggie interrupted. "I won't be working in the factory itself. Mr. Smythe has hired me to work in the office. I'll be taking care of the accounts, making sure the orders are filled properly, ordering supplies, tracking each batch that goes through the factory, that sort of thing. I won't be in any danger at all."

Shaking her head, Mrs. Gilley frowned. "You'll still be working close to the factory, won't you? Isn't the office close by?"

Maggie sighed. "It's in the same block, but not in the same building. Besides, they wouldn't allow women to work there if it wasn't safe, would they? In any of the posters around town recruiting women to work there, have you ever seen any of them that mentioned that it's a dangerous environment?"

Mrs. Gilley's frown deepened. "No, but..."

"No buts," Maggie interrupted. "The money is good and I'll not be in harm's way, so just give me your blessing and I'll start work tomorrow." She gave her mother a winning smile.

With a deep sigh of resignation, Mrs. Gilley hugged her daughter. "Congratulations." Her normally cheerful voice didn't sound so cheerful, but Maggie wasn't to be deterred.

"It's going to be just fine, Mama," she said. "You'll see."

The next morning, Maggie made her way to the factory, excited to start on her new adventure. She turned a corner and saw Shelly walking ahead of her.

"Good morning, Shelly," she called.

Her friend turned around and waved. "Hi, Mags! What are you doing in these parts this time of the day?"

Catching up to her, Maggie replied. "I'm starting at the factory today."

"Really? I've been there a month. What section will you be working in?" Shelly asked.

"I'll be in the office," Maggie smiled.

"Lucky girl. I'm in the filling department." Shelly made a face. "The work's tough, but I'm getting used to it. Beth is there, too."

"Beth's working with you? Wow. Maybe we can eat lunch together?" Maggie suggested hopefully.

"Not a chance, friend," Shelly replied. "We don't get a lunch break."

"No break?" Maggie was shocked.

"No break. We eat our sandwiches standing on the line. The work doesn't stop just because we're hungry," she laughed wryly.

"Wow. That sounds awful."

"It's not so bad. There are other women who have it worse." Shelly shrugged. "Anyway, I need to run. Talk to you later, Mags. Good luck on your first day," she called over her shoulder, then rushed off.

Maggie entered the office and spotted Mr. Smythe leaning over a clerk sitting at a desk in the corner. She politely cleared her throat and then waited quietly. After a few moments, he looked up and motioned her over.

"Take a look at this, Mrs. Bennett," he said, pointing to the papers they were working on. "See if you can spot the mistake."

She leaned over, reading the paper carefully. In just a few moments, she spotted it.

"Here," she pointed. "The six and the nine have been reversed."

The clerk glared up at her, but remained silent.

"By jove, that's it!" Mr. Smythe agreed. "Good work, Mrs. Bennett."

He glanced down at the clerk. "Make sure you haven't made that same mistake elsewhere. I want the corrected order on my desk in one hour."

Looking up at Maggie he motioned, "Come. Your desk will be over here."

She followed him to a small desk sitting under a window across the room. He pulled the chair out for her and she sat down. Taking a stack of papers from a nearby desk, he sat them in front of her.

"These are the requisitions for the supplies we'll need next week. I want you to check them over for mistakes, then put them in this stack to be processed. Understand?"

"Yes, sir," she nodded.

He left her to her work and she began. It was tedious work, checking all the numbers on each page, but she was thorough and found several errors. Setting them aside, she determined to ask Mr. Smythe about them when the stack was completed.

Two hours later, she picked up both stacks of papers, placing the completed ones in the pile to be processed and taking the ones with mistakes to her supervisor's office.

She knocked on the open door and entered when he motioned. When he finished the note he was writing, he looked up.

"Yes?"

"These requisitions have errors. How would you like me to handle them?" she asked.

"The clerks have to sign their names to the bottom of the first page. Find the name, find the man, and return it to him for correction." With that, he went back to his work, waving his hand in dismissal.

Maggie stifled a sigh, then turned to find the men in question. It didn't take long, but she was met with scowls and frowns. One man even swore at her.

When she returned to her desk, there was a stack of munitions orders for her to check. She went right to work, again finding some errors in the lot. She put the finished ones in the To Be Processed pile, and returned the flawed ones to the clerks who'd prepared them, none of which greeted her with any professionalism or politeness. This pattern followed for the entire day.

When her shift was over, she tidied her desk, pushed her chair in and put on her hat. As she was donning her coat, one clerk brushed past her and whispered, "Watch yourself, sister. Don't be acting superior with us or you'll be sorry."

Shocked that anyone would speak to her so, she stared at his retreating back, her mouth half-open. As he closed the door, she shook her head. She was just doing her job, after all. What did he expect? Was she to ignore the mistakes she found? It was apparent that Mr. Smythe expected her to find the mistakes so they could be corrected. It didn't make sense that the clerks would find offense at that. Did it?

Walking home, she continued to be baffled by their behavior. As she turned onto her street, she took a deep breath and blew it out hard, trying to let go of the frustration she felt. No sense in worrying Mama or Katie. Besides, it was just her first day. The men would become used to her in time, wouldn't they?

Two weeks later, Maggie was preparing to go home after another uncomfortable day at the office with the male clerks, when Mr. Smythe called her into his office.

"Mrs. Bennett," he began. "I'm afraid I'm quite disappointed in your performance."

Confused, Maggie asked why. She'd been working hard and had found many mistakes that might otherwise have gone unnoticed.

"We seem to have developed quite a bottle-neck and the blockage seems to be your desk. The men are starting to complain. Orders are not going out in a timely manner and requisitions are slow to be processed. You do not seem to be doing your job, Mrs. Bennett, and if it continues, I'm going to have to let you go." His voice was stern, but Maggie was more incensed than hurt.

"Pardon me for saying so, sir, but I'm not the problem here," she stated matter-of-factly.

"Excuse me?" The boss was obviously not used to being questioned.

"I said, I'm not the problem here." Maggie stood her ground.

"Pray tell, who would you blame then?" he asked.

"The problem, sir, is that the men won't listen to me. I take their work, I find mistakes, I return it to them for correction. That's my job. But instead of correcting the errors I point out, they return the paperwork to me the next day with the same errors. Nothing changed. Nothing corrected. What am I to do, sir, if the men won't take correction?" Maggie felt proud that her voice stayed calm even though she was quaking inside.

"You mean to tell me the clerks are not correcting the work you send back?"

"That's right, sir."

Mr. Smythe pursed his lips and nodded slowly. "Let's test your theory, Mrs. Bennett. Tomorrow, when you find one that needs correcting, bring it to me. I'll look it over, then you can return it to the clerk who signed it. If he returns it to you uncorrected, I want you to bring it to me again. At that point, I will handle it personally."

"Thank you, sir. I'll do just that," Maggie was elated. Maybe the work would go easier now. One could hope!

Stepping lighter than she had in days, Maggie almost whistled on her way home. Turning the first corner, she noticed someone bending over on the side of the street, retching. Rushing to help, she recognized her friend, Shelly.

"Shelly, what's wrong?" she called before she even reached her.

Shelly didn't answer, just continued to retch and cough. Finally, the spasms eased and she caught her breath. Standing slowly, she turned and looked at Maggie.

Maggie gasped. "Shelly, your face is yellow!" she cried.

Nodding, Shelly held up her hands. "I know. My hands, too. In fact, everything is yellow."

"And you're sick!" Maggie put her arm around her friend, walking slowly beside her.

Again, Shelly nodded. "Been that way for two days now."

"You can't work when you're sick," Maggie admonished.

"I have to," her friend said. "We need the money."

"But…" Maggie began.

"I have to," Shelly repeated.

Maggie frowned, but kept silent for a few blocks, then asked, "What else are you feeling besides sick to your stomach?"

Shelly shrugged, "Headaches, dizziness sometimes, food tastes like metal, nothing much to worry about."

"Sounds like a lot to worry about, to me," Maggie said dourly. "Have you seen a doctor?"

"I saw the company doctor yesterday. He said it was a normal initial reaction to working with TNT and that my body would become used to it in time."

Shaking her head, Maggie helped her up the steps to her apartment. "I wish you would take a day or two off, Shell. Perhaps you'd feel better if you did."

"I'll think about it, Mags" her friend answered, but Maggie knew she wouldn't.

She wondered if there were other girls who were sick like Shelly. *Doesn't seem right,* she thought.

Chapter Ten

December 15, 1914

"Did you hear?" Fritz asked as he entered their tent.

"Hear what?" Friedrich answered his question with a question. He tried once more to tie the knot tightly around the brown paper package in his lap, but once again, it slipped and wouldn't hold the package tightly enough.

Fritz rustled the newspaper in his hand. "The Pope is calling for a truce. Listen to this:

Pope Benedict XV has called for an official truce between Germany and Britain, and asked 'that the guns may fall silent at least upon the night the angels sang'.

"Now what do you think of that?" He slapped the newspaper into his opposite hand for emphasis.

"Hey, Fritz," Friedrich called. "Lend me your finger for a moment."

Fritz obliged, holding the knot while Friedrich finished tying it. "Did you hear what I said? The Pope is calling for a Christmas truce. Wouldn't that be wonderful?"

Friedrich smiled. "I think it will be a miracle if anyone listens to a man so far away from here."

"A man? A man?" Fritz was livid. "How dare you call the Holy

Pope a mere man!"

Holding his hands up in surrender, Friedrich ducked his head. "I'm sorry. I didn't mean to offend. But not everyone sees him the way you do."

Fritz just frowned and turned away. Then, apparently his curiosity got the better of him and he turned back.

"What's in the package?" he asked.

Friedrich smiled. "It's a music box for Gerdie, and a rattle for the baby."

"Did she have a boy or girl?"

Laughing, Friedrich shook his head. "She hasn't had it yet, as far as I know."

"Oh," Fritz was puzzled. "So, you got the baby a gift even though it's not born yet?"

"Well, sure. He'll probably be here before Christmas, so he will need a Christmas gift."

"He?" Fritz's eyebrows raised.

Again, Friedrich laughed. "Hopeful thinking, *kumpel*, but I'll be just as happy if he turns out to be a she."

"Must be tough to be so far away," Fritz observed.

Sighing, Friedrich nodded. "It's the hardest thing I've ever done."

"Mail call," a voice shouted from outside their tent.

"*Verdammt*," Friedrich muttered under his breath.

"What's wrong?" Fritz asked, concerned.

"Gotta run. I don't want to miss the mail truck," Friedrich called over his shoulder.

That evening, Friedrich thought about Fritz's excitement over the newspaper article. He felt badly that he'd offended his friend, but the truth was that it was unlikely that anyone in authority would honor the pope's request. *That's just reality,* he thought.

The next day, however, Friedrich had occasion to rethink his opinion. He was on guard duty just before dinner. Everything was quiet, with no movement on either side of No Man's Land. That had become an unspoken agreement the past couple of weeks, no firing from either side during mealtime. Still, he was watchful, as usual. One never knew when the Tommies might get it in their minds to attack.

He'd just finished a visual pass of the enemy side of No Man's Land when a movement caught his eye. Nearly two meters away, he saw two German soldiers poke their heads up from their trench with their hands in the air.

What are they doing? Friedrich thought and readied his rifle. He watched them, ready to defend them if necessary. When no one fired on them, they climbed out of the trench and hurried to several of their wounded and dead comrades. They started pulling them back towards their lines, looking this way and that, like they expected to be fired on at any moment.

Instead, there was movement on the British side. Three Brits mirrored the movements of their German counterparts. They rose with hands in the air, then climbed out and began retrieving their own wounded and dead.

The German soldiers paused and watched them for a minute, then beckoned them over. Friedrich watched in amazement as the Germans and British soldiers began helping each other bury their dead. It was as if there was no war being fought. They were just five men working together.

After a few minutes, several others on both sides came out to help. When the dead were all safely buried, the soldiers on both sides talked for a few minutes, some exchanging cigarettes, chatting as if they were old friends.

Then, suddenly, as if someone rang a school bell to recall frolicking students, the soldiers on both sides turned and jogged back to their trenches. No shots were fired, no alarms were sounded, but that moment of peaceful coexistence was over.

Friedrich marveled at the sight. It seemed too ironic for words. There, two nights before, they had been having a terrific battle, and then today, there they were smoking each other's cigarettes as if there was no such thing as war.

Later that week, he received the first of several Christmas packages. He didn't know who it was from, as it wasn't labeled with a return address. Inside was a little note wishing him a Merry Christmas and hoping he would enjoy this little *Liebesgaben*.

Hm, he thought, *I would enjoy it more if I knew who this "loving gift" was from.* Still, the cigar and chocolate did taste fine.

Herr Otto pulled a small box from his vest pocket and handed it to Gerdie.

Opening the box, Gerdie gasped. Inside was a simple, but lovely ring. "It's beautiful! She will love it. But how could you afford it?" Her hand flew to her mouth in embarrassment at her rudeness.

But Herr Otto smiled gently. "I sold my pipe. Do you really think she will like it?" he asked, unsure.

"Oh, yes. I have no doubt about that." Gerdie nodded emphatically. "And I'm sure when you look at it on her finger, you'll not miss your pipe at all. When will you give it to her?"

"Christmas Eve," he smiled. "Then, if she likes it, I'm going to ask her to marry me."

"What? That's wonderful," Gerdie exclaimed. "What an excellent Christmas gift."

"I hope she will accept," he said simply.

"The gift or the proposal?" she asked, smiling.

"Both," he grinned.

"Somehow, I don't think you need to worry. She's in love with you, you know."

"She is?" he asked, his face showing the hope he obviously felt.

"Oh, yes. I have no doubt she'll accept," Gerdie was quite certain. In her many talks with Frau Schmidt, there was no trace of the guilt over their relationship that had plagued her earlier.

"Then perhaps we can celebrate a new year with a new marriage?" Herr Otto's eyes twinkled merrily.

"That sounds like a perfect time to me," Gerdie agreed, then gasped and clutched her swollen belly.

"What's wrong?" Herr Otto's concern was evident as he jumped out of his chair and moved toward her.

She held up a hand to stop him. "It's okay," she panted. "It's easing up."

"What was it?" he asked, still concerned.

"Just a preparatory contraction," she tried to reassure him. "I've been having them frequently lately, but Frau Schmidt says it's just my body preparing for the birth. It's nothing to worry about."

Herr Otto didn't look convinced. "If you're sure. Do you need anything? Water? Food?"

Gerdie smiled, "Some fresh water would be lovely." Handing him her cup, she gasped again and dropped the cup, spilling what was left in it all over the bed and floor.

This time, Herr Otto wasn't to be deterred. He rushed over and helped her lie back on the pillow. "That doesn't look like any preparatory contraction to me," he muttered.

Taking a deep breath, Gerdie started to speak. Instead, her eyes grew wide and she looked at her belly.

Herr Otto instinctively looked, too, but didn't see anything but the wet bedclothes from her spilled water cup.

"What is it?" he asked.

Gerdie looked up and smiled a knowing smile. "Would you please tell Frau Schmidt that it's time?"

"What? Now? How do you know?" Herr Otto's deep voice almost squeaked with anxiety.

"Trust me, Herr Otto," she grinned. "A mother knows."

Just then, another contraction hit and she took a deep breath, trying not to fight it. "Please, will you hurry?" she managed through the pain.

"Of course!" he said, as he grabbed his hat and coat from the hook, throwing them on as he ran out the door.

Reaching Frau Schmidt's apartment, he pounded on the door.

"Come quick!" Herr Otto's voice was frantic. "It's time!"

He heard someone pounding on the floor above and a cranky voice yell, "Keep it quiet down there! I'm trying to sleep."

Ignoring Frau Schultz, he pounded again. "Frau Schmidt, please come! Gerdie says it's time!"

Suddenly, the door opened and Frau Schmidt rushed out, holding the bag she'd packed for just this occasion. "I'm coming, Herr Otto."

"Hurry!" he insisted.

Smiling a little, Frau Schmidt nodded as she passed him in the doorway. "Babies take a while to be born, Herr Otto. Don't worry. We'll arrive in time."

"But…" he protested.

"Come along," she called over her shoulder. "I'll need you to boil some water for me."

Seventeen hours later, Gerdie was bathed in sweat. To her, it seemed as though this baby would never arrive. She was tired and alternated between feeling too hot and feeling too cold. Every time she'd start to relax and drift into a half-sleep, another contraction would force her awake again.

Frau Schmidt was by her side constantly, bathing her forehead, patting her hand, rubbing her back, giving her sips of water, and anything else that seemed like it would soothe her.

"Will it ever end?" Gerdie moaned after another long contraction.

"*Ja, mein mädchen*. It will end once the baby is here," she crooned.

"I don't think I can do this," Gerdie gasped after another hard contraction.

"But you can. The female body was made for this task. Try to relax and allow it to happen as it should," Frau Schmidt bathed her forehead and neck once again.

Herr Otto poked his head in the doorway with a questioning look on his face, but Frau Schmidt shook her head and he disappeared again.

When the next contraction was over, Gerdie accepted the sip of water Frau Schmidt offered her, then lay back panting, eyes closed.

Suddenly, her eyes popped open.

"What's that?" she asked, frightened.

"What's what, Gerdie?" Frau Schmidt asked.

"This feels different. Oh… oh… oh…!"

Frau Schmidt smiled. "It's time, *kleine mutter*. It won't be long now."

"Won't be long…" turned out to be two more hours, and even Frau Schmidt was becoming concerned. Gerdie was so tired, and each time she pushed, she seemed to be weaker than before. She was sipping beef broth between contractions, but it didn't seem to help.

Finally, however, the moment arrived.

"Breathe, Gerdie," Frau Schmidt instructed.

Gerdie tried to take a deep breath, but the contraction consumed her and she cried out as she succumbed to its power. This time, the baby slipped out into Frau Schmidt's waiting hands.

Plopping her head back on the pillow, breathing hard, Gerdie closed her eyes and whispered, "*Endlich*, finally."

She thought she never wanted to move again, but when Frau Schmidt laid the little squirming bundle in her arms, her face softened into a tender smile, tears filled her eyes and she kissed the wet little head. "*Willkommen in der welt, mein kleiner.* Welcome to the world."

"Ooo la la," Budgy exclaimed as he admired the seal on the small oblong package he'd just received.

"What's that?" Thomas asked.

Budgy held up the package and showed him the royal seal. "It's from Princess Mary herself," he gloated.

Thomas laughed. "We all got them, Budgy."

"I don't care," he sounded defensive. "When I tell my grandchildren about this, I don't have to tell them that she sent the same bloody package to every bloody soldier in the bloody army, do I?"

Shaking his head, Thomas had to agree. "No, you can tell your stories any way you like. Of course, the history books might disagree with your version."

"What history book writer is going to care what we received for Christmas this year?" Budgy asked, incredulous at the very idea.

"I don't know," Thomas shrugged, "but you never know, they might."

He turned to his own royal Christmas package and opened it. It contained a tin box embossed with an image of the princess and other military and imperial symbols. Inside was an ounce of tobacco, a packet of cigarettes in a yellow monogrammed wrapper, a cigarette lighter, chocolates, a photograph and a Christmas card from Princess Mary which read, "May God protect you and bring you home safe."

Thomas smiled at the sentiment and said a quick prayer that the princess's Christmas wish would come true.

"Hey, it's a plum pudding," Budgy exclaimed, opening his second package.

"Who's that one from?" Thomas asked.

Budgy looked at the paper he'd discarded. "Says it's from the *Daily Mail*."

"That's nice of them," Thomas commented smiling.

"Yup," Budgy took a huge bite, then looked at his friend. "I'll share if you'll take my guard shift tonight."

Thomas laughed. "On Christmas Eve?" Then he sobered. "I heard some of the fellows talking and they say the krauts might use the holiday to catch us with our pants down, so to speak. Guard duty might be risky tonight."

"So, you're holding out for more than a little nibble?" Budgy cocked his head and pursed his lips.

"No, but…" Thomas started to protest, then caught Budgy's playful look. "…but maybe for half?" he tried, jokingly.

"Done!" Budgy yelled, handing him the box.

"Wait, I didn't…"

"Too late, Tommy-boy. A deal's a deal," Budgy chuckled as he left the dugout.

How did that happen? Thomas wondered as he took a bite of the pudding.

Later that evening, as he climbed the parapet, he was met with a strange sight. The guard on duty was staring at a plain brown box with a puzzled look on his face.

"What's wrong, Eric?" Thomas asked.

"Something extraordinary," the young private responded. "I was watching like usual and I see this kraut stand up with his hands in the air. I get ready to shoot in case it's a trick and he lifts something out, then ducks back down. The something moves and I take aim to shoot, but then realize it's a dog. I can't shoot a dog!"

"I wouldn't, either." Thomas agreed.

"So, this dog comes ambling through No Man's Land right up

to the parapet. I look down and he's got something strapped to his back. I climb down to see what it is and it's this box. When I unstrapped the box, the dog ambles back the way he came, but the kraut yells something at him and he sits down. Right there in the middle of No Man's Land. See? He's still there."

Thomas looked and sure enough, there was a large, yellow dog, just sitting between the two barbed wire barriers. Looking back, he asked, "So what's in the box?"

"I was afraid to open it. What do you think we should do?"

Thomas frowned. He didn't know what to do either.

"Maybe we should take this to the colonel," Thomas suggested.

"Yes. Good plan. So, you take it to him and let him decide what to do." Eric shoved the box into Thomas's hands. "I'll stay here until you get back. But hurry. This might be the beginning of some strange new diversion. They might attack at any moment."

Not knowing what else to do, Thomas climbed back down and ran to find the Colonel. Upon reaching him, he tried to talk, but found he was out of breath.

"Colonel?" he finally panted.

"What is it, Private? Calm down and tell me what's going on," the colonel ordered.

"It's this, sir. The guard didn't know how to respond, so he sent me to deliver it to you." He handed the colonel the box.

The colonel opened it and found it contained a splendid chocolate cake and a note, which read:

"We propose having a concert tonight as it is our Captain's birthday, and we cordially invite you to attend, provided you will give us your word of honour as guests that you agree to cease all hostilities between 7:30 and 8:30... When you see us light the candles and footlights at the edge of our trench at 7:30 sharp, you can safely put your heads above your trenches, and we shall do the same, and begin the concert."

Nodding, the colonel penned a quick note, then looked around for something to put it in. His eyes landed on the Christmas tin he'd received. Opening it to be sure the cigarettes, tobacco and chocolate were in sufficient supply, he shoved the note into the tin and gave it to Thomas.

"Private, see that this is delivered to the sender of this invitation," he ordered. "Then pass the word that we are going to enjoy a concert tonight and all hostilities will cease between 7:30 and 8:30. Is that understood?"

"Yes, sir." Thomas snapped off a salute and headed back. He found Eric pacing in the small confines of the parapet.

"Well? What was it?" he asked.

"It was a cake," Thomas announced.

Eric frowned. "A cake?"

Thomas nodded. "Yes, a cake and an invitation to stop shooting and listen to a concert tonight between 7:30 and 8:30."

"That makes no sense," Eric shook his head.

Shrugging, Thomas replied, "Maybe not, but we're to find a way to get this reply back to the krauts who sent the invitation."

"How are we supposed to do that?" Eric groused.

"I wonder," Thomas looked at the dog, still sitting halfway between the trenches. He whistled and the dog looked up, then trotted over. Thomas climbed down and tied the reply around the dog's neck.

"Go home, boy," he ordered, pointing towards the enemy lines.

Obediently, the dog loped back the way he'd come. After a few moments, a German soldier poked his head up and gave the thumbs up sign.

"I guess the concert is on," Thomas commented as he ascended the parapet again. "I'm on duty here, so it's up to you to spread the word."

"Thanks," Eric said sarcastically.

"Any time," Thomas grinned.

As promised, all hostilities ceased precisely at 7:30 p.m. A few tentative heads poked out of the British trenches. When they saw German heads poking up, as well, facing away from them, they motioned for others to join them.

Thomas, who was still on guard duty, leaned on the parapet railing. He wasn't disappointed. A double quartet of German soldiers sang a variety of songs for the next hour. The British applauded each song.

Just before the last number, a big voice called from the German parapets, "Blease come mit us into the chorus."

A killjoy on the British side shouted back, "We'd rather die than sing German."

In reply, the big voice boomed, in English, "It vould kill us if you did."

The concert ended with *"Die Wacht am Rhien"*, and the Germans applauded and cheered their favorite patriotic song. Soon after, the trench footlights went out. A few shots deliberately aimed at the heavy clouds ended the extraordinary evening.

Chapter Eleven

December 24, 1914

"Fritz, come and look." Friedrich was standing in the entrance of the dugout looking out.

"Mmm," Fritz mumbled, half-asleep.

"Fritz," Friedrich called again. "Come see. You won't believe this."

Fritz rolled out of bed and stumbled to the entrance. Rubbing his eyes, he looked out at a white wonderland where only mud and muck had stood the day before.

"Looks like it froze," he commented.

"Then snowed a little," Friedrich added with a smile. "It looks like Christmas to me."

Grinning, Fritz agreed. "Now all we need are Tannenbaum and Schnapps."

"Keep dreaming, *kumpel*," Friedrich laughed.

"A man has to dream, or he dies inside," Fritz pursed his lips. "I choose to dream."

Friedrich nodded. "That's a good philosophy. So, let's take our dreams to the mess tent and see what's for breakfast."

The two joined several others on their way to eat, their mood was jolly and light, which was amazing considering how many of their number had been maimed or killed in the past few weeks.

As they finished eating, someone announced, "Mail call." A mass exodus ensued as each soldier left their meal in the hopes they would have a Christmas package or letter from a loved one. The Christmas *pflegepakets* were welcome, but a soldier could only use so many bars of soap. The cigarettes and matches were put to good use, but there were never enough of those. Besides, those packages didn't mean as much as that personal touch from someone they knew at home.

"Gunderson."

"Schneider."

"Fischer."

On and on, as each name was called, the soldier attached to that name would make his way to the front of the group to collect his mail.

Friedrich tried to be patient, but he knew that his Gerdie was due to give birth at any time. Surely there would be word today!

"Weber."

"Meyer."

"Wagner."

Fritz let out a single whoop, then made his own way to the front. He had a package and a letter. As he passed Friedrich, he grinned. "It's from my father. I'd bet real money he's sent us some Schnapps. Join me later for a drink?"

Friedrich nodded, then turned back to listen.

"Hoffman."

"Schäfer."

Then there was a pause. Thinking there were no more letters, Friedrich turned away, his heart sinking. No word. *That either means she hasn't had the baby yet, or there's something terribly wrong and no one has the heart to tell me,* he thought.

He'd taken several steps back towards his dugout when he heard, "Krause."

Grinning from ear to ear, Friedrich rushed up and snatched his letter. Calling *"Danke"* over his shoulder, he rushed off to find a quiet corner to read. He settled for the dugout he shared with Fritz.

"I told you my father would come through!" Fritz called as he came in. He held up a silver flask, then took a long draught, wiped his mouth, puffed on the cigar in his hand, then sighed a contented smile. "Schnapps and tobacco. Takes away all your troubles, *kumpel!* Want some?"

"Maybe later," Friedrich waved him off with a grin. "I received a letter from home."

"Suit yourself," Fritz went back to his pleasures as Friedrich settled himself on the blankets across the dugout.

December 16, 1914

Dear Friedrich,

I'm happy to tell you that Gerdie gave birth to a beautiful baby boy last night. He is healthy and strong. He nurses well and has a healthy set of lungs on him. She has named him Karl after your father.

Gerdie is recovering slowly, but her color is better this morning and I expect she will be as strong as ever in no time. She has promised to write you soon.

Merry Christmas and may you find your way home to us soon.

Sincerely,
Frau Klara Schmidt

P.S. Herr Otto sends his Christmas greetings as well.

"*Hurra!*" Friedrich hollered.

Fritz looked up, startled.

"I have a son!" Friedrich explained. "Gerdie had a baby boy!"

"*Glückwünsche!* This calls for a drink," he offered the flask to the new papa, who accepted it gratefully.

Taking a long swig, Friedrich grinned. "I can't believe it! I'm a papa. I'm going to share the news," he announced as he stood.

"Shout it from the parapets, *kumpel*," Fritz encouraged.

"I just might do that," he said as he left.

Before he took two steps out of his dugout however, a private handed him a small fir tree. Puzzled, he asked, "What's this?"

"*Tannenbaum*," the man answered. "We got a whole truck full. Pass it down, there's more coming."

Turning, he saw another private waiting for him to pass the tree to him. The line of trees being passed down the trenches from man to man seemed to stretch on for miles. An hour later, the man on his left said, "Keep that one, we have ours."

The fir tree in his hand was small, but nicely shaped, with

branches that turned slightly upward, dark blue-green needles, and a wonderful scent. It would make a lovely Christmas tree.

He poked his head into the dugout and called to Fritz. "Hey, you remember your Christmas wish?"

Obviously feeling the effects of the first half of his wish, he nodded sleepily. "*Tannenbaum* and *Schnapps*."

"Well, come and see our tree, *kumpel*," Friedrich laughed.

Fritz's eyes popped open and he stumbled out. He grinned as he looked at the small tree and laughed when Friedrich showed him the box of little candles that he'd just been handed.

"We'll have a festive Christmas in our dugout, after all!" Fritz gloated. "Let's just hope Tommy doesn't decide to attack while we're celebrating."

Friedrich frowned. That was a possibility. "I wonder if the Brits celebrate Christmas like we do," he mused.

"*Ja*," Fritz answered, digging through his things for a bit of string. "My cousin worked as a waiter in Ketner's in London for a while. He said they go all out when it comes to Christmas and New Year's celebrations."

"Maybe we should offer a truce then," Friedrich suggested. "Just for the holiday."

Fritz's eyes grew wide. "That's brilliant, *kumpel*. But doesn't that have to come from the generals or the Kaiser or someone with authority?"

Shrugging, Friedrich shook his head. "I don't see why. We're the ones on the front lines. We're the ones who decide to shoot or not. They may give the orders, but we decide whether to follow them."

Fritz frowned. "Sounds like you're headed for a court-martial and firing squad, Friedrich."

He thought about that for a moment, then shook his head. "They wouldn't dare. Not on Christmas."

Now it was Fritz's turn to shrug. "So, what do you have in mind?"

94

"Remind me again why we're here?" Thomas asked Budgy as they stood guard on the parapet.

"Because the generals think the Germans will use Christmas as an excuse to launch an offensive," Budgy recited without much emotion. "They think the Germans will think we're vulnerable because we'll be busy celebrating instead of standing guard."

Thomas frowned. "So, no celebrations? Instead we stand guard even though there hasn't been much fighting the past couple of weeks?"

Budgy nodded. "That's the story."

Sighing, Thomas rubbed his eyes. "Well, it beats slogging around in the mud, I suppose. But the sun on the snow is sure bright in my eyes."

Budgy looked at the sun sitting low in the west. "It won't be shining much longer. Hang in there, Tommy-boy."

They stood without saying much as random gunfire punctuated the winter scene. As the sun slowly set, the gunfire grew more sporadic, and as the last of the sun's rays glistened on the tops of the trees, it suddenly stopped. The silence was as eerie as the twilight that changed the landscape from brilliant white to a dull purple-grey, dotted with mysterious shadows.

Then, as if someone turned out all the lights, everything was black except for the stars that twinkled high above. The silence continued and Thomas found himself feeling tense and fingering the trigger of his rifle nervously.

Abruptly, Thomas blinked his eyes as he thought he saw something in the distance. He looked again, but the apparition was still there.

"Budgy, look there. What's that?" he pointed.

His friend looked, squinted, then pointed himself. "There, another one. What is it?"

The pinpricks of light began appearing all along the German line. Thomas was baffled and kept squinting his eyes to try and see clearer in the darkness.

"Christmas trees!" Budgy suddenly announced. "The krauts are putting up Christmas trees!"

"What? Where would they get Christmas trees?" Thomas wanted

to know. But he looked closer and sure enough, there were dozens of little fir trees lit by candles or lanterns dotting the line that marked the Germans' trench.

As he looked, he realized the night wasn't silent anymore. Quietly at first, then growing louder, he heard German voices singing, "*Stille nacht, heilige nacht…*"

"What's that they're singing?" he asked. Budgy, who knew a little German, translated.

"They're singing 'Silent Night, Holy Night'," he said.

"It's beautiful," Thomas whispered in awe. He looked up at the stars and saw a soft first-quarter moon just beginning to rise. It leant a magical quality to the snow-covered No Man's Land.

As the song finished, there was spontaneous applause from the British trenches. Thomas smiled. The generals certainly wouldn't approve of British soldiers applauding German soldiers! *But if we can't be home, what a wonderful way to spend Christmas Eve*, he thought.

With a smile, Thomas poked Budgy, then started singing, "The first Nowell, the angels did say…"

Budgy joined in, and by the second line, many of their comrades started singing, as well. It wasn't as beautifully harmonized as the Germans' song, but they sang with heart and soul and the Germans applauded loudly.

The Germans' next song was "*O Tannenbaum, O Tannenbaum*".

The British replied with "O Come All Ye Faithful".

But they were surprised when the Germans joined in singing the words in Latin. "*Adeste fideles…*"

Tears filled Thomas's eyes as he realized the significance of this event. Who would have ever thought that British and German soldiers would be harmonizing Christmas carols across No Man's Land?

As the last notes died, someone on the German side called, "English, come over! You no shoot, we no shoot."

Thomas looked at Budgy, suddenly suspicious. Then Budgy called, "You come over here!"

To their astonishment, two figures rose from the German trench, their arms raised. They climbed over their barbed wire and advanced.

"Do you see any guns?" Budgy asked.

Thomas shook his head. "No. Do you think it's a trick?"

Before Budgy could answer, one of the Germans called, "Send an officer to talk."

Thomas raised his rifle to the ready, but the captain, who was standing at the base of the parapet, called out, "Hold your fire."

He then climbed out of the trench and advanced to meet the Germans halfway. Thomas heard them talking, but couldn't make out what they were saying.

A few minutes later, the captain came back with a German cigar in his mouth and announced, "We've agreed there will be no shooting before midnight tomorrow, but sentries are to remain on duty, and the rest of you, stay alert."

Thomas and Budgy kept their eyes open and could see small groups of two or three men starting out of trenches on either side. In a matter of minutes, there were soldiers on both sides in No Man's Land, shaking hands with the same men they'd been trying to kill just a few hours earlier. It was a sight to behold.

Before long, a bonfire was built, and around it, the soldiers mingled. British khaki and German grey. Thomas snickered as he noticed the Germans were better dressed, with fresh uniforms for the holiday. As he listened, he noted that only a handful of Brits knew German, but there were many Germans who knew English.

"Budgy," he asked. "Why do the Germans know English so well?"

"Many of them have worked in England," he stated matter-of-factly. "My own nanny was German. They also work as waiters, maids, and sometimes in the mines. Perhaps one of them waited on you and you didn't even realize it?" he suggested.

"Perhaps," Thomas nodded.

The evening progressed and it wasn't until the wee hours of the morning that they allowed the bonfire to die. Thomas and Budgy had been relieved and were settling in to sleep when Thomas had a thought.

"I wonder if the Germans will honor the truce until tomorrow midnight as they promised," he said aloud.

"I hope so," Budgy answered sleepily. "I could use a day of rest."

Gerdie sat in the rocking chair, nursing Karl. She stared into his little face and still couldn't believe that she had a son. It had been two weeks, but she was still in awe of this little person who'd become so much a part of her heart and soul already.

As she nursed, she hummed *"O Tannenbaum"*. Leaning her head back, she rested against the back of the chair and looked at the little Christmas tree Herr Otto had set up in the corner of her room. Frau Schmidt had decorated it with popcorn, cranberries, ribbons, and candles. The older couple were planning to celebrate with her later this evening. She wasn't well enough to go to Christmas mass, but they would have their own commemoration here.

She happened to know a little secret that Herr Otto had shared with her the day before. That made her even more excited for the evening to come. It was lovely of him to let her share in their special time. She smiled and looked back at the baby who had fallen asleep.

Frau Schmidt came in and smiled down at her. "He looks content," she remarked.

"He is. He is a good baby and only cries when he's hungry or needs to be changed."

Nodding, Frau Schmidt offered to take him.

"I can manage," Gerdie said. "Thank you, anyway."

She stood with only a little difficulty and carried her baby to the cradle. As she laid him in it, she whispered, "Come, Karl. We should nap now. It's going to be an eventful night!"

Frau Schmidt fluffed her pillows and helped her lie back. "Would you like another blanket?"

Gerdie shook her head. "No. I have my shawl if I get chilled. Why don't you go home? I'm sure you have much to prepare for this evening's celebration. I'm just going to nap and rest."

Watching her closely, Frau Schmidt finally nodded. "All right, but I won't be gone long. Most of the cooking will have to be done here, anyway. Have a good rest."

Gerdie smiled at her friend's retreating back. She didn't know what she would have done without Frau Schmidt or Herr Otto these past months. She said a short, but sincere prayer of gratitude for her dear friends. No sooner had she muttered amen then her eyes closed and she fell into a deep, restful sleep.

A few hours later, she awoke to the wonderful aroma of roast duck and mulled wine. She smiled as she sat up and stretched. Swinging her legs over the side of the bed, she stood and turned in one fluid motion... and stumbled as the room spun around her. Her right side hit the little cradle as she fell, which caused Karl to start crying.

"*Was ist passiert?*" Klara called as she rushed into the room. "What's happened?"

Gerdie was sitting on the floor next to the cradle, shushing the baby. Looking up, she smiled wryly.

"It's nothing. I kicked the cradle as I tried to walk around the bed. I guess I don't have my balance yet," she chuckled, trying to ease Frau Schmidt's mind.

Klara didn't look convinced, but after a moment's hesitation, she returned Gerdie's smile.

"Perhaps he would be better soothed if you were to rock him?" she offered.

"Good idea," Gerdie agreed. With a bit of effort, she stood cautiously and stepped to the rocking chair, sitting carefully.

Klara lifted Karl out of the cradle and handed him to his mother. Gerdie smiled tenderly at him, pulled him close, and began humming.

"*Alles ist gut?*" Klara asked. "All is well?"

Gerdie nodded, not looking up, but continuing to hum as the infant settled into her bosom.

"Then I will finish our dinner preparations."

After Frau Schmidt left, Gerdie allowed herself a shaky breath, mentally checking herself for injury. Everything seemed to hurt, but her right side was especially painful when she tried to breathe deeply. She closed her eyes and controlled the urge to cry out. After a few shallow breaths, the pain eased a bit and she could breathe more normally. Looking down at her son, she smiled again.

"*Mutter* needs to be more careful," she told him. "I have a bit of healing to do before I'll be ready to jump out of bed like that."

A few moments later, she heard the front door open and Herr Otto's voice wishing Frau Schmidt a merry Christmas, followed by a returned greeting from Klara. Gerdie heard them talking, but couldn't hear what they were saying. It didn't matter. She was content to sit quietly, rocking her now sleeping baby.

Before she knew it, Frau Schmidt was gently shaking her awake.

"Wake up, *mein leibchin*," she called softly. "Dinner is ready. Shall I bring it in?"

Sleepily, Gerdie nodded. "That would be lovely."

"I thought so," Klara grinned. She looked at the doorway and Herr Otto, dressed in an apron and chef's hat came in carrying a large tray laden with the most delicious-looking food.

Gerdie laughed at the elderly gentleman, then closed her eyes and inhaled the savory aromas deeply. She caught her breath, hoping her face didn't show the pain that suddenly flared in her side. Breathing out slowly, she opened her eyes.

Her friends were busy filling plates from the tray that Herr Otto had placed on the small table. Mentally, Gerdie breathed a sigh of relief. Apparently, she'd hid her pain successfully. *No need to worry them on this festive occasion,* she thought.

They sat and ate, talked, and ate some more, then Frau Schmidt asked if anyone was ready for dessert. Both Herr Otto and Gerdie groaned and held their bellies.

Klara laughed and suggested they wait a bit and let their dinner digest. Everyone agreed.

"Won't you play for us, Herr Otto?" Gerdie suggested. "You did bring your violin, didn't you?"

He just grinned and stepped into the living area, returning with the old violin in his hands. "What would you like to hear?"

The evening was delightful as they alternated between singing the carols they all loved, and listening to Herr Otto's skillful playing of them. Finally, he put the violin back in its case and sighed. "I would enjoy playing all night if these stiff old fingers would cooperate."

"It was wonderful," Klara reached over and patted his arm. "*Danke.*"

"Shall we open gifts?" Gerdie asked, suddenly anxious to share her Christmas tokens with her friends. Instructing Herr Otto to open the little drawer in her bedside table, she reached for the small packages hidden there. Glancing at them, she handed one back to him and one to Frau Schmidt.

"How…?" Frau Schmidt started to ask, then gasped as a white handkerchief with delicate crochet edging fell into her lap. "When? How?" she repeated.

"It was my grandmother's," Gerdie said simply. "I know she would be pleased if you would accept this token of my love and gratitude."

Tears filled Klara's eyes as she stepped over to give Gerdie a gentle hug. "I would be pleased to carry it with me. Thank you," she said simply.

Gerdie smiled and turned to Herr Otto. "That was my father's. I hope you enjoy it as much as he did."

Herr Otto opened the package and grinned. The pipe was hand-carved from a cherry wood burl. It had a silver cover in the shape of a seashell. "I've been needing a new pipe since mine fell into the river last fall," he admitted.

Frau Schmidt frowned. "How did your pipe fall into the river, might I ask?"

He just grinned and winked at Gerdie. "I was looking at my reflection and smiling. I guess I smiled too big because my pipe fell right out of my mouth into the river. I saw it a week later, though. A big trout surfaced near the bench we always sit on and it was puffing away, happy as could be."

Returning his grin, Frau Schmidt flapped her hand at him, dismissing his tall tale. "Your stories get taller by the day."

He laughed and leaned over to give her a peck on the cheek. She blushed and made a sound that nearly sounded like a schoolgirl giggle.

I guess old people can fall in love, too, Gerdie thought with a chuckle.

Klara reached behind the door and pulled out a package wrapped in brown paper, handing it over to Gerdie.

Opening it, Gerdie grinned. "You hid that there when I was sleeping, didn't you?"

The older woman nodded and smiled.

Gerdie caught her breath as a soft little blanket fell into her hands. She knew that her baby would enjoy it for many years. "How did you know I wanted a soft blanket for my son?" she asked, smiling at Klara.

"Oh, *mein liebling*, I was a mother once, you know."

Gerdie's smile faded a little as she recalled that Klara's son had been killed in the Franco-Prussian War. This blanket must have been his. "I'm sorry," she whispered.

"*Nein, nein,*" Klara shook her head. "It was many years ago and I have long since spent my tears over him. Now, I will enjoy seeing Karl wrapped in it."

She reached into her other apron pocket and took out another package, handing it to Herr Otto.

"You shouldn't have," he protested. "You can't afford to buy me anything."

"It's too late," she laughed. "The money is spent and I can't take it back. So, you might as well enjoy it."

He opened the package, threw back his head and guffawed loudly, startling Karl who began to cry.

Gerdie cuddled him and he quickly quieted. "What is it?" she asked, curious about what had caused such a reaction.

Herr Otto held the package out to show her. It contained a sizable portion of pipe tobacco. Gerdie chuckled, trying not to disturb her baby again.

"I didn't realize you'd lost your pipe," Klara grinned. "But now it doesn't matter since you have such a fine new one."

It was Herr Otto's turn. He handed Gerdie a beautiful wooden rattle for Karl. She beamed and immediately rattled it in front of the sleeping baby, who only squirmed a little, then settled back to sleep. They all laughed.

Finally, Herr Otto turned to Klara. He suddenly looked nervous as he faced her.

"*Mein Klara,*" he began. "These past four months, I have been happier than I have in years. My neighbors are talking about the new, happy man that moved into my apartment."

Klara and Gerdie chuckled.

"There is only one thing that would make me happier." He reached into the little pocket of his vest, then dropped from his stool onto one knee.

Klara's eyes grew wide as her hand flew to her chest. Her eyes glistened with tears, but her mouth held a smile of hope.

"Klara Schmidt… *mein Klara.*" Suddenly, he seemed unable to speak as the tears in his eyes started down his grizzled cheeks. He swallowed hard and tried again.

"*Mein Klara,* the only thing that would make me happier is if you would consent to be my wife." He said it in a rush, then opened his hand to reveal a simple, silver ring.

Klara was crying openly now. She put out a finger and gingerly touched the ring in his palm. "It would be my honor to become your wife."

As if the weight of the world had slipped from his shoulders, Gustav Otto took the tiny ring and slipped it onto Klara's left ring finger. They kissed tenderly and neither noticed the young mother in the rocking chair, tears coursing freely down her cheeks, as well. She kissed the top of her baby's head.

As she watched the happy couple hugging each other, sharing tender kisses, she thought of her Freidrich and her tears flowed freely again. She'd had no gift for him, and that pained her.

Karl stirred in her arms and began rooting around, looking for the milk he could smell so close. She chuckled through her tears and prepared to nurse him.

"You are right, *mein kleiner.* You are his Christmas gift this year."

She looked out the tiny window at the stars. One seemed to be brighter than the others, and she smiled.

"One more gift, *meine geliebte,*" she whispered. Her voice started softly, then grew strong and sweet as she began to sing.

> "*Stille nacht, Heilige Nacht*
> *Alles schläft, einsam wacht*
> *Nur das traute hochheilige Paar,*
> *Holder Knabe im lockigen Haar,*
> *Schlaf in himmlischer Ruh*
> *Schlaf in himmlischer Ruh.*"

On the last verse, Klara and Gustav joined in, drawing closer to her as they offered their gift of song for the soldier they loved who was so far away.

"Would you like to sit up a bit and look at the Christmas tree?" Maggie asked hopefully.

Shelly shook her head no. "I just want to rest for a while," she said, her voice quiet and a bit gravelly.

"Shall I sit with you?" Maggie asked again.

Opening her eyes to look at her friend, Shelly nodded. "I'd like that. Will you sing to me?"

Maggie smiled. That, she could do. She started with "Once in Royal David's City".

The next few hours crawled by with Maggie singing Christmas carols, hymns and popular songs until Shelly finally fell asleep. As Maggie prepared to leave, Shelly's mother tucked the blankets up under her daughter's chin, then turned to hug Maggie.

"Thank you for all you are doing for her," she said, her voice filled with tears.

"I'm not doing much," Maggie protested. "Does she seem to be getting any better?"

Shelly's mother hesitated, then nodded. "I think so. I hope so. But I don't want her working in that plant ever again!"

It was Maggie's turn to nod. "I don't blame you for that," she agreed.

As she let herself out and closed the door behind her, she absentmindedly started humming the last carol she'd sung to Shelly. The hum evolved into words and tears came to her eyes as she sang, her voice husky with emotion.

"Silent night, Holy night,
All is calm, all is bright

'Round yon virgin, mother and child
Holy Infant so tender and mild.
Sleep in heavenly peace,
Sleep in heavenly peace."

That song is for my soldier, sweet Thomas. I hope you are sleeping peacefully tonight, she thought.

As she walked, she wondered if Thomas had received her letter yet, and if so, what must he be thinking about on this Christmas Eve. Maggie smiled as she thought of his reaction when he learned the news.

She looked up at the stars and was struck by the silence of the night. The sky glittering brilliantly with starlight and the moon gave a soft glow to everything. Walking slowly, she wondered if Thomas was looking up at the same stars. On a whim, she made a Christmas wish, for a swift end to the war and a happy, healthy husband for the New Year.

Chapter Twelve

December 25, 1914

"*Frohe Weihnachten*," Friedrich grinned as Fritz just covered his head with his blanket. "Merry Christmas, *kumpel*," he tried again. "Come, let us see if the Brits will keep the truce today."

He shook his head, as it was apparent that Fritz wasn't going to join him. Standing in the doorway of their dugout, he looked up and down the trench. As dawn began brightening the eastern sky, he could see German soldiers beginning to poke their heads up over the side of the trench.

"What do you see?" he called to one nearby.

"Nothing yet," was the answer.

"Have you wished them a Merry Christmas?" he asked.

"Not yet," came the reply.

Laughing, Friedrich stepped up on the firing-step, and called, "Merry Christmas, English!"

After a moment, he heard, "You, too."

A flash of inspiration hit him and he called, "Today, let us bury our dead together."

The Brits agreed, and soon, soldiers on both sides crawled out of their trenches, shovels in hand. For several hours, they worked side by side to dig through the frozen ground to bury the dead that dotted No Man's Land.

When there were no more bodies to bury, they shook hands and began exchanging gifts of cigarettes, plum puddings, sausages, buttons, and hats.

As Friedrich shook hands and passed out chocolate to various British soldiers, one took his hand and didn't let go. He looked into the young man's eyes and couldn't seem to look away.

He pointed to himself. "Friedrich. I'm Friedrich."

The private pointed to his own chest. "Thomas. Do you speak English?"

"A little," Friedrich admitted.

Thomas smiled. "Then, Merry Christmas."

Returning his smile, Friedrich answered, "Merry Christmas to you."

Thomas handed him a plum pudding.

Friedrich grinned. He didn't have anything of such value, so he took the helmet off his head and tried to place it on Thomas's.

Laughing, Thomas took off his cap and placed it on Friedrich's head. Then he put the helmet on his own.

As he did, Friedrich noticed the ring on his finger. Pointing, he asked, "You married?"

Thomas nodded. "You?"

Friedrich nodded. "Nearly six years."

Smiling, Thomas replied, "We got married just before I came here, four months ago."

"Ah, no children then?"

"Not yet. When I get home, we'll start our family. Do you have children?"

"Yes!" Friedrich pulled out the letter and began translating it as best he could.

Thomas listened and understood Friedrich's broken English. He clapped Friedrich on the shoulder. "You have a son? Congratulations!"

Just then, Thomas heard his name called and turned around. A young corporal jogged up to them.

"Are you Private Thomas Bennett?" he asked.

Thomas nodded.

"This was tucked between my letters," the corporal said as he handed him an envelope. "That's you, right?"

Glancing at the return envelope, Thomas's face broke into a

huge grin.

"Sure is! Thanks!" he exclaimed happily.

"From your wife?" Friedrich asked.

Thomas nodded, tearing the envelope open. He glanced through, then stopped and began to read more slowly, not believing his eyes.

Friedrich started to leave, but Thomas put a hand out to stop him, eyes never leaving the paper.

A moment later, Thomas shoved his fist in the air and started dancing around, whooping and hollering.

Friedrich grinned and asked, "Good news?"

"The best," Thomas chortled. "I'm going to be a father, Friedrich! My Maggie is going to have our baby!"

He re-read the letter again, this time aloud so Friedrich could hear.

December 15, 1914

My dearest Thomas,

I pray this letter finds you healthy and safe. I, myself, have not been feeling my best of late. It is nothing to worry about, I just feel a little nauseous from time to time. The doctor says there's no need for concern and I should be feeling better in time… about five months' time.

I am hoping this reaches you for Christmas, because I have the best Christmas present for you. If you haven't guessed already, I am expecting a baby in the spring. Our baby! Can you believe it, darling? We had only one night to spend together as husband and wife, yet, we manage to create a new little life in that one glorious night.

I am so happy I could cry. In fact, I have cried… several times.

Now my prayers include your safe return and that you return home in time to see our baby born. Keep your head down, my love. I need you now more than ever.

Merry Christmas, darling!

With all my love,
Maggie

This time, Friedrich clapped him on the back, handed him a cigar, and said, *"Glückwünsche*! Congratulations!"

"Thank you," Thomas replied, still in shock over the news.

Friedrich looked out over the No Man's Land and smiled. Everywhere he looked, he could see Germans and English talking and exchanging gifts. He saw cameras out as soldiers took pictures with the very men they'd been shooting at two days ago.

Far down the way, barely visible through the mist, he saw Scottish and German soldiers playing football.

"Hey, Thomas," he elbowed his new friend. "Want to play some football?"

Thomas looked up from his letter and grinned. "That's a great idea."

They jogged down to the impromptu game and asked if they could join in. Everyone assented and the match was underway.

From what Friedrich could see, the goals were marked with hats, the ball was made with what looked like a ration tin wrapped in socks, and there was no referee. It seemed to be just an old-fashioned kick-about, and everyone was having fun. The frozen ground made staying on their feet challenging, but everyone played with great enthusiasm.

The highlight of the game, however, was when a gust of wind revealed that the Scots wore no drawers under their kilts. All the Germans hooted and whistled every time they caught an impudent glimpse of a posterior belonging to one of yesterday's enemies.

An hour later, however, the German commander sent an order that the game must stop.

Friedrich and Thomas wandered back to the place they'd first met. Each man felt unwilling to end this unexpected fraternization.

"You worked before the army?" Friedrich asked.

"I delivered groceries in the neighborhood for our grocer, Mr. Martin," Thomas admitted. "I had a bicycle that was the fastest in town. He helped me outfit it with a basket and I was in business. It didn't pay much, but many of the widows made sure I was filled with tea and crumpets before they'd let me go back to the store."

Friedrich laughed pointing to himself. "Barber. Our soldiers… best haircuts in all Germany," he boasted.

Thomas reached up and felt the longer hairs on the back of his head.

"Would you consider cutting my hair before some general decides this truce is over?" he asked.

Grinning, Friedrich nodded.

Reaching into his jacket pocket, he pulled out a pair of scissors.

Thomas laughed. "Aren't you afraid you'll puncture your heart keeping those in there?"

Friedrich raised an eyebrow and reached into the pocket again, this time pulling out a leather pouch. He slid the scissors, point down, into the pouch and then put them back into his pocket.

"Clever bloke!" Thomas exclaimed.

Giving him a little bow of thanks, Friedrich motioned for Thomas to sit on a burned-out log nearby.

The next half hour they spent comparing lives, wives, parents, and siblings. They talked about work, worries, and war. They compared newspaper articles about the war.

Friedrich howled with laughter at a London newspaper article and assured Thomas that France was finished and Russia nearly beaten, too.

Thomas told him that was nonsense, to which Friedrich replied, "You believe your newspapers. I'll believe ours."

Thomas wouldn't let it go so easily, however. "As you can see, we have both been lied to by our press agents. You are not the 'savage barbarians' we've read so much about. We are not so easily beaten as you've read. We are both simple men with homes and families, hopes and fears, principles, and love of country. In other words, we are more alike than we are different. Why are we led to believe otherwise?"

Friedrich had no answer. He sat for a long moment and watched the sun as it began to set. He watched the men on both sides beginning to make their way back to their trenches. Finally, he asked what Thomas had been asking in his heart, "My God, why cannot we have peace and all go home?"

Thomas told him gently, "That you must ask your emperor, my German friend."

Friedrich looked at him searchingly. "Perhaps, *mein kumpel,* but also, we must ask our hearts."

He paused, then continued. "Today we have peace. Tomorrow you fight for your country and I fight for mine. Good luck."

Each man raised his head as two shots were fired into the air from the British parapet, then two more from the German side. The truce was officially over. They shook hands and parted company, each trudging back to the now-familiar trenches.

As he entered the German trench, Friedrich was met by a corporal who'd chosen not to participate in the illicit truce. Friedrich saluted the young man, who saluted back, then said, "You should be ashamed of yourself, Private. Such a thing should not happen in wartime. Have you no German sense of honor?"

Friedrich wasn't sure how to respond, so he said nothing. The young corporal huffed at Friedrich's silence, then moved on.

After he left, Friedrich couldn't help but wonder what would happen if the spirit shown during this Christmas truce were to be caught up by the nations of the world. He knew that disputes always arise, but what if the leaders were to offer well wishes in place of warnings? Songs in place of slurs? Presents in place of reprisals? Would not all war end at once?

As he sat heavily on his cot, he looked at the cap that Thomas had given him, marveling as he stuck a finger through the bullet hole he found in it. He whispered to himself, "All nations say they want peace. Yet on this Christmas night, I wonder if we want it quite enough."

Across No Man's Land, Thomas was writing a letter to Maggie. He wrote,

Today I have discovered war's most amazing paradox. I have been ordered to shoot the Germans on sight. Yet for the past twenty-four hours, I have seen enemies in war celebrating together as friends the birth of the Prince of Peace. In forty-eight hours' time, I have seen blood and peace, enmity and fraternity, all on the same soil. I believe that if left to ourselves, there would not be another shot fired. It makes no sense, Maggie. War makes no sense.

Frau Schmidt peeked through the curtain. Seeing that Gerdie was awake, she came in and started straightening the blankets. "*Frohe Weihnachten, mein liebling*," she said cheerfully.

"Merry Christmas to you, too. I thought you'd be snuggling with your fiancé this morning," she teased.

Klara blushed a little and waved off the teasing comment. "Plenty of time for that once we're married."

"Have you talked about a date, yet?"

"No. We want to see that you are well on your feet first. You have to be well enough to stand with me, you know," she said almost shyly.

"Me? You want me to stand with you?" Gerdie's face showed her surprise.

"Of course," Klara nodded. "You are like a daughter to me and since my boy can't be there…" Her voice trailed off.

"I'd be honored to stand with you," Gerdie said sincerely.

Klara beamed. "Oh, good! If we are lucky, maybe Friedrich will be home and can stand with Gustav."

"That would be wonderful." Gerdie's voice was wistful. She started to take a deep breath, but the pain in her side caused her to whimper instead.

"What's wrong?" Klara was suddenly concerned. "You are in pain?"

"It's nothing," Gerdie tried to reassure her. "A little pain in my side that catches me off-guard sometimes."

"How long has that been there?"

Gerdie shrugged. "Not long. It will pass."

"May I look?" Klara asked. "Perhaps you bruised it when you fell yesterday."

Realizing she couldn't hide the truth anymore, Gerdie nodded.

Klara moved the blankets and lifted the new mother's gown. Gently, she probed Gerdie's side until Gerdie flinched and gasped.

Returning the gown and blankets to their original positions, Klara was suddenly all business.

"There is a bruise there," she said matter-of-factly. "You most likely bruised a rib when you hit the cradle. We'll keep you in bed a few days, and if it doesn't feel better, we should consider sending for the doctor."

Gerdie shook her head. "I can't afford a doctor. I'll be fine."

"We'll see," Klara patted her shoulder. "Now, would you like some breakfast?"

"Maybe a little," Gerdie agreed with a small smile.

"*Gut*. I'll bring you a tray in a few minutes."

As she left the sleeping area, Klara's pasted-on smile faded and tears filled her eyes. Gustav, who was sitting at the table drinking his coffee, looked up. Instantly, he crossed the small space to fold her into his arms, letting her bury her face in his chest so her sobs wouldn't be heard.

"There, there, *mein Klara*," he soothed softly. "What is it?"

After a few moments, Klara took a shaky breath and tried to calm herself. When she could talk again, she motioned for him to follow her outside.

Adjusting her shawl around her, she didn't speak for a moment. When she did, her voice was low and filled with emotion.

"Remember when Gerdie fell yesterday?"

"Yes," he nodded.

"I'm afraid she injured something inside. She is dizzy when she stands, her belly is more tender than I think it should be, especially her right side. She's started running a little fever, but none of these things are necessarily serious by themselves. It's the combination that worries me."

"We should go for the doctor, then," Gustav started to move toward the street, but Klara put her hand on his arm to stop him.

"It won't do any good. We can't afford to pay the doctor and if he recommends surgery, we can't pay for that, either."

"I'll find a way," Gustav insisted. "We have to help her."

Klara sighed. "At this point, the best we can do is keep her comfortable and pray her body heals itself. I know a poultice recipe that may help with the pain. I'll try that and see what happens. We need to keep her quiet, though. She should stay in bed for the next few days and not move around any more than is necessary."

Nodding, Gustav frowned. "That won't be easy. She has a little one to care for."

"I know. We'll take over as much of that as we can, so she can rest. Do you recall how to change a diaper?"

Gustav's face showed his horror at the very idea.

Klara laughed. "I thought not. Do not worry, *mein Gustav*. I will take care of the diapers. You just stand ready to help Gerdie if she needs to turn or get up for any reason."

The relief on the old man's face was nearly as funny as his horror had been the moment before. "I can do that."

"Merry Christmas, Mama," Katie was fairly bouncing with excitement. It didn't seem to faze her that she'd been up so late the night before.

"Merry Christmas, Katie," her mother answered, kissing her on top of her head.

"Can we open the rest of the presents now?"

Mrs. Gilley laughed. "You have to wait for Maggie. She'll be disappointed if you start without her."

"Well, where is she, anyway?" The five-year-old nearly stomped her foot with impatience.

"She went to deliver some Christmas treats to the neighbors for me."

"How long will she be gone?" Katie pouted.

"How long will who be gone?" Maggie asked as she closed the front door behind her.

"You!" Katie squealed. "Merry Christmas, Maggie!"

Hugging her tightly, Maggie grinned. "Merry Christmas to you, too, little sister."

"Can we open the presents now?" Katie asked her mother.

Laughing, Mrs. Gilley agreed. "I'm sure you'd survive if I made you eat breakfast first, but I wouldn't enjoy my meal with you pouting all through it."

"Hurray!" Katie bounded over to the tiny tree and began picking up the few gifts that adorned the base of it.

"This one's for you, Mama," she announced, "and this one's for Maggie."

"Is this from you, Katie?" Maggie asked.

"Yes, I made it myself." The little girl's voice was proud.

Opening the small gift, Maggie gasped a little at the button necklace. It was lopsided and the buttons were too big, but obviously made with such love that it touched Maggie's heart deeply. Tears filled her eyes as she reached out for her little sister.

"Why are you crying, Maggie? It wasn't supposed to make you cry!"

"These are happy, grateful tears," Maggie assured her as she tied the necklace around her neck. "I'm grateful for the present and grateful that you're my sister."

They hugged each other tightly for a moment before turning to their mother.

"Your turn, Mama," Maggie urged.

Mrs. Gilley slowly untied the string around her gift, peering at Katie all the while. Each tiny tug of the string caused Katie to squirm and wiggle.

"Oh, please do hurry, Mama," she finally cried. "I can't wait for you to see!"

Laughing, Mrs. Gilley gave a final hard tug and the string fell away. She tore at the paper until it fell away revealing another button necklace. Then she stopped and placed her hand to her mouth.

"What's wrong, Mama? Don't you like it?"

Mrs. Gilley smiled through her tears. "I love it, Katie! It's just what I wanted."

Katie threw her arms around her mother and squeezed with all her might. "I knew you'd like it!"

"Now, poppet," Mrs. Gilley grinned. "Your turn."

Pulling a larger box from the back of the tree, she handed it to her daughter.

Katie sat on the floor and tugged at the string, finally pulling it off. As she opened the box, she gasped.

"Oh, Mama! It's the coat I wanted from Mr. Giles' store! Thank you, thank you!" She jumped up and hugged her with the precious coat in between them.

Mrs. Gilley laughed. "Try it on now. Let's see how you look."

Katie donned the knee-length, double-breasted brown wool coat. With her tongue sticking out in great concentration, she carefully buttoned the large buttons on the right. Upon completion of this monumental task, she looked up, grinned, and twirled in front of them. "It's perfect!" she exclaimed.

Pursing her lips, Mrs. Gilley considered it for a moment. "I don't know. Maybe the color isn't right?"

"Oh no, Mama! It's just right!"

"I really think the collar is too big," her mother teased again. "What do you think, Maggie?"

"You're right. Definitely too big. And the buttons are too small," Maggie joined in the fun.

Katie stopped in front of them and this time she really stomped her foot. "They are not! This coat is perfect and I'm going to wear it all the time."

"What?" Her mother looked shocked. "Even in bed?"

"Even in the bath?" Maggie looked equally horrified.

Laughing, Katie relaxed. "Well, maybe not in bed or in the bath. But every time I go outside I'll wear it!"

"Now that's a splendid idea," Mrs. Gilley nodded her approval. "Why don't we have some breakfast and then go see if we can scrape up enough snow for a little Christmas snowman?"

"Yippee!" Katie squealed as she dashed towards the kitchen.

As Maggie stood, she put her arm around her mother.

"Thank you for helping me buy the coat for her," Mrs. Gilley said.

"I was happy to contribute," Maggie assured her. "She needed a new coat, so why not give her the one she wanted?"

She fingered the little locket at her throat. "Thank you for the locket, Mama. I know you've cherished it since your grandmother gave it to you. It means so much that you'd trust me with it."

Mrs. Gilley smiled. "She'd be proud to see you wearing it. And proud of the resourceful woman you've become."

"Well, I have a little something for you, as well." Maggie reached inside her skirt pocket and pulled out an envelope.

"What's this?"

"Just open it," Maggie laughed.

Mrs. Gilley carefully opened the envelope and her eyes grew wide as she saw the contents.

"Where did you get so much money?" she asked.

"I've been saving it."

"But you need it for you and the baby!" her mother protested.

"I have another little nest-egg for the baby. This is for you to buy new shoes, or a new hat, or a new dress. Whatever you want, but it has to be for you."

"Oh, Maggie," Mrs. Gilley breathed. "I don't think I could spend so much on just myself."

"Try, Mama," Maggie chuckled. "You just try."

"Aren't you two coming? I'm hungry and I want to build a snowman," Katie complained from the kitchen table.

The two women laughed and joined her for a simple Christmas breakfast.

When they'd finished eating, they put on their coats, hats, and mittens, wrapping scarves around their necks. Opening the front door, they gasped in unison. There was a light dusting of snow on the ground. Just enough to lend an ethereal quality to the Nash Mills streets.

"It's beautiful," Mrs. Gilley sighed.

Katie didn't wait long to admire the scene, though. She dashed out and started gathering the snow. When it wouldn't stick together, she threw it down in disgust.

"This isn't snowman snow," she grumbled. "It won't stick."

Maggie laughed and reached down for a handful. "Maybe not, but we can still have a snow fight."

She threw the handful of snow at her sister whose frown turned upside down in a heartbeat. She gathered her own handful of snow and threw it back at Maggie.

After a few minutes, they stopped, looked at each other, and nodded.

Mrs. Gilley, who'd been enjoying the spectacle, realized something was up. "Oh no," she protested. "Don't get me..."

Just then, both girls threw snow at her. It covered her hair, coat, and face. "All right, then," she said, bending down. "If that's the game, then I'm in!"

The next half hour they laughed and ran down the street, throwing handfuls of snow at each other. Finally, they slowed down and started walking back. They found an untouched patch of snow in a neighbor's tiny yard.

"Do you think Mr. Grimes would mind if I made a snow angel?" Katie asked.

"That all depends," a gruff voice answered from the doorway.

"Depends on what?" Katie asked.

"Depends on whether you're willing to sing for the privilege."

"Sing?"

"Sing. I haven't heard a single carol today and I'd like to hear one or two, if you don't mind," the old gentleman answered.

Katie looked at her mother and sister. "Will you sing with me?"

Both women nodded and they began to serenade their neighbor and friend, starting with "The First Noel". After several carols, Maggie had an idea.

"Why don't we end with "Angels We Have Heard on High", while Katie makes you a Christmas snow angel, Mr. Grimes?"

He nodded and Maggie began to sing as her sister laid carefully on the pristine snow. Mrs. Gilley joined in while Katie slowly moved her arms over her head, then down to her sides. Her legs spread out as far as she could spread them, then she pulled them back in. Over and over, she repeated the movements until the carol ended.

Maggie helped her up and Mr. Giles came down to admire her work.

"It's beautiful," he nodded. "A perfect decoration for this Christmas day. Merry Christmas to you all."

With that, he turned and hobbled back into his house, closing the door behind him.

"That was fun," Katie announced. "Maybe there are other neighbors who'd like to hear Christmas songs?"

"I think you're on to something," Maggie smiled, and her mother nodded.

The rest of the morning, they walked up and down the street, caroling at every door while Katie made Christmas angels on every patch of unspoiled snow she could find. Most neighbors opened their doors and enjoyed their music. Some joined in and a few even joined their growing choir. By the time the sun was high enough to start melting the snow, there were nearly a dozen friends and neighbors with them.

"You are all invited to our place for tea and Christmas cake," Mrs. Gilley announced.

Laughing and chatting together, the group climbed the steps to their apartment. While Mrs. Gilley went to put the tea on to brew, her guests made themselves comfortable, enjoying the rare opportunity to visit.

The afternoon passed quickly, and before anyone realized, the sun set and the holiday was over. One by one, their guests left and the apartment was once again quiet, with only the three of them sitting by the Christmas tree. It seemed a little barren after all the hubbub of the impromptu celebration, but as they gazed at the candles and the few handmade ornaments, they felt grateful for such a wonderful Christmas day.

"Tell us about Daddy? About your first Christmas together," Maggie asked.

"Oh my, that was a few days ago, wasn't it?" Mrs. Gilley chuckled. "I remember we didn't have much money, so we decided to make each other gifts. Like Katiedid this year.

"Our wedding was in November, so Christmas wasn't far off. Your daddy was apprenticed at the cobbler's near where we lived."

Katie's brow furrowed. "What's a 'prentis?"

"An apprentice is someone who's learning a trade that they can do for money when they become skilled at it. Your daddy was learning to make and repair shoes."

"Everybody needs shoes," Katie observed.

"Yes, they do. That's why he thought it would be a good trade to learn. But they don't pay apprentices very much, so we didn't have much to live on. I was working as a seamstress so I had a little, but it wasn't enough to pay the bills and afford Christmas gifts, too."

"So, you were creative?" Katie grinned.

"Yes, we were," her mother nodded. "For my gift to him, I knitted a little baby sweater out of an old pair of socks. I had worn a hole in the toe, so rather than darn them again, I unraveled them, washed the yarn, and knitted the sweater."

"A baby sweater? Why would he want a baby sweater?"

"Because we were going to have a baby," Mrs. Gilley grinned. "That was my way of telling him he was going to be a daddy."

Katie's eyes grew wide. "You were going to have Maggie, right?"

"That's right, and your daddy didn't know yet."

"What did he give you?"

"He was creative, too. He asked if he could have the scraps of leather from the shoes he made. With that, he stitched me a colorful pair of boots that I wore for many years. Even when we could afford new boots, I still wore the ones he made for me."

"Because he made them, right?"

"Exactly. They meant more than any store-bought boots he could give me."

"What about your first Christmas after Maggie was born? What did you give each other then?" Katie was stalling, but her mother didn't mind.

Story after story fell softly from Mrs. Gilley's lips with Maggie hanging on every word. She'd heard them all before, but they never failed to bring joy and comfort. She was glad Katie wanted to hear them, too.

That is, until unexpectedly, a quiet little snore interrupted the tale-telling. They both laughed softly as they looked at Katie, lying under the Christmas tree, fast asleep.

"We'd better put our stories, and your sister, to bed," Mrs. Gilley chuckled.

"Thank you, Mama, for sharing those stories with me again. Merry Christmas."

"Merry Christmas, Maggie, and may the years bring you many happy stories to share with your little one.

Chapter Thirteen

December 26, 1914

Friedrich woke to the sound of gunfire. He and Fritz were due to be rotated to the rear tomorrow, but today, it looked like they would have to fight. He groaned.

"You okay, *kumpel?*" Fritz asked.

Nodding, then shaking his head, Friedrich groaned again. "I'm fine physically, but I don't think I can go back to this *verdammt* war again."

"It does seem strange to think about shooting those men when yesterday we were playing football with them," Fritz agreed. "But we're soldiers and we follow orders. So, if we're ordered to shoot, we shoot."

Friedrich looked at him and sighed. "So it would seem. I'm just not sure I can do it."

"Well, you'd better figure it out soon," Fritz said. "It's time to roll out for stand-to. If no one fires, you should be safe from having to make that choice today. If they do…"

He left the implication hanging in the air.

Friedrich groaned again, but sat up and put his boots on.

"It seems we are not fighting the same war as our superiors anymore," he commented.

"I think you're right," Fritz agreed. "For us the past twenty-four hours have been a light shining in the darkest depths of war. But I'm afraid those higher up see the truce more as a tale of subversion."

"Perhaps," Friedrich answered.

As they stood along the firing-step, Friedrich prayed the Brits wouldn't fire. He truly did not know how he would respond. They stood for an hour and no sound was heard on either side.

Friedrich breathed a sigh of relief when the signal came to stand down. He smiled at Fritz and they stepped down, prepared to enjoy breakfast in peace.

They relaxed too soon, however, as a British shell exploded a few meters to their left. The men flattened themselves against the wall of the trench and took a moment to gather their wits about them.

The second shell exploded off to their right. Friedrich turned to face the enemy, his gun loaded. But as he rose to fire, he caught a glimpse of a German helmet just showing above the British trench. The memories from the past twenty-four hours flooded his mind, especially the time he'd spent with Thomas. Tears filled his eyes and he found he could not fire at these good, decent men who were just following orders.

The young corporal who'd disapproved of the truce came down the line and noticed Friedrich and several others were not firing.

"The order is to fire, men!" he shouted. "Fire!"

Knowing that disobeying a direct order could lead to court-martial and possibly the firing squad, Friedrich stood, turned, and raised his rifle, aiming it at the men labeled "enemy".

"I said FIRE!" the corporal shouted again.

Friedrich fired, but deliberately raised his gun a fraction of an inch at the last second, knowing the ball would fly high over the heads of the Tommies.

"Tommies." That word brought all the memories back once again. His new friend, Thomas, was over there somewhere. In fact, Friedrich was wearing Thomas's cap. How could he fire on someone he'd just made friends with?

"FIRE!" came the order again.

Again, Friedrich fired, but aimed just a little to the right. He hoped no one would notice his deliberate attempt to save English lives.

Unfortunately, someone did.

"Private, let me see your weapon." It was the same trigger-happy corporal. He took Friedrich's rifle, peered through the sight, then raised it over the edge of the trench. He pulled the trigger, and watched as a British soldier fell.

"Your rifle seems to be working well," the corporal commented. "So, either you need more training on aiming, or you are deliberately missing your target, Private. Which do you suppose is the case?"

For a split second, Friedrich entertained the notion of showing this upstart corporal just how good his aim really was... by aiming at him. But, the following thought was of Gerdie and his son waiting at home.

"I suppose I need more training, sir," he answered.

"Then more training you shall have," the corporal said. "Starting now."

To Friedrich's dismay, the corporal stood by his side on the firing-step and showed him how to aim properly. Friedrich tried to aim just to the side, or above, or below the British soldier the corporal wanted him to shoot. But each time, the corporal corrected his aim.

Finally, the corporal ordered him to fire and Friedrich pulled the trigger. The man in the opposite trench fell and Friedrich immediately turned and retched... all over the young corporal's shoes.

"*Dummkopf!*" he shouted. "You did that deliberately!"

Friedrich tried to apologize, but felt the bile rise in his throat again. He turned just far enough to avoid the corporal's shoes this time.

Fritz, who had witnessed the entire episode, dared to speak up at that moment. "I'm sorry, sir, but I'm afraid my friend has eaten some of the Tommy's food and it has made him ill."

The corporal looked at Fritz, then at Friedrich. He scowled. "Serves him right. Get him back to the dugout. We'll rotate him out this afternoon so he can get medical help."

With that, Corporal Adolph Hitler stomped away.

Fritz watched him go, then reached for Friedrich's arm. "Come on, *kumpel*," he said. "Let's get you somewhere more comfortable."

Once he was settled on the blankets, Friedrich tried to thank his friend, but Fritz cut him off.

"While I applaud your ethics, your timing stinks. You're going to

123

get yourself court-martialed if you're not careful," he cautioned. "You'd better get yourself together before we're rotated back to the front line."

Friedrich nodded and watched his friend go back to the shooting. He was right, of course, but Friedrich still didn't know how he could bring himself to fire willingly on those good men in the opposing trench.

He thought about Corporal Hitler and sighed deeply. It was that kind of thinking that started wars and kept them going. *Sadly, that little corporal with the silly mustache is going to cause a lot of trouble someday*, he thought. *Maybe I should have shot him, after all.*

With that thought, he shook his head and tried somewhat successfully to turn his mind to something more pleasant… his Gerdie and their son.

"I'm worried about her," Herr Otto frowned. "She's not eating enough and she seems so tired all the time."

Frau Schmidt nodded her agreement. "I thought at first it was just the normal recovery from having a baby. Then when she fell Christmas Eve, I am certain she injured something inside. She's not regaining her strength as fast as I'd like."

"Perhaps we should fetch a doctor?" Herr Otto offered.

"She would never agree to it. Doctors cost money, and we both know she has none."

Herr Otto nodded sadly, "And we have none to give her."

With a heavy sigh, Frau Schmidt glanced at the curtain dividing the sleeping area from the living area. "Could you make some of that rich beef broth you made last week? Perhaps make it extra strong this time. That may help improve her constitution."

"Of course," Herr Otto nodded. "I'll stop at the butcher for a soup bone with a bit of meat on it."

"*Gut*," Frau Schmidt smiled. "You're a good man, Herr Otto."

He smiled shyly. "Surely you can call me Gustav now that we are to be married."

Cocking her head, Frau Schmidt looked at him. "I fell in love with you as Herr Otto. It seems strange to think of you as Gustav now."

Leaning down to take her hand, he smiled softly. "In my mind, you have become *mein Klara*. I cannot imagine you as anything else."

Frau Schmidt smiled. "That sounds nice. *Mein Klara. Mein Gustav."* She pursed her lips. "I think I could get used to that."

Gustav kissed the back of her hand, then stepped away. "I hope so," he said. "Have a good night, and I'll bring some broth with me when I come in the morning."

"*Gut,*" Klara smiled, then pushed back the curtain to check on Gerdie as he closed the door behind him.

Gerdie lay with her eyes closed, so Klara tiptoed to the cradle to peek at Karl. He stirred a little as she adjusted the blanket, but settled back to sleep almost immediately.

"How is he?" Gerdie whispered from the bed.

"He's sleeping soundly," Klara told her. "How are you feeling?"

"As sleepy as he is," she admitted. "Why am I so tired, Frau Schmidt? I don't think I should be this tired."

"Having a baby is hard work," Frau Schmidt hedged. "Your body needs time to recover."

"But I just don't feel quite right," Gerdie frowned. "I'm too tired. I can't even hold my baby for long without fear of dropping him when I fall asleep unexpectedly. And my side still hurts."

"Shall we call for the doctor, then?"

Gerdie thought for a moment, then shook her head. "No. There is no money. Besides, all new mothers are tired. You said so, yourself."

"That I did. I'm sure you'll recover in time and be just fine." Klara was afraid this might be a lie, but didn't want the new mother to worry.

Gerdie yawned. "If you're certain," she said, her eyes drooping. "I'll try not to worry then."

With that, she fell asleep again and Klara Schmidt tucked the blanket around her. Her own worry lines were deepening these days.

"Bad news, Tommy-boy," Budgy said as he entered the dugout. "Word just came down that anyone caught disobeying orders to fire will be court-martialed."

Thomas leaned his head against the wall of the dugout. "I was afraid of that."

"Me, too," his friend nodded. "I really started to like those krauts. They're not bad fellows after all."

"No, they're not. What are we going to do, Budgy?" he asked.

"I don't know yet," Budgy admitted. "But we have guard duty tonight."

Thomas sighed. He truly didn't want to shoot the Germans any more. His entire perspective of war had changed. He hadn't liked it before, and that was when the "enemy" was a faceless, nameless "barbarian" who deserved to be shot for invading their ally's country.

Now, they were men who had names and faces and families. Men who were simply following orders.

"Hey, Budgy," he called as they made their way to the parapet. "I have an idea."

"What's that?"

"Let's put all the generals into a boxing ring and let them use fisticuffs to resolve it. Winner gets the country."

Budgy laughed. "That's not a bad idea, Tommy-boy. Why don't you suggest that at the next war-planning meeting?"

Thomas punched his friend in the arm. "Very funny."

The night was quiet except for a few shots fired far down the line. Thomas felt grateful that his ethics weren't being put to the test tonight. He spent the evening scanning No Man's Land and thinking about Maggie and the baby she held in her womb. Each time he thought of her, he smiled. He was going to be a father!

Just as dawn was about to break, Budgy nudged him and pointed. "What's that?"

Thomas peered into the blue-gray shadows and could just make out the figure of a man crawling under the German barbed wire towards the British trenches.

"What's he doing?" Thomas whispered.

"I don't know, but it doesn't look good," Budgy whispered back.

Just then, Captain Bloem poked his head above the edge of the parapet. "How goes it, men?" he asked.

"Sh," both Budgy and Thomas hissed in unison.

Raising an eyebrow, the captain continued up the ladder and climbed into the watchtower.

"What do you see?" he whispered.

Budgy pointed. By this time, the German soldier was halfway across No Man's Land. They still had no idea what his intentions were.

"Shoot him!" hissed the captain.

"But, sir…" Thomas began.

"He's nearly to our trenches! Shoot him!"

Thomas raised his rifle and put the German into his sights. But he couldn't pull the trigger. All he could think about was Friedrich and the other soldiers he'd met Christmas Day. He couldn't bring himself to take a life after getting to know them, if only for a few hours.

Captain Bloem looked at Thomas and glared. "Soldier, if you don't fire, I will have no choice but to put you in front of a court-martial."

Thomas stared back at him and made his choice. He lowered his rifle and stood at attention. "Then you must court-martial me, sir. For I will not fire."

The look on the captain's face spoke volumes. It was dark and angry and promised dire consequences for Thomas's decision.

He turned to Budgy. "Then you must fire, Private."

Budgy looked from the captain to Thomas to the man who was nearly across No Man's Land, then back at the captain again.

"No, sir," he said firmly. "I stand with Private Bennett."

Swearing, the captain grabbed Thomas's rifle, aimed, and fired. The German jerked once, then lay still. Thomas frowned and looked at the toes of his boots.

Captain Bloem then turned on Thomas and Budgy. "You two

will face a court-martial at the first opportunity. Meanwhile, you will be held in the guard room."

He leaned over the railing and yelled at a soldier below. "Find the Battle Police and have them report, on the double."

"Yes, sir," came a muffled response.

As the sun peeked over the horizon and illuminated No Man's Land with streaks of yellow and orange. Thomas couldn't help but look out at the dead soldier lying so close to their lines. As the light grew, his mouth dropped open and he nudged Budgy, nodding towards the sight.

Budgy looked and gasped.

"What was that?" the captain whirled and glared at Budgy. "Do you have something to say?"

"No, sir," Budgy shook his head.

Thomas couldn't take any more, however, and spoke up. "I do, sir."

"Well, what is it?" the captain snapped.

"If you'll look at the German, sir," Thomas pointed.

"What about him?"

"He was only trying to retrieve his football, sir," Thomas said softly.

"What?" The captain's voice was unreadable. "What? A football?"

He looked and stood still for several long seconds. Then he straightened his back and turned to face them.

"Nonetheless, you two disobeyed a direct order to fire. That man might have been sent to spy on our trenches, see where our guns are placed. You have no proof he was after the ball." His voice grew stronger and louder with each sentence. "I'll see to it that neither of you ever see the light of freedom again!"

At that moment, the Battle Police arrived and the captain pointed at Thomas and Budgy. "Hold them for court-martial," he ordered.

As the guards led Thomas and Budgy away, Thomas noticed that few soldiers would meet their gaze. It was heartbreaking that he and his friend would be an example of what happens when good men refused to obey orders from heartless brass hats.

"I wonder how Thomas spent his day," Maggie mused the next morning as she tidied the kitchen after breakfast. "I hope he had some peace yesterday, even if he couldn't be here to celebrate with us."

Mrs. Gilley smiled. "Somehow, I think he found a way to celebrate. He isn't the type to let a holiday pass without enjoying it."

Maggie sighed. "If the Germans allowed that," she muttered.

Looking thoughtful, her mother faced her. "What are you most afraid of, Maggie?"

Startled by the question, she looked up. "What? Why do you ask that, Mama?"

"I have found in my life, that when I begin worrying, I only waste time and make myself unhappy. So, I've devised a method for eliminating worry from my life."

"What's that?" Maggie was truly curious now. How could anyone learn to eliminate worry from their lives?

"When I recognize the seeds of worry starting, I ask myself what I'm most afraid will happen. I think hard about it. Once I have identified my greatest fear, I ask myself what I would do if it were actually to happen. I really work to put a plan in my mind. Then I go on to the next fear and do the same thing. Once I have a plan in mind for each fear, each worry, I find I don't have a reason to worry any longer."

"Oh, Mama. Does that really work?"

"It does for me," Mrs. Gilley nodded. "Come sit with me and tell me what you are most afraid of, Maggie."

Joining her mother at the table, Maggie thought hard. "I guess I'm most afraid that Thomas will be killed and I'll never see him again."

Mrs. Gilley patted her hand. "I can understand that fear. What would you do if you received that letter saying he'd been killed?"

Tears filled Maggie's eyes as she thought about that. "I'd cry, probably for days or weeks. I just don't know how I could go on living."

"Those are intense feelings," her mother agreed. "But what about the child growing inside you? Doesn't it deserve a mother, even if it can't have a father?"

Putting her hand protectively on her slightly swollen belly, Maggie looked down, then answered softly. "Yes. Yes, it does."

"So, then, what will you do?" Mrs. Gilley was persistent.

Maggie thought, then a determined look graced her face. "I will continue to work and save until the baby is born. Then I will raise our child the way I know Thomas would want me to, with love and respect and lots of laughter."

"Good. Now what's your next fear?"

For the next hour, they discussed potential worries and what they might do about them.

"Now, daughter mine, how do you feel?"

Examining her emotions, Maggie was surprised to find she was no longer worried. She had plans in mind and she could face anything that happened.

Standing, Maggie hugged her mother. "Thank you, Mama. I needed your reassurance. I miss him so, and when I miss him too much, I can't seem to stop my mind from worrying. But now, I have a plan for that, as well. That's the best gift you could have given me." She laughed and continued, "And Christmas is already over!"

Chapter Fourteen

January 12, 1915

Friedrich held the knife in one hand and a potato in the other. He'd received a reprimand upon reporting at the rear. Apparently, Corporal Hitler had filed a complaint against him for "showing disrespect to an officer".

He stifled a smile. Although it hadn't been planned, Friedrich found it quite appropriate and more than a little amusing that he'd vomited all over the little Corporal's shoes. The captain had issued a formal reprimand and assigned him to *küche pflicht* for the next month. He didn't mind kitchen duty. Truthfully, he was getting rather good at it.

Hefting the potato and smiling, he began peeling furiously. Peeling potatoes, he could do. Shooting good English soldiers, maybe not. Ah well, he had a month before they'd rotate him up and the chances of having to fight so far to the rear were slim.

From what he'd heard, the English were suffering for supplies and this was hampering their war effort. He hadn't heard of any German advances, either, so the rear trenches were quiet.

Friedrich finished with the potatoes and put them in a large pot to boil. He looked at Sergeant Haas who was supervising him. That was the harder challenge of this disciplinary action. Sergeant Haas and he hadn't exactly seen eye to eye over the past few months. The sergeant nodded towards the mess tent and Friedrich carried the pot of potatoes inside.

A bit later, standing behind the row of nearly inedible food, he served spoonful after spoonful of something that looked like a cross between sloppy mortar and huge bird droppings. He knew the potatoes were for the noon meal, but they looked much more appetizing than this. Still, this was his task, and he was grateful. There were worse tasks to which he could be assigned.

When the breakfast rush was over and most of the soldiers had left for their assigned duties, Friedrich took a bucket and rag and began wiping down the tables. As he worked, he overheard a conversation that disturbed him. Two privates had apparently been recently rotated to the rear and were discussing the last battle.

The first private reported, "…it wasn't even noon yet and we were sent into a regular storm of bullets by the major. These red tabs send their men forward in a most ridiculous way. They themselves remain far behind the lines, safely under cover. It's scandalous. Enormous losses on our side are partly from the fire of our own people, for our leaders neither know where the enemy lies, nor where our own troops are, so we are often fired on by our own men. It is a marvel to me that we have got so far as we have."

The second private nodded his agreement. "When our Captain fell, there was no one to give the orders. So, we remained the rest of our day under cover. The next day, another attack was ordered. It wasn't successful either. It cost us many lives and at least fifty of our men are now prisoners."

Private One shook his head, "It is simply ridiculous, this leadership. If only I had known it before. My opinion of the German officers has changed! The officers have no idea what goes on at the front trenches. They stay safely behind where it is safe, while in the front trenches, we are either searching for things to do, or are dodging shells and shrapnel without ceasing. It's too much to bear."

"What astonishes me," Private Two commented, "Is how quickly I've become accustomed to it all. The first day I went into the fight with some nervousness, but determined to do my duty. Yesterday, as we advanced, when my comrades right and left fell dead and wounded, I felt quite indifferent. That seems rather horrible to me, to have no feeling about it at all."

"I see that everywhere I turn," Private One nodded. "In fact, the only emotional response these days seems to be when the Kaiser sent a message of congratulations to our Commander-in-Chief. It caused the liveliest satisfaction amongst our ranks. Are you going to the cockroach races this afternoon? It should be great fun."

"I wouldn't miss it. I've put money on Private Newman's roach."

As the two soldiers left the tent, Friedrich closed his eyes and said a quick prayer. "God, don't let me become so numb that I forget what's important. Please bring me home safely and soon to my Gerdie and my son."

He finished the tables, but wasn't focused on his task. His mind was with his sweet wife in Düsseldorf.

Oh, Gerdie, how I long to see you, to clasp you in my arms… and I long with all my heart to see my son. How I love him already. What hopes I have for him! What a strong, kind boy he will be.

"Please, Gerdie," Frau Schmidt begged. "You must eat something to regain your strength. Just a few sips of broth, *bitte*."

Gerdie tried to open her mouth obediently, but after one swallow, she frowned and shook her head.

"Doesn't it taste good to you?" Frau Schmidt asked.

Shaking her head a little, Gerdie tried to answer. "Tastes fine. Too tired. Later," she whispered, then turned her head and fell asleep.

With a deep sigh, Klara stood and looked down at her. She was so gaunt, so pale. It was heartbreaking to see her like this and know there was nothing she could do.

A soft sound came from the cradle and she leaned over to soothe little Karl.

"Hush, hush, *mein kleiner*," she cooed. "*Deine mutter* is sleeping now. Sh… sh…"

The baby relaxed at the sound of her voice. With one last look at the still sleeping Gerdie, she moved through the curtain into the living area and sat at the kitchen table, her head in her hands.

After a few minutes, the door opened and Herr Otto came in. He took one look at her, crossed the room in three steps, and knelt beside her, taking her in his arms.

"What's wrong, *mein Klara?*" he asked, his voice filled with concern.

Klara turned and put her arms around his neck, laid her head on his shoulder, and wept bitter tears.

"She's dying, *mein Gustav*," she cried, "and I can't make her live."

Holding her close, Gustav didn't say a word. He just stroked her hair and patted her back, letting her cry it out.

After there were no more tears, Klara sat back and blew her nose. She looked forlornly at the new love in her life. "What are we going to do?"

"We are going to continue trying to keep her alive," Gustav said pragmatically.

"I mean, what if she dies? What will we do then?" Klara insisted.

Gustav sat back on his heels, looked at the curtain dividing the room, then looked back at Klara.

"We will care for the baby until Freidrich returns," he said. "That is what friends do for each other. They care for each other, and each other's families."

"But, we are old and tired," Klara pointed out. "Can we really care for a tiny little one?"

Gustav smiled. "With each other to lean on, we can do anything that is required, *mein liebling.*"

Klara couldn't help but return his smile, although her mind was still filled with doubts about their abilities. "We will do our best, *mein Gustav*," she promised.

Thomas and Budgy were led into the small room, both in shackles. Thomas wasn't sure why they were shackled. Neither he nor Budgy were violent, and neither planned to try and run away. Still, here they were, shackled, standing in front of three officers who sat behind a long table. Beside them stood their Prisoner's Friend, a corporal who'd been assigned to defend them. However, after speaking with him for a few minutes before the General Field Court-Martial began, Thomas was less than optimistic. He was assigned their case just twenty minutes before and didn't seem to have a clue what he was going to do.

After shuffling papers for a few minutes, the colonel looked up, banged his gavel, and announced, "This court-martial is now in session. Private Thomas Bennett and Private George Ellis, you are charged with Insubordination, Disobeying a Direct Order from a Commanding Officer, and Cowardice in the Line of Duty. How do you plead?"

Their court appointed "friend" stepped forward and replied for them, "They plead guilty, sir."

"What?" Thomas was shocked. "No, sir, we plead innocent."

The colonel pounded his gavel on the table. "Silence. The prisoner will be silent!"

"But…" Thomas began to protest.

"I said, silence," the colonel insisted. "You have been assigned a Prisoner's Friend to speak for you. So, unless you want to dismiss him and defend yourself, you will be silent."

Thomas gritted his teeth, thought for a moment. "Then I wish to dismiss him, sir. From this point forward, I will speak for myself."

The corporal tried to get his attention, but Thomas ignored him. Budgy tried to kick him in the shins, but his shackles made that impossible.

Looking at the paper in front of him, the colonel asked, "Does Private Ellis feel the same?"

Budgy looked at Thomas, then at the corporal, then back at Thomas. With a huge sigh, he nodded. "I do, sir."

The colonel frowned. "You realize that this greatly lessens your chances for leniency from this court-martial?"

Thomas's eyebrows shot up. "May I ask why, sir? Why should wanting to speak for ourselves lessen our chances for leniency?"

The colonel didn't hesitate. "By denying yourselves of the privilege of a Prisoner's Friend, you have demonstrated that you have no respect for this court-martial and the officers who are serving here. That demonstrates a distinct lack of respect for military discipline. It's soldiers like you who undermine the very fabric of His Majesty's military, which makes you all but a traitor to the Crown. And you expect leniency from this court-martial?"

The colonel's voice rose with each sentence. It was apparent to Thomas that he'd already tried and convicted them in his own mind. This would be tough, but Thomas was determined to tell his side of the story.

"No, sir," he answered. "I don't expect leniency from this august group of officers. I expect fairness. If this court will allow me to tell my side of the events leading up to this court-martial, I will accept whatever disciplinary action this court-martial decides is fair."

"Do you agree with that, Private Ellis?" the colonel asked.

After a look of trepidation crossed his face, Budgy again nodded. "I do, sir."

"So be it," the colonel declared. "Corporal Harris, you are dismissed."

The corporal stepped back, saluted, then left the room.

When the door closed behind him, the colonel turned to Captain Bloem. "You may begin, Captain."

Glaring at Thomas and Budgy, the captain stepped forward and began.

"The night after Christmas, I was inspecting the trenches, as I usually do when arriving at a new command."

"Where were you previously?" the Colonel interrupted.

"Settling into my tent, sir. I'd been rotated up that afternoon and hadn't yet had the opportunity to inspect my unit."

"I see. Go on."

"I reached the second parapet and noticed that the two privates on guard were watching something rather intently. So, I decided to investigate. I called up to ask what they were looking at. Both privates told me to shut up.

"Of course, I climbed the ladder since the men obviously weren't going to tell me what they were looking at. As I reached the top, I looked out and saw a kraut crawling through No Man's Land straight for our trenches. Yet, neither of these so-called soldiers were doing anything to stop him.

"I ordered them to shoot, but they argued with me. I ordered them a second time and one of them raised his rifle, but then lowered it. I warned him that he was facing a court-martial, but he belligerently refused and dared me to court-martial him.

"I turned to the other private and ordered him to fire. But he aggressively told me to mind my own business. He had no intention of firing.

"So, I took matters into my own hands. I grabbed a rifle and shot that kraut dead on the spot. Then I ordered the Battle Police to put these two mutineers under arrest.

"I don't know exactly what that kraut was doing, but I'm sure it was no good. He most likely was a spy sent to see where our big guns are placed. But these two directly disobeyed my order to fire on him. It's cowards like them that will keep us from winning this war, unless we slap them down hard. They are guilty of treason, and I want them sentenced to death. They deserve nothing less."

When he was finished, he stepped back with a look of arrogance and superiority. It was obvious he thought he'd already won his case and they were headed for a firing squad.

The colonel looked at Thomas and ordered, "Tell your story, Private Bennett."

Thomas took a moment to gather his thoughts, then began. "I'm sure each of you officers has heard stories of the Christmas Truce that occurred two weeks ago. May I ask if any of you were witness to that truce?"

The three officers looked at each other and then shook their heads no.

"Then let me tell you what we experienced during those twenty-four glorious hours," Thomas began to lose his nervousness and shared his story freely, without embellishment, but with all the heart and soul he could muster.

As he finished, he looked each officer in the eye. "Now I ask you, sirs. After spending time with such fine, upstanding young men, learning how alike we are, hearing about their families, their hopes, their dreams, and their goals for life, could you in good conscience shoot one down in cold blood?

"That German soldier wasn't trying to spy on us. He wasn't trying to sneak into our trenches. He was trying to retrieve his football. The very one he had kicked around with our own boys the day before. He was no threat to us. There was no reason to shoot him. Yet Captain Bloem insisted that we shoot.

"I understand the need for military discipline and the importance of obedience. But is it wise to have an army made of men who follow orders blindly? Who are expected to obey officers who have not been on the front lines, who don't know the enemy the way we do? Is it wise to expect common foot soldiers to turn off their minds and their emotions and become killing machines?

"If that's the way it needs to be, then what do those 'killing machines' do after the war is over? How can you send them home to wives and families after they've turned off their minds and their hearts? How can they adjust back to civilian life after witnessing and inflicting the horrors of war on other human beings, men who happen to be affiliated with the opposite side in this war?

"I am here to tell you, sirs, that those German soldiers don't want to fight a war any more than we do. They follow orders, but maybe not so blindly now. We follow orders, too. But maybe not so blindly now.

"I couldn't shoot an innocent man who was simply trying to retrieve his football. He wasn't shooting at me. He wasn't shooting at any of our men. He wasn't a threat to anyone in that moment. That's why we didn't follow orders, sirs. Are we guilty of refusing an order? Yes, sirs. Are we guilty of treason? No, sirs. That's all I have to say, sirs. We stand ready for your judgement."

"Do you have anything to add, Private Ellis?" the colonel asked.

Budgy shook his head. "No, sirs. I believe Private Bennett has spoken eloquently and his words reflect my own feelings quite well."

All three officers sat with deadpan faces for several moments before turning to confer with each other. Thomas couldn't tell if he'd reached them or not. It was a little unnerving.

Budgy leaned his head toward Thomas. "What do you think? Are they going to put us before a firing squad?"

Thomas shrugged. "I don't know. I hope not."

The clock on the wall ticked mercilessly as the officers whispered back and forth. Budgy fidgeted with the chains at his wrists. Thomas stood as still as he could, but after a while, his back and shoulders began to ache from having his arms shackled in front of him for so long.

Nearly an hour later, the officers finally sat back and looked at the prisoners.

"We find your story compelling," the colonel said. "However, it does not excuse you from directly disobeying an order from a superior officer. Because no one was in actual danger, we will forgo the firing squad. However, because your actions could lead other soldiers in your unit to think it's permissible to disobey orders, we need to make an example of you.

"You are hereby sentenced to twenty days of field discipline and hard labor over the course of the next twenty-eight days, to begin immediately following this court-martial. That will be followed by thirty days of restricted movement under strict guard. If, during those fifty-eight days, you prove that you can and will follow any orders given you, you may be reinstated to full freedom within the regulations afforded you as privates in His Majesty's military. This court-martial is adjourned."

The colonel slammed his gavel twice on the table, and the officers stood and left the room. Captain Bloem turned and smirked at them.

"See you at the binding," he sneered, then left the room, as well.

Budgy's shoulders sagged. "Field discipline and hard labor? That seems a bit excessive, don't you think?"

Thomas shook his head. "Help me out here, Budgy. What is field discipline?"

"Well, Tommy-boy," Budgy frowned. "in this case, they have sentenced us to the fullest extent. For the next twenty-eight days, they will bind us to a pole, or some other object, with our hands above our heads for two hours each day. There will be two days in the middle where we won't be bound. That's the field discipline part. When we aren't bound, the captain will assign us to whatever hard labor he deems appropriate."

"I'm sorry." Thomas's voice was full of regret. "I thought maybe if they heard the whole story that they'd understand. Maybe we should have kept the Prisoner's Friend after all."

"No," Budgy disagreed. "The story needed to be told and you told it well. I think they just need someone to prove their point; that military discipline is all-important and nobody better disobey orders ever."

Thomas sighed. "I'm afraid you're right. So, we do our best to put up with it all, then try to stay out of trouble until we can go home again."

"Right," Budgy agreed as the Battle Police led them out of the room for their first day of field discipline and hard labor.

"How are you feeling?" Maggie's face showed only concern.

"I'm getting better, slowly," Shelly still looked tired and pale, but a bit less yellow than before.

Maggie smiled. "I'm glad. Would you like a little surprise?"

"A surprise?" Shelly laughed. "You know how I love surprises."

After a bit of effort, Maggie had helped Shelly to move to an armchair and arranged a blanket around her legs.

"All set?"

"I'm ready." Shelly's face looked brighter already. Maggie was certain the surprise would cheer her even more.

"Okay, close your eyes and wait just a moment," she directed.

After a moment, Shelly called, "Can I open my eyes yet?"

Maggie laughed from across the room. "In a moment. Patience, Shelly. This is a practice in patience."

"I'm finished learning patience," Shelly teased.

That's more like the Shelly I know, Maggie thought.

"All right, you can open your eyes."

Shelly opened her eyes and blinked a couple of times, then looked around the room… and squealed with joy.

"Beth!" She held out her arms and leaned forward.

Beth stepped over and tried to lean down to hug her friend, but then stood up and laughed.

"Sorry, Shelly. I'm not bending so well these days," she grinned.

That's when Shelly gasped. Reaching out, she gingerly touched Beth's belly.

"Has it really been so long? I'd heard that you were pregnant, but I didn't know you were so far along."

"Seven months," Beth announced proudly.

Shelly sighed, happily. "That's wonderful, Beth!" Then her expression changed to one of concern. "Are you still working at the munitions factory?"

Beth shook her head. "Yes, but I'm doing a different job now. After you became ill, Michael insisted that I quit. I knew we couldn't afford for me to quit, so I asked if I could change departments. I'm putting pins in the firing mechanisms now. I can sit down to work, or stand up if I feel like it. It's still a little stressful, but safer… except when I drop a pin on the floor." She laughed as she pretended to try and pick up a pin off the floor.

Shelly and Maggie both laughed with her. They spent the next few hours chatting and gossiping together. When Shelly began to yawn, Maggie stood up and helped Beth to stand.

"We'll let you get your beauty rest now," Maggie smiled.

Shelly smiled and her eyes filled with tears. "I'm so glad you both came. It felt good to laugh again."

Beth reached down and patted her shoulder. "Then we must do this again soon," she grinned.

"We will," Maggie promised.

As they left Shelly's room, Maggie turned back and waved. She was pleased to see that Shelly still had a smile on her face, and looked better than she had in weeks. The visit was good for her. *Yes,* she thought, *we'll definitely do this again soon.*

Chapter Fifteen

February 10, 1915

"Krause."

Friedrich grinned as he made his way to the front of the group of soldiers assembled for mail call. He hadn't heard from Gerdie for a while, so he was excited to see what she had to say.

He was supposed to go on kitchen duty in a few minutes, so he took his letter to the bench outside the cook tent and sat down. Glancing at the front of the envelope, he was puzzled. This was not Gerdie's neat handwriting. Oh, it was neat enough, but it definitely wasn't hers.

January 26, 1915

Dear Friedrich,

My heart aches to have to tell you sad news this day. Your sweet Gerdie died in my arms yesterday. It was no one's fault. She simply did not have the strength to recover from childbirth. She will be buried in the Nordfriedhof next to her father.

Do not worry about little Karl. Herr Otto and I will care for him until you return. We are praying you will return safe and soon.

Sincerely,
Frau Klara Schmidt

Friedrich sat staring at the pages, unable to cry, unable to move or consciously process what he'd just read. He had no idea how long he sat there. When Sergeant Haas came looking for him, he wasn't prepared to deal with the realities of his life here in Belgium. His mind and heart were with his dead wife and half-orphaned son in Germany.

"Private," the sergeant barked. "You're late for your shift."

Looking up at him, bewildered, Friedrich said nothing.

"Private," the sergeant barked again. "I said you're late."

When Friedrich didn't move, Sergeant Haas yelled, "*Aufmerksamkeit!*"

Still, Friedrich sat, staring at him with a dazed look.

Unwilling to be disobeyed by a private who'd already been reprimanded for disobedience, the sergeant grabbed Friedrich's arm and tried to force him to stand.

That was the last straw. Friedrich yanked his arm out of reach and in one fluid motion punched his superior officer across the jaw, dropping him to the ground. The look on his face was no longer one of bewilderment. He was angry. More than angry. His heart was full of rage. Rage at the sergeant. Rage at the army. Rage at the damned war that kept him from being at his wife's side when she needed him most.

Without conscious thought, Friedrich kicked out at the man on the ground, his boot connecting with the sergeant's ribs. Not once, but twice, and pulling back for a third kick when another private grabbed him by the arms and tried to pull him away.

Friedrich pulled back to punch this man, as well, but a third man grabbed his arm, preventing him from following through.

Struggling to break free, he managed to get one arm loose and elbowed someone in the stomach. His legs were still trying to kick as he threw his head back, connecting solidly with someone's face.

What followed required six large men to hold down the distraught soldier. They finally managed to restrain him, but he wasn't ready to surrender. He struggled and fought until Fritz wormed into the fray.

Tapping the soldier on his right, he nodded that the man should make way for him. Obediently, the man slid back a few inches. Fritz filled the now empty inches and placed one knee on Friedrich's shoulder, throwing the other leg over his torso. Lowering down so he was sitting on his chest, he leaned down so he was nose-to-nose with his friend.

"*Kumpel!*" he shouted. "You must listen to me!"

Still Friedrich fought the men holding him.

"Friedrich!" Fritz tried again. "Stop! Let's work this out together."

When it was apparent that Friedrich couldn't hear him, Fritz sat back up, frowned, then slapped his friend hard across the face.

Friedrich blinked twice, shook his head, and finally made conscious eye contact with Fritz.

Holding Friedrich's face with the palms of his hands, Fritz's voice became quiet and soothing.

"Friedrich, *kumpel,*" he said. "It's going to be all right. But you have to stop fighting so we can work this through."

Trying to shake his head no, Friedrich whispered hoarsely, "No. No, Fritz. It's not going to be all right. She's dead. My Gerdie is dead."

Tears flowed freely then and Friedrich stopped fighting the men who were still holding him down.

Fritz nodded that they could release their hold and all but two stepped away. Those two remained close to Friedrich's shoulders, in case they should be needed again.

Shifting his weight off Friedrich's chest, Fritz sat on the ground beside him, pulling his friend into his arms.

"I'm so sorry, *kumpel,*" he whispered. "I'm so sorry."

He didn't have long to comfort the grieving soldier, however. Sergeant Haas recovered and stumbled over to where they were sitting.

"I want that man arrested!" he yelled. "I want him executed for striking an officer!"

The two soldiers standing nearby looked at each other, unsure what to do.

"I said, I want him arrested!" the sergeant yelled again.

This time, the soldiers moved, somewhat slowly, but they moved to take Friedrich gently by the arms and help him up.

This time, Friedrich let them take him without a fight. They escorted him to the guard tent with Fritz following behind. *This is not going to go well,* Fritz thought. *Not well at all.*

Thomas tried not to groan as his hands were taken up and around behind the pole he'd become so familiar with. The private administering the discipline today was no rooky and seemed to enjoy his assignment a little too much. After tying Thomas's hands together, he pulled them well up, straining and cramping the muscles.

After nineteen days of this, with two days off in the middle, Thomas wondered that his muscles weren't used to it yet. *Maybe that's what the days off were for,* he thought. To keep us from getting too accustomed to it.

Without thinking, he tried to ease the tension on his arms by putting more weight on his feet, but only his toes could reach the ground and his calves soon began to cramp.

A fine choice, he thought for the hundredth time. Cramps in my arms or cramps in my legs. He closed his eyes and took a couple of deep breaths, willing his muscles to relax as much as possible. That helped a bit and he opened his eyes again.

Turning his head to the left, he could see Budgy, and the look on his face told him that his friend was faring no better than he.

"You okay?" he asked.

Budgy groaned a little. "I think that private enjoys this duty too much. My toes are barely scraping the ground today."

"Just try to breathe and remember that we only have today and tomorrow, then we're done with this torment."

"Right," Budgy breathed. "I'm looking forward to a little restricted movement right now."

Thomas started to chuckle, but caught his breath as the motion created a new cramp in his shoulder. A movement to his right caught his attention. The private who'd strung them up was talking with another soldier. Thomas couldn't tell who it was, but the voice sounded familiar.

"But, sir, I haven't been on duty that long," the binding private complained. "These two have only been bound for fifteen minutes and I'd like to see them through it, if you don't mind, sir."

"Orders are orders." The officer's voice was stern. "The captain wants you to relieve the guard at the south parapet now. That's an order, Private."

"Yes, sir. Just make sure these two stay put for the full two hours. The captain wants no quarter given."

"You're giving me instructions, Private? I've guarded many men serving field discipline. I certainly know what's expected. Dismissed."

Thomas closed his eyes again, his breath shallow, as a new cramp grabbed his back.

"Painful, huh?" the new voice said.

Opening his eyes, Thomas saw a middle-aged second lieutenant with a little mustache and bushy eyebrows looking up at him.

"Yes, sir," he answered when he could speak. "But I think it's supposed to be that way."

Nodding, the second lieutenant lit up a cigarette, puffed a few times, then looked back up at Thomas. "You smoke?" he asked.

"Never took it up," Thomas answered.

"It helps relieve tension," the officer stated matter-of-factly. "But if you've never smoked, now might not be the time. If you coughed..." He left the sentence unfinished but Thomas filled in the blanks for himself.

Wandering over to Budgy, he asked the same question. "What about you, Private? You smoke?" he asked.

Budgy tried to nod, but caught his breath as the movement obviously caused him pain.

Without a word, the officer put the cigarette to Budgy's lips. Two drags on the cigarette and Budgy's face looked noticeably more relaxed. He looked down at the man and gave him a half-smile of gratitude. "Thanks," he whispered.

"You're welcome. Just don't tell anyone. If you do, I'll be the one bound to that pole, never mind that I'm an officer."

With that, he moved off to the designated guard position and finished his cigarette, watching a unit practicing bayonet drills a few yards away.

Thomas was impressed with the officer's compassionate action, and the nonchalance with which he exercised it. "Sir?" he called softly.

"Yes?" The second lieutenant looked back over his shoulder.

"What's your name, sir?" Thomas asked.

"Brooke. Alan Brooke," he answered simply, then returned his gaze to the drills.

Thomas knew he would never forget the compassionate second lieutenant. *He'll either get caught being kind and be punished, or he'll advance quickly in the ranks,* Thomas thought. *I hope he advances. We need more officers like him.*

Maggie stood at the window and watched the rain fall. She didn't really see it, though. She didn't feel the cold pane against her hand. She didn't hear the thunder. Her mind was far away in Belgium.

It had been nearly a month since she'd had a letter from Thomas, and she was worried. She tried not to let herself worry, tried to apply her mother's advice, but today, it wasn't working. So, she stood and stared out the window.

She didn't feel Katie touch her arm at first, but slowly became aware as Katie's touch became more insistent.

"Maggie," Katie called again. "Maggie, are you all right?"

Slowly, as if from a deep sleep, Maggie brought herself back to her true location and looked down at her little sister. She forced a smile. "Why yes, Katie. I'm all right."

Katie frowned. "You don't look all right, and it took forever to get your attention."

"I'm sorry, sis. I was thinking about Thomas."

Katie's frown deepened. "I miss him, too. Do you think he's okay?"

Nodding in spite of her own fears, Maggie drew Katie into a hug.

"I'm sure he's just fine. I think he's just busy trying to drive the Germans out of France."

"Why'd those nasty ol' Germans have to come into France anyway?" Katie pouted.

"I don't know," Maggie answered truthfully. "I don't know why some people think they need more than they already have."

"Well, I hate them!" Katie announced, stomping her foot.

Pulling back to look her sister in the eye, Maggie shook her head. "I don't think that's a good thing, poppet. Hate doesn't help anybody. It doesn't help you, or me, or Mama, or Thomas. It just makes you and those around you feel bad. Hating the Germans doesn't make them go back to Germany. Hating them doesn't stop the war. It doesn't stop the fighting. It only spreads the sadness and anger."

"I can't help it," Katie insisted. "They marched into France and started fighting and made my Thomas go away. So, I hate them!"

"Hm," Maggie thought fast. "How would you feel if I took your doll?" She reached over and took the doll from Katie's hand.

Katie looked shocked, then frowned again. "Why'd you do that?"

"Because I wanted it," Maggie said simply.

"But it's my doll," Katie protested.

"I know. But I want it."

Katie frowned. "That's not very nice, Maggie."

"I know that, too. But I want it."

"Please give it back."

"No, I don't think I will. I want it."

Katie's frown turned angry and she reached for the doll.

"But it's my doll and you shouldn't take it."

"I know. But I want it," Maggie continued to insist, holding the doll high out of Katie's reach.

Katie started to cry just as her mother came in.

"What's wrong, Katie?" she asked putting her arm around her daughter.

"Maggie took my doll and won't give it back," Katie cried.

Mrs. Gilley looked up at Maggie surprised. "Is this true?"

Maggie winked at her mother and admitted that it was true. Mrs. Gilley cocked her head, obviously trying to figure out what Maggie was up to.

"Well, I don't think that was very nice," she said, a bit hesitantly.

Maggie nodded slightly, hoping her mother would get the idea that she should continue to play along.

"I know. But I want it," she repeated.

"See, Mommy? She won't give it back," Katie cried.

Mrs. Gilley stood up and faced Maggie. She winked and then frowned. "Maggie, you are not being a very nice sister. You should give Katie her doll back right now."

"But I don't want to. I want it," Maggie said again.

Mrs. Gilley held out her hand. "Give me the doll, Maggie."

Maggie frowned, then handed over the doll. Her mother then gave it back to Katie, who hugged it tightly.

"Thank you, Mommy," she sniffled.

Maggie smiled at her mother, then knelt beside Katie. Her voice was soft as she spoke.

"I'm sorry I took your doll, Katie. You were angry with me, weren't you?"

Katie nodded. "I was very angry!"

"But you couldn't get your doll yourself, could you?"

Katie shook her head, her tears beginning to subside.

"I'll bet you're glad Mommy came to help you, aren't you?"

Katie nodded, still hugging her doll tightly.

"Well, the Germans have taken some of the land that the people of France own. The French people can't get it back by themselves, so they asked us to help them. That's why our soldiers are over there. They are trying to make the Germans go back to Germany so the French people can have their land back. Does that make sense?"

Katie looked up, her eyes wide. She thought for a moment, then nodded. "That's why I hate the Germans!"

Mrs. Gilley spoke up then. "Katie, did it help you get your doll back when you cried and were angry?"

Shaking her head, Katie looked at her mother.

"Being angry and hating the Germans won't make them do what we want, either. It just makes us all feel bad."

"That's what Maggie said," Katie looked from one to the other. "But I can't help it."

"Of course, you can," Mrs. Gilley said. "What's your favorite song?"

"'Wiggly Woo'," Katie said without thinking.

"Fun choice. Can you sing it for me?"

Again, Katie nodded. She puffed up her little chest and started singing. After a few lines, Maggie and Mrs. Gilley joined her.

When the song was finished, they were all smiling. Mrs. Gilley took Katie's hand and looked her in the eye. "Do you want to know what I do when I'm feeling angry?"

Katie nodded, more relaxed now.

"I sing. I sing whatever comes into my mind and I keep singing until those angry feelings go away. I do that when I'm sad, or when life feels like it's just too hard. Or when it doesn't make sense. Like when I think about why the Germans wanted to invade France at all. It doesn't make sense and makes me feel angry. So, I sing. Would you like to try that when you feel like you hate the Germans?"

Thinking hard, Katie finally nodded. "So, when I feel angry or hate the Germans, I should just start singing?"

"That's right. Sing until those ugly feelings go away. It won't make the Germans go home, but it will make you and those around you feel better. Does that make sense?"

"Yes. I think my doll needs a nap now. She's very tired." With that pronouncement, Katie went to her room and closed the door.

"She has a lot to think about," Mrs. Gilley noted.

"Yes. Thank you for going along, Mother," Maggie smiled.

Her mother smiled back. "I wasn't sure what you were doing at first, but I trusted that you had a reason for acting like a spoiled six-year-old."

Maggie laughed. "I'm so glad you trusted me."

"What's not to trust?" Mrs. Gilley stood and hugged her. "You're going to make a great mother," she said, glancing down at Maggie's pregnant belly.

"I hope so. I certainly hope so."

Chapter Sixteen

March 15, 1915

Friedrich stood at attention while the panel deciding his fate conferred. The panel consisted of Commander Möhler, Captain Berger, and Captain Roth. The first two he knew only by reputation. The third was a captain he'd served under before being assigned to Belgium. He knew Captain Roth to be a fair and honest man. Commander Möhler had a reputation for being a "by the book" officer. He knew nothing about Captain Berger and no one he spoke to had heard of him, either.

As he stood, he felt the malevolence of the sergeant he'd struck. If the sergeant had his way, he'd be tortured, crucified, burned at the stake, then drawn and quartered for good measure.

Friedrich still didn't remember much of what he'd done that day. All he remembered was the horrible pain of learning that his sweet Gerdie was dead and the intense longing to be there with his son. Nothing else registered. He vaguely remembered the sergeant pulling his arm. The next thing he could recall was Fritz sitting on his chest looking down at him with so much worry and concern that Friedrich couldn't help but respond to him.

Since then, he'd spent the past month in the guard tent, eating cold meals, sitting on the hard dirt floor, and worrying that he'd done something that would make his son an orphan.

Fritz had visited him as often as they'd let him, but they wouldn't allow any mail, or reading material of any kind. They brought him a basin of cold water to wash his face and hands in a couple of times a week. But other than that, he was left alone to stew and worry about the consequences of what he'd done.

He brought his attention back to the panel. The captain he knew seemed to be arguing with the other two. They were whispering, so he couldn't hear what they were saying, but it didn't look like it was going in his favor. Inwardly, he groaned. What had he done?

Allowing his mind to wander, he thought about Herr Otto and Frau Schmidt. They were such dear friends! *It's too bad they are so old,* he thought. *They would make wonderful parents for Karl.*

That thought stabbed him in the heart and it was all he could do to continue standing at attention. He wanted to crumple into a little ball on the floor and sob like a baby himself. But he stiffened his back, clenched his jaw, and told himself to be strong for Karl. His son needed him, and if there was any way, he would survive to raise his son to manhood.

"Private Krause," Commander Möhler brought his attention back to the room. "Your actions of January 12 were deplorable and not worthy of a soldier of the Imperial German Army. We know of the unusual circumstances regarding your outburst…"

"Attack, sir!" Sergeant Haas interrupted as he stood and started to move towards the table where the panel was seated. "The man attacked me maliciously. He is a disgrace to the uniform and should be shot!"

"Enough!" Commander Möhler bellowed. "You had your chance to speak and you did so quite eloquently. Now you will sit down, be silent, and hear our verdict. Is that understood?"

The sergeant had enough good sense to shut his mouth and sit down, but not without glaring at Friedrich in the process.

Friedrich kept his eyes forward, using every bit of willpower he had to keep still. All his senses wanted to finish the job he'd started a month ago, beating the *verdammt* sergeant to a pulp. But that wouldn't do anyone any good, least of all, his son.

"Regarding your outburst on January 12," Commander Möhler continued. "We understand the unusual circumstances. However, this is not the first time you've disrespected a superior officer. In fact, you were on kitchen duty specifically as a disciplinary action for disrespecting an officer at the front line. Is that not correct?" he asked.

"That is correct, sir," Friedrich admitted.

"Would you care to tell us why you have a problem disobeying the officers placed over you?"

Shocked that he was given an opportunity to speak, Friedrich made eye contact with the commander, then the other two in turn.

He licked his lips, took a deep breath, and asked, "Excuse me, sir, but are you truly wanting an honest answer to that question?"

"I am," Commander Möhler replied.

Friedrich glanced at the floor, gathering his thoughts. "Well, sir, it's difficult for me to see why we are fighting this war at all. After getting to know some of the Brits at Christmas…"

"Wait," Captain Berger interrupted, "you were part of that unauthorized truce?"

Nodding, Friedrich continued. "Yes, sir, I was. It didn't seem right to fight while we should be celebrating the birth of Jesus. It's a sacred day, sir. So, someone down the line, I don't know who, arranged for a temporary truce for Christmas Eve and Christmas Day. Somewhere in that time, some of our soldiers and some of theirs ventured into No Man's Land and started talking. After a while, others followed suit. Then, it seemed like the thing to do, celebrate the holiday with them."

"How did you come to that conclusion, Private?" Captain Berger asked.

Friedrich thought for a moment, then answered, "I'm not sure I really thought about it. I just saw others talking and laughing and it seemed like a good idea."

Captain Roth had his own question then. "And does it seem like a good idea now?"

Without hesitation, Friedrich nodded. "Yes, sir, it does. You see, sir, I learned something while I was out there talking with the enemy. I learned that those men fighting on the other side are no different than us. Oh, they speak a different language and celebrate their holidays a bit differently, but they are good, decent men who are trying to do the best they can. They have families, wives, and children that they love. They have hopes and dreams. They have frustrations and things that make them angry. They play games and talk about politics. In every way that's important, they are just like us. So why are we shooting at them? Why are we trying to kill them? Is it so that some leader somewhere can say his country is bigger than theirs? Is it so someone can say they rule over them? Is it..." he paused.

"Go on," the captain said.

Friedrich looked at him for a moment, then continued. "Is it so our venerable Kaiser can increase his empire? How much land, how many people must one man rule in order to feel he has enough? Is it really so important that he rule the entire world? Is it worth the lives of men, women, and children on both sides of this damned war?"

Looking at the floor to hide his tears, he swallowed hard. Then deciding he was in it up to his eyeballs already, he took a deep breath, then searched each officer's face individually.

"As you know, I recently lost my wife. My three-month-old son is being cared for by elderly neighbors. He has no mother, and his father is here in Belgium, trying to do my duty, but feeling all the while that I should be in Germany raising my son myself. If you were to put yourself in my shoes, could you say honestly that you wouldn't have responded as I did? Could you blindly put aside your feelings about your wife and child and go about your duties as though nothing had happened?

"Am I sorry for what I did? Yes. Would I do it again? Given the same circumstances, yes, I would, because the honest truth is that my emotions, my feelings, my very soul are in torment. I cannot be a good soldier when my heart and mind are more than three hundred kilometers away in Germany. If that makes me a disgrace to the uniform, sir, then I admit that I'm a disgrace. But I cannot change the way I feel or how I think."

Pursing his lips, Commander Möhler, motioned to the other two and they put their heads together in a brief conference.

Sergeant Haas leaned over and whispered, "You're going to die! They are going to shoot you at dawn."

Friedrich heard him, but refused to acknowledge that he was even in the room.

After a few moments, the panel faced front again.

"Private Krause," Commander Möhler addressed him, "this court-martial panel has determined that you are under extreme mental and emotional duress and are not fit for duty. We are prepared to offer you a choice. You may remain part of this Imperial Army, but will serve the next five years in prison, after which you will rejoin your unit and fight the remainder of your tour of duty in whatever battles and wars your superiors command."

Friedrich's heart fell, but he clenched his jaw tighter, trying to keep control of his emotions.

"Or…" the commander paused to be certain he had Friedrich's full attention. "Or you may accept a dishonorable discharge and return to your son on the next transport."

"Bear in mind," he cautioned, "a dishonorable discharge will follow you for the rest of your life. It may make it difficult to find work, housing, or other necessities as loyal Germans discover what you've done. However, if that is your choice, we will see that you are returned to your son as quickly as possible. What is your decision?"

Friedrich thought his knees would buckle under him. He steadied himself against the table and offered a timid smile to the panel.

"With your consent, sirs, I will accept the dishonorable discharge and return to my son as soon as possible," he answered, his voice husky with emotion.

"What?" The sergeant was livid. "How can you…"

"Be careful, Sergeant," Commander Möhler warned. "We are inclined to hold you in contempt if you finish that question."

Clamping his mouth shut, Sergeant Haas glared at the panel, then at Friedrich, then stomped out of the room.

Suppressing a grin, the commander clapped his gavel on the table. "This court-martial is adjourned."

Fritz, who'd been sitting behind Friedrich, stood and clapped him on the shoulder.

"Congratulations, *kumpel*," he said. "You're on your way home!"

"Thanks, Fritz," Friedrich smiled, feeling hopeful for the first time in months. "I'm really going home!"

"Ugh," Budgy groaned, rolling out from under his blankets as the bugle sounded stand-to. "I truly did not miss our morning routines here."

Thomas smiled. "Neither did I, my friend, but here we are. Just think, though, today is our first day of real freedom. Once stand-to's are finished, we can go to breakfast without an escort, and between drills we can do whatever we want."

Grinning, Budgy pushed himself to a crouch as he tried to stretch in the cramped quarters of the front-line dugout. "That's right! I think we should find some other war-weary souls and scare up a game of rugby or something."

"Rugby?" Thomas laughed. "Why not polo or cricket?"

"We have no horses for polo, and my cricket wicket is bent beyond repair," Budgy quipped.

They laughed together as they grabbed their rifles and made a beeline for the fire-step. They watched carefully, as the battle the day before had been less than successful and the word down the line was that the Germans weren't as surprised as the British officers had hoped.

All was quiet. Nothing moved in No Man's Land. No one on either side seemed to even breathe. Thomas thought about Friedrich and was grateful he'd been assigned here in Neuve Chapelle instead of back in Ypres. The chances were slim that he'd have to fire on his new German friend.

He took a deep breath. It still bothered him that he'd had to fire on other German soldiers in the battle yesterday. The only thing that kept him from rebelling again was the thought of sweet Maggie and their unborn child. During his field discipline, he'd decided he'd do anything to get back home to them safely, including firing on men he knew well didn't want to fight any more than he did.

The increased size of No Man's Land created by yesterday's battle made it a bit more difficult to see what the Germans were doing. Still, Thomas peered into the early morning light and tried to be vigilant.

As the sun rose over the horizon, Thomas squinted his eyes involuntarily as something on the other side reflected the morning sun. Blinking rapidly, then willing his eyes to stay open, he tried to figure out what had momentarily blinded him.

Frustrated, he looked over at Budgy. "Did you see that?" he whispered.

"The reflection? Yeah," Budgy whispered back.

"What was it?"

Budgy just shrugged.

Turning back to his vigil, Thomas took a deep breath and let it out slowly, willing his pounding heart to slow. One breath. Two. But his third breath was interrupted by the whip and crack of enemy machine guns opening up with deadly effect. Soldiers on either side of him were mowed down as they stood to return fire.

Thomas kept his head down until there was a break in the firing, at which point he peeked over the edge of the trench. The sun's early morning rays gleamed off the German's barbed wire defenses. It was evident that the bombardment of the day before had not even touched them. Instead of being broken up, the wire and the thick hedge looked just the same as they had before the bombardment.

He saw two British soldiers lying half out of the trench. It seemed as though they were trying to advance, but Thomas hadn't heard any such order.

"Hey, Budgy," he turned to his buddy. "Did you hear an order…"

His question was cut short by the sight of Budgy lying with one arm hanging limply at his side.

"I think I've been shot," Budgy mumbled, then swallowed hard. "I can't feel my arm."

"Lie still," Thomas ordered as he stood to look for someone to help him carry his friend out of the line of fire.

Just then, Thomas's world turned upside down as a shell exploded a few yards away. Everything seemed to move in slow motion as his mind tried to grasp what was happening. He marveled that his brown boots were such a stark contrast to the blue of the early morning sky. Then he wondered why his feet were in the air at all. They should be on the ground, shouldn't they? But his musings in that horrible moment were cut short as he saw his right foot fly off, seemingly under its own power, while the rest of him continued falling to the ground.

As his head hit the edge of the firing-step, he heard Budgy scream. That was the last sound his mind registered as Private Thomas Bennett lost consciousness.

Katie screamed as she grabbed the table. Her dinner plate slid off into her lap as another loud boom resounded through the apartment. She screamed again.

Maggie tried hard to keep her feet, but the second explosion sent her to the floor.

"What was that?" Katie asked, her voice shrill with fear.

"I don't..." Maggie began, then stopped, her eyes widening as the realization dawned. "The factory," she whispered.

Katie slid off her chair and tried to help Maggie stand. They ran to the front door. The scene outside was unbelievable. People were running through the street, some towards the factory, but most were running away. Some had children in tow. Others were frantically scrambling over flowerbeds and low fences in their hurry to get away.

"What's happened?" Maggie shouted to the crowd.

"Fire at the factory!" one man shouted back, not slowing his run.

Maggie's hand flew to her mouth. She started to move toward the factory, but Katie stopped her.

"We can't go there, Maggie," she said. "The fire is there."

"But Mother..." Maggie began, then looked toward the factory and stopped, not wanting to scare her little sister more than she was already.

The entire sky was alight with bright orange and red. Yellow-grey smoke billowed up, filling the air with an acrid smell.

Tears filled her eyes as she watched, helpless to do anything. She thought of the school, not two blocks away from the factory where her mother was helping set up for the winter carnival, which was to be held the next day.

"Maggie, come on!" Katie pulled at her sleeve. Maggie wanted to run and save her mother, but she couldn't leave Katie. She knew her first duty was to her little sister. Reaching inside the door, she grabbed their coats. She helped Katie put hers on, and the two of them joined the crowd fleeing the scene of devastation.

They were hampered a bit by Maggie's seven-month pregnant belly. After only a few minutes of running, Maggie had to stop to catch her breath.

As they rested, Katie suddenly grew frantic. "What about Mommy?" she cried.

Maggie took in a deep breath to steady her voice. "Mommy is at the school, not at the factory, so she's safe." She hoped that was not a lie.

They continued on, following the crowd to a railway bridge some distance from their home. As the crowd found shelter under the bridge, Maggie could hear the fear in so many voices. Mothers trying to calm their children. Children whimpering in terror and cold.

One woman tried to calm children that were obviously not her own. The little ones kept calling, "Mommy! Mommy!" and the woman stroked their hair and tried to soothe them. "Mommy will find us soon," she crooned.

Suddenly, another huge explosion rocked the ground beneath their feet. Screams filled the air, and one poor woman went berserk. A man followed her and tried to bring her back.

"It's just like Silvertown!" she screamed, breaking away. "We'll all be killed!"

The man ran after her. They were soon lost from sight as smoke filled the air like fog.

A couple stumbled into their crowded shelter, crying. They had been to the cinema and felt the explosions. They rushed out and tried to return to their home, but they were stopped by police who told them to go back because it was a danger zone. Apparently, they didn't budge, even when the woman kept insisting that they must get through because their children were there.

Katie coughed and Maggie showed her how to wrap her scarf around her mouth and nose to help filter out the smoke. Katie looked up at Maggie, tears in her eyes.

"Is Mommy going to be all right?" she asked.

Maggie pasted a smiled on her face under her scarf, hoping it reached her eyes.

"I'm sure she will be," she said.

Katie thought for a moment. "Is this a good time to sing?"

This time, Maggie's smile did reach her eyes. "I think this is an excellent time to sing."

Leaning her head against Maggie's chest, Katie began softly singing "Sleep my Child". Maggie joined her. A few moments later, others joined in. By the time the song was over, the mood under the bridge was calmer. Even the frightened children seemed to respond to the music.

Maggie looked at Katie, who was lying still against her chest. She was grateful that they were safe and prayed that their mother was, as well.

Several hours later, the sky began to lose some of its color and Maggie decided it was probably safe to return home. She roused Katie from her fitful sleep, and they began the trek back to their apartment.

As they arrived, they were relieved to find their mother just leaving. They rushed to embrace her, as she rushed to embrace them. After a few moments of hugging and checking for wounds, Mrs. Gilley ushered them inside.

"I'm going to make some tea and we can compare stories," she said, trying to sound calm. Her voice quivered, though. It was obvious she was still quite shaken.

When the tea was ready, they sat around the table while they told of their escape and about the people under the bridge. When Katie and Maggie were finished, Mrs. Gilley shared her experience.

"We were just finishing with the decorations when we felt the first explosion. The glass in the windows shattered into the room and peppered us.

"Oh, Mother! Were you cut badly?"

"Oh no, Maggie. Just a few small cuts here and there from glass shards. But poor Mrs. Taylor was standing on the ladder putting up the snowflakes. She fell off, and I'm certain her arm is broken. I was standing on the floor and nearly lost my balance, but caught myself with a nearby desk.

"I knelt to help her when the second explosion hit. I didn't realize how off-balance one is when kneeling, but I was thrown forward and landed on top of her, poor woman."

Katie started to giggle at the thought of her mother lying on top of the teacher. When her mother frowned, she stopped.

"Maybe I'll be able to laugh about it later, Katie, but right now, it doesn't seem funny to me."

"I'm sorry, Mommy." Katie looked chastened.

Mrs. Gilley hugged her daughter. "That's all right, poppet. I suppose laughter is a better way to release tension than crying or throwing things."

They chuckled together and Mrs. Gilley continued her story.

"We managed to stand and made our way to the door, but it wouldn't open. No matter how hard we tried, it wouldn't budge. We think the building shifted and the door was jammed in the opening.

"We looked around and saw the broken windows. There were jagged edges where the glass broke, so I took my coat and tried to knock them out. It worked on the larger pieces, but I couldn't get the smaller ones to break off.

"So, I laid my coat on the bottom edge. We brought a chair over and I climbed up to see how far it was to the ground.

"Isn't Mrs. Taylor's room on the third floor?" Maggie asked.

"Yes. That was my concern. It's a long way down from the third floor."

"What did you do?" Katie asked, totally immersed in the story.

"We got creative," Mrs. Gilley smiled. "There were some jump ropes and trundle hoops in the closet. We tied a rope between each hoop until there were no more left. Then we tied a rope to a table leg and to the first hoop.

"And you climbed down?" Katie's eyes were large with excitement.

"Yes, we did. Unfortunately, they didn't quite reach the ground, and poor Mrs. Taylor had a difficult time climbing with only one good arm."

"How did she manage?" Maggie wanted to know.

"Well, I went first and when I was standing on the second hoop, she threw her leg over the edge and found the first hoop with her foot. I had my hands on the sides of that hoop so she didn't step on my fingers. She hooked her good elbow to the edge of the window. When she was set, I moved down to the next hoop and then she stepped down to the hoop my hands were on."

"How did she do that? How could she move down without holding on with both hands?" Shock showed on Maggie's face.

Her mother laughed. "She balanced against my arms while she moved her arm to the next hoop. We managed quite well, except the smoke kept us coughing, which made us stop for a few moments to catch our breaths."

"When we reached the last hoop, we realized there was still two meters left to the ground. It doesn't sound that far to say it, but looking down, that was maybe the scariest moment."

"Oh no," Katie breathed.

"There was nothing to do but let ourselves drop. I landed and then fell backwards onto my... well, my backside. No harm done there except to my pride," she grinned as she rubbed her hip.

"What about Mrs. Taylor?" Maggie asked.

"Sadly, she broke her ankle and her other wrist when she landed."

"How's she going to teach school with a broken ankle and two broken arms?" Katie cried.

"Well, poppet, she's not. In fact, I'm pretty certain there will be no school until they replace the windows."

Katie nodded her understanding.

"I sat with her until help came. Two men made a makeshift stretcher with their coats and two heavy limbs that had blown off the trees. Those sweet men carried her all the way to the hospital," Mrs. Gilley's voice held awe and admiration.

"That's ten blocks!" Maggie exclaimed.

"Yes, and they just kept trudging along, even while they were coughing."

"Amazing."

"The hospital was in chaos. There were so many people there with injuries of various kinds. Those with lesser injuries, like Mrs. Taylor, were asked to wait while they treated the ones who'd actually been at the factory."

"Were there many?" Maggie asked.

Her mother nodded. "Sadly, yes. Some burned so badly, you couldn't tell if they were men or women."

"Oh my." Tears filled Maggie's eyes as she thought of all the workers on the night shift. So many lives lost. So many whose lives would never be the same again.

"Do they know what caused it?" she asked.

"The police and firemen at the hospital were saying the first explosion was due to a picric acid leak. The second was actually the gas storage tanks half a block away."

"It doesn't make much sense to have a munitions factory so close to gas storage tanks," Maggie frowned.

"Or so close to a school!" Katie added. "What if it happened when school was in session?"

"It does seem crazy that the government allowed the factory in the middle of town," Maggie commented.

"Remember," Mrs. Gilley admonished, "the building itself wasn't designed as a munitions factory. It was a mill before, and they converted it into the factory when the war started. A fireman said the one of the major problems was the floors were wooden, and obviously having picric acid near wood is very dangerous. Another problem was that the walls of the building didn't go right to the very top so the fire spread very rapidly."

Maggie frowned. "I believe the owners of the factory knew about this. I've seen invoices going through our office for modifications to the factory itself. Apparently, they didn't happen fast enough."

"So much TNT must be unstable," Mrs. Gilley noted. "It's no wonder it went up so fast."

Katie looked at Maggie, her eyes wide. "Does that mean you don't have a job anymore, since the factory burned down?"

Maggie sighed. "I don't know, poppet. I'll have to see what I can find out tomorrow. Meanwhile, I think it's time for some sleep for all of us."

"Agreed," her mother nodded.

Katie looked nervous. "Can I sleep with you, Mommy?" she asked.

Smiling fondly at her, Mrs. Gilley nodded and started to stand. "Oh," she winced. "This old body isn't used to climbing out of windows from the third floor."

Maggie helped her mother up, then hugged her tightly. "I'm just glad you're safe."

"And I'm glad you two are safe," she replied, pulling them both into a hug.

Chapter Seventeen

April 11, 1915

The rhythmic clickety-clack of the rails lulled Friedrich's tired brain into a half-sleep, half-stupor state. He didn't notice when the lieutenant sat beside him. He didn't see the scenery passing outside the window. He didn't hear the conductor asking for tickets. He was tired, oh so very tired, and just wanted to be home holding his baby son in his arms. Then, perhaps then, he could properly grieve the loss of his dear wife.

Until then, he was resigned to sit and stare out the window without seeing anything. His new seatmate had other ideas, though.

"Excuse me, Private," he asked politely. "Do you have a light?"

"Hm?" Friedrich stirred. "A light?"

"Yes. Do you have a light for my cigarette? I seem to have lost my matches."

"Oh," Friedrich roused enough to reach into his pocket for the small box of matches. Handing it over, he suddenly recognized the man's rank and fumbled trying to salute while still holding the matches.

Smiling, the lieutenant took the little box. "At ease, soldier. We've both been discharged, so no need to salute now. In fact, I suppose neither of us should be in uniform at all."

Friedrich thought about that for a moment. "I suppose you're right. But I don't have any civilian clothes with me, so it would have been difficult to change."

The older man nodded, puffing his cigarette. "Same story here. Were you wounded?"

Frowning, Friedrich shook his head. "No. My wife died and I am going home to raise my baby boy."

"I'm sorry to hear that. I didn't realize they would discharge a man for that."

With a wry smile, Friedrich decided he might as well start setting the record straight. He'd have to face the repercussions of his dishonorable discharge sooner or later.

"They don't. When I found out my wife had died, a nasty sergeant tried to make me follow through with my duties and I... I hit him... more than once. It took several men to pull me off him, in fact."

Friedrich was surprised to see that there was no judgement on the older man's face. "I can't say I blame you for that. I might have done the same thing."

He held out his hand. "I'm Johann Bergman, formerly with the 57th division."

Friedrich shook his hand, grateful that the former lieutenant didn't seem to be judging him. "I'm Friedrich Krause. Formerly with the 92nd. It's nice to meet you. So, what takes you away from the fighting?"

Johann pointed at his right knee. "Wounded at Champagne. And I must admit, I'm glad it's over for me. But I'm a bit apprehensive, too."

"Apprehensive? Why?"

Sighing, he put out his cigarette and leaned back. "I've been fighting wars for a long time. Nearly twenty years ago, I signed up as a private in the Bafut War. Since then, I served in the Herero War, the Second Samoan Civil War, and now this one. I'm not sure how I'll handle civilian life after so many years of conflict. To think that I shall not walk among machine guns again and never hear another shell burst is simply unimaginable."

"I didn't think of that," Friedrich admitted. "I haven't been out that long, so perhaps it will be easier for me."

Johann looked at him. "I hope it will. You deserve to raise your son without the nightmares that follow so many battles."

He sighed. "I'm just not certain what's to become of us old-timers. We have lived this life for so long. Now we shall have to start all over again."

"What's your plan once you get home? How will you start over?" Friedrich was curious how an older veteran soldier would begin life again.

Thinking for a moment, Johann shook his head. "I'm not sure I have a plan. I will spend some time getting to know my wife again. Then perhaps I'll open a little cobbler shop. I was learning the trade when I first enlisted. In fact, in my first two units, I spent most of my time repairing the boots of the men in my unit."

"That's a useful skill," Friedrich was impressed. "I am hoping to open my own barber shop."

"Oh?" Johann's eyebrows raised. "Perhaps you'd consent to give my hair a trim before we arrive?"

Friedrich laughed. "Of course. But I won't guarantee the results. The rocking of the train will make it hard to hold my scissors steady."

Johann joined in his laughter. "I didn't take that into consideration. I may be putting my life at risk if we do it on the train. I think I'll pass."

"I don't blame you," Friedrich smiled, then he sighed as the face of a certain English soldier came into his head.

"What is it? Your face suddenly looks sad."

"I was just remembering the last haircut I gave. He was an English soldier that I met during the Christmas Truce."

"I heard about that. We didn't see any such truce in our area. What was it like?"

Friedrich took a moment to find the right words. "It was incredible. To be talking with, playing with, eating with men we had tried to kill just the day before, was an experience not to be forgotten. I learned so much about them from that brief encounter."

"What did you learn?"

"I learned that they are men, just as we are. They have families, homes, work, beliefs… so many things are similar. There are some differences, certainly. Their foods are different. They don't dress as we do. Their language is different. But in all the ways that make us men, they are the same. They complain about the officers over them…" Friedrich's eyes grew wide as he remembered who he was talking to.

Johan smiled. "Go on. I'm well aware that officers are the enlisted man's nemesis, nearly as much as the enemy we are fighting."

Friedrich relaxed a bit. "It all comes down to the fact that they are just men. Human beings who are in a terrible situation, just as we are. It was hard to think of shooting at them the next day, I'll tell you."

"Did you?" Johann asked, his face intent. "Did you shoot them?"

Friedrich shook his head. "No. I tried, but found I kept seeing the English soldier's face and just couldn't shoot at them. As I stood on the firing-step the next day, with bullets whizzing all around me, I felt the fear of death, as I had so many times before. A corporal came along and ordered me to shoot. After I fired and killed one of them, I vomited. I felt physically ill. My knees were shaking and I was quite frankly ashamed of myself.

"Some of my comrades were absolutely undisturbed by what had happened. One boasted he had killed a Tommy with the butt of his rifle, another had strangled a captain, a French captain. A third had hit somebody over the head with his spade.

"These were ordinary men, Johann," Friedrich's face was a study in bewilderment. "One was a train conductor, another a commercial traveler, two were students, and the rest were farm workers, ordinary people who never would have thought to do any harm to anyone. How is it that they became so cruel?"

Johann looked at a young boy playing with a wooden car in the seat across the aisle. When he spoke, his voice was husky and low. "I remember when they trained me to become an officer. We were told that the good soldier kills without thinking of his adversary as a human being. The very moment he sees in him a fellow man, he is not a good soldier anymore."

Friedrich nodded. "Perhaps you are right. I shook the hands of several English soldiers. I walked and talked with them. I played football with them. After that, I could no longer shoot at them.

"The Englishman, Thomas, whose hair I cut was just a poor boy who had to fight, who had to go in with the most cruel weapons against men who have nothing against him personally, who only wore the uniform of another nation, who spoke another language. But he was a man who had a father and mother, a wife at home who he'd just learned was expecting a baby. He was going to be a new father, just as I am a new father. We had more in common than we had differences."

Johann's face had a far-away look. "Sometimes, in the beginning, I would wake up at night drenched in sweat because I saw the eyes of my fallen adversary, of the enemy, and I tried to convince myself what would have happened to me if I wouldn't have thrust my sword first into his belly. I wondered what it was that made we soldiers stab each other, strangle each other, and go for each other like mad dogs. What was it that made us, who had nothing against them personally, fight with them to the very end, dying for what?"

"We are civilized people, are we not?" Friedrich asked, sincerely.

"So we tell ourselves," Johann nodded. "But I wonder if the culture we boast so much about is only a very thin lacquer which chips off the moment we come in contact with cruel things like real war."

"I disagree," Friedrich shook his head. "I think when we meet the enemy face-to-face, when we learn to know them, the civilized part of us resurfaces. When we know that they are men like we are, we are not so quick to do them harm. I would hope that they would feel the same.

"Perhaps every war should start with a Christmas truce. Perhaps that would end, or at least shorten, the conflicts, saving many lives that would otherwise be lost to that insanity we call war."

Looking out the window, Johan was silent for a moment. "Perhaps. But I'm guessing the officers in charge are thinking it wasn't wise for the officers in your area to allow the fraternization at all."

"Perhaps not wise for the war's sake, but it was the best part of this *verdammt* war for me," Friedrich declared in all seriousness.

Regarding him, Johann nodded. "I can understand that. For me, the best part was the friends I've made along the way. Fine fellows I've shared experiences with that will live in my memory as long as life shall last."

"I made one such friend. Fritz. I won't forget him any time soon. We protected each other from danger, shared food and sleep."

"I know. My comrades and I have seen thousands wounded and dying. We've had good times and bad ones together. But now we must start a new life, make new friends, overcome new challenges."

Friedrich suddenly sat up straight and looked intently out the window. "That's Ypres. We fought there."

"It's certainly seen better days, hasn't it?" Johann commented.

"Yes. It's taken as much of a beating as the soldiers who fought there. I wonder how any of us survived?"

"I would guess a lot of luck, good hearing, and a keen sense of danger. That's how any good soldier survives war."

"But, what was it for?" Friedrich turned to him. "What have we got for it? Or anyone else for that matter? What is so important that so many good men have to die, on both sides of No Man's Land?"

Johan shook his head. "I have no answer for that one, my friend. No answer at all. Let's just hope we have lived through it all for a good purpose."

Loud pounding from the floor above made Karl cry all the louder.

Klara looked up and glared, willing her displeasure to seep through the ceiling into the grouchy woman's living room.

"*Stille, stille, mein kleiner,*" she crooned. "It's just cranky Frau Schultz. If you can stop crying, she will stop pounding."

Humming a lullaby, Frau Schmidt walked the floor, patting Karl's back and hoping he would quit crying soon. Ever since his mother had died, the infant was inconsolable. Herr Otto brought fresh goat's milk every day for him, but it was almost as if the little one knew his mother was gone and refused to be comforted by anyone else.

It had been a month since Gerdie's death. Klara and Gustav had shared the responsibility of caring for little Karl. The hard work of caring for a baby, and the lack of sleep were beginning to take their toll on both of them. Klara prayed once again that Friedrich would find his way home swiftly and safely.

At last, Karl's crying slowed and finally stopped as he fell asleep. Klara breathed a slow sigh of relief and dropped into the rocking chair. Gustav had brought it over, along with the trunk containing Gerdie and Friedrich's belongings. Their landlord had insisted they move everything out right away so he could rent the room as quickly as possible. It hadn't seemed right to disturb their belongings when Friedrich wasn't there to say yea or nay. But there was no choice, so they gathered what they could and moved it into Frau Schmidt's apartment.

Klara was rocking and beginning to nod when a loud knock woke her and the baby abruptly.

"*Potzblitz!*" Frau Schmidt muttered under her breath as Karl resumed crying. "*Kommen,*" she called. "Coming."

Holding the infant in one arm, she managed to open the door and step back. Her eyes widened when she saw the *polizei* at the door.

"Yes, sir," she said, bewildered. "Is there something wrong?"

"I'm afraid so, frau," he said. "We've received several complaints about a baby crying non-stop here."

Frau Schmidt frowned, thinking *verdammt* Frau Schultz. "I'm sorry, sir," she ducked her head. "The poor *kleiner* has lost his mother. His father is fighting in Belgium and he is all alone in the world. I've taken him in just until his father returns, and am doing my best to care for him, but he struggles without his mother."

The policeman frowned. "I'm sorry to hear that. Does your landlord know you have an infant here?"

Klara's eyebrows raised as she tried to look innocent. "I didn't think to tell him. Will that be a problem, do you think?"

Shrugging, the officer shook his head. "I don't know. It depends on how he has classified these apartments. If they are classified as No Children or Pets, then yes, it will be a problem."

Klara sighed. "I suppose I should contact him then."

"That would be a good idea," the policeman said. "I will have to file a report, and he will receive a copy since the complaint was filed on one of his tenants. It would be better if you talked to him before he receives that report. Meanwhile, try to keep the baby quiet until this is resolved."

"I will," Klara nodded. "Thank you, sir."

She started to close the door when she saw Gustav pass the policeman on the street. Waiting for him to approach, she gritted her teeth, seething inside as she continued to rock and pat Karl.

"You look angry, *mein Klara*," Gustav remarked.

"Perhaps because I am!" she exploded, handing him the still-crying baby.

His eyebrows raised and he escorted her inside carrying the baby.

"Tell me what's happened?" he requested after he had her sitting comfortably in the rocking chair. He stood by the window and bounced Karl gently, trying to calm him.

"It's that *alte hexe*, Frau Schultz," she hissed. "She's filed a formal complaint to the *polizei*. Now, I must talk to the landlord and see if he'll allow me to keep Karl here, even though the apartments are classified No Children No Pets."

"What if he won't allow it?" Gustav asked, concerned. "I live in a Male Only building, so *der kliener* can't stay with me."

"Why not?" Klara asked, momentarily hopeful. "He's a male."

Gustav chuckled, "Yes, but the youngest male there is 44. I don't think he'd fit in very well."

Klara sighed. "I just don't see what the problem is. He'll adjust in time, and we'll teach him to be quiet as a mouse. Frau Schultz will never know he's here. If only she'd be a little more patient!"

With that, she pounded the arm of the rocking chair, then stood up, pacing the floor. Ranting about uncharitable neighbors, she continued pacing, growing more agitated with each sentence.

Gustav frowned as he watched her. He'd never seen his Klara act this way. It wasn't like her to carry on so. He continued to bounce and rock the baby as he tried to find words to soothe his beloved fiancée.

Suddenly, Klara stopped, a bewildered look on her face.

"What is it?" Gustav asked.

"I don't know," she shook her head. "I just feel strange... Oh!"

She clutched her chest, gasped, and collapsed on the floor.

Gustav stood for a moment, unable to believe what he was seeing. When Karl wailed again, he looked down at the crying boy then back at his beloved lying still on the floor.

"I'm sorry, *mein kleiner*," he said as he crossed the small room. "*Mein Klara* needs me."

When the baby was safely in the cradle, he rushed to Klara's side and knelt over her. She was clutching her chest, sweating and pale. He shook her gently and called her name.

"Klara," he whispered, then repeated it louder when she didn't respond. "Klara, don't leave me!"

Sunlight filtered through the dingy window, moving slowly across his blankets as Thomas opened his eyes and blinked at the brightness. Confused, he tried to look around as his eyes adjusted, but every little move made his breath catch as the pain in his head intensified.

Breathing shallow, to minimize the pain, he tried to be content with moving only his eyes. He couldn't remember where he was or how he'd arrived here.

The room was large and seemed rather dingy. As he moved his eyes to the right, he saw a wood-paneled wall. To his left, he couldn't see much except what looked like more wall that seemed to extend forever. *That doesn't make sense*, he thought. *Tents don't have wooden walls.*

A few moments later, a woman in a starched white uniform with a red cross on the bib of her apron appeared in his line of sight.

"Oh, good," she cooed. "You're awake. I'll just tell the doctor."

She's far too perky for this place, Thomas thought, frowning.

After a moment, an army doctor appeared with the perky nurse by his side.

"Welcome back," he said, then referred to the clipboard he carried. "Private Bennett, is it?"

Thomas tried to nod, but winced as the pain shot through his head again.

"Don't try to move. You've had quite a nasty blow to the head, among other things," the doctor warned. "You'd be better off just lying still for a few days. Let yourself heal."

"What happened? Where am I?" Thomas whispered, surprised that he had no voice.

"You are in the Casualty Clearing Station at Remmy Farm near Ypres, Belgium."

"You were wounded, soldier," the perky nurse said, patting his arm. "But you're going to be just fine."

Thomas closed his eyes and it all came flooding back; the gunfire, artillery, an explosion, Budgy...

"My friend?" he tried to ask.

"Friend?" the doctor looked puzzled. "What's his name?"

"Budgy... wait, Private Ellis," he amended. "He may have come here with me."

Nodding, the doctor began writing. "I'll see what I can find out. Meanwhile, let's look under those bandages."

Gently, more gently than Thomas expected, he lifted the bandages and peered under, pursing his lips as he examined the wound. Then nodding, he turned to the nurse.

"It's beginning to heal, but I want these bandages changed twice a day for the next few days. We don't want infection to set in."

Looking back at Thomas, he smiled. "You're lucky, son. As Nurse Morrow said, you're going to be just fine."

"Thank you," Thomas whispered, his voice starting to kick in a little.

When the doctor and nurse were gone, Thomas spent a few minutes testing his range of motion. First his head, which he couldn't move very far before the headache flared. Next, his shoulders, arms, and hands. All seemed to be in working order. He lifted his right hand and felt the bandages on his head. They seemed enormous to him, but he thought perhaps it was to protect the wound.

Dropping his hand to his side, he took a couple of deep breaths. That caused his ribs to ache a little, but it didn't seem that any ribs were broken.

Next, he tried to bend his knees, which tested both his knees and his hips. He couldn't see them because lifting his head hurt, but he could feel them move fairly easily. So far, so good. His right leg was sore and his foot hurt, but both ankles seemed to be moving well and his toes tingled. Probably from being still for so long.

He took another deep breath and sighed, closing his eyes. It was amazing how that little bit of movement had tired him out. *No harm in a little nap*, he thought, allowing himself to drift off to sleep.

At the other end of the ward, the doctor and nurse were discussing him.

"Why didn't you tell him, doctor?" she asked.

"He wasn't ready," was his answer. "We'll let him heal a bit before we burden him with the bad news."

Maggie couldn't decide whether to be relieved, angry, or worried. She looked at the letter again, re-reading it for perhaps the dozenth time.

April 14, 1915

My dearest Maggie,

I hope this finds you well, and that our baby is growing healthy and strong inside you.

I have news that needs sharing, my love. I want you to sit down and make sure you are not alone when you read this.

No, no, there is no reason to panic or get hysterical. (I've heard that pregnant women sometimes get hysterical.)

There's no easy way to say this, but I've been wounded. I am recovering in a Casualty Clearing Station at Remmy Farm. They are taking good care of me here.

I have a concussion and the doctors are not letting me move around much right now, so a nurse is writing this for me. But my head will heal and I'm going to be just fine. So, no worrying, understood? Worrying won't do you or our baby any good at all.

Say hello to your mother and Katie for me. Have Katie give you a big hug from me, will you?

Don't worry, sweetheart. I'm healing nicely.

All my love,
Thomas

On the one hand, she was relieved to finally hear from him. She was relieved that he was alive and in a hospital, safe from harm.

She was angry that he didn't say whether he would be coming home or not. She was angry that he'd been sent to Belgium and that he'd been wounded. It almost made her want to echo Katie's sentiment, *I hate those Germans*. Almost.

She was worried that he might be sent back to the fighting. She was worried, too, because he didn't say how bad the concussion was. She thought there might be residual effects from concussions, but she wasn't sure. *I'll have to ask Dr. Williams about that,* she thought.

"Maggie! Maggie!" Katie shouted as the door slammed behind her. "Come quick!"

"What is it, poppet?" Maggie asked looking up from her letter.

"It's Beth. She's in the park and can't stand up! Come quick!"

Grabbing her sweater off the hook as she ran, Maggie flew down the steps and up the street, with Katie close behind.

The "park" wasn't really a park at all. A generous neighbor had taken down the fence surrounding his yard and invited the neighbors to come and enjoy his flowers. He'd even put a couple of benches near the flowerbeds so the neighbors could relax as they took in the scents, sights, and sounds of his beautiful little garden.

Maggie often found herself wandering among the flowers, enjoying their colors and fragrant scents. It wasn't surprising that Beth was there, since she lived only two doors down.

As she approached, she saw Beth lying on the ground near one of the benches. She was trying to sit up, but her face was etched in pain.

"Beth, are you hurt?" Maggie called as she drew closer.

Shaking her head no, Beth continued to try and sit up.

Kneeling beside her, Maggie gently pushed her back. "Don't try to get up just yet," she admonished as she removed her sweater and rolled it up, placing it under Beth's head. "Tell me what happened."

Beth laid back and took a shaky breath. "I was enjoying Mr. Carlisle's daffodils when I felt my belly tighten. I've felt it before, but this was different. It was more intense and lasted longer. I didn't think much about it, but it happened again, and then again. So, I started to stand up to go home and rest. Then it was like someone stabbed me in the gut."

She paused and grimaced as another contraction started. Maggie put a hand on her belly and felt how tight it was. "How often are the contractions coming, Beth?" she asked when it had passed.

"Every couple of minutes now," Beth answered, panting a little.

Maggie looked up at her sister. "Katie, I need you to be brave and fast. Can you do that?"

Katie nodded, eyes wide, but a determined look on her face.

"I need you to first go get Dr. Williams. Tell him Beth is having her baby and we need him right now. Then run home and get Mother. Tell her we need towels, sheets, whatever she can grab and carry. Got that?"

Katie nodded again and then ran toward the doctor's office.

Maggie reached into her pocket and took out her handkerchief. She wiped the sweat from Beth's brow and tried to reassure her.

"Do you need some help?" a kind voice asked from behind her. She looked up and saw Mr. Carlisle. "I'm not sure."

She turned and asked Beth, "Do you think you can walk? Maybe we can get you into the house."

Just then, Beth's face screwed up in pain and she groaned.

Looking back at Mr. Carlisle, then at the small crowd that was gathering, she had a brilliant idea.

"Mr. Carlisle, would you bring as many blankets and sheets as you have available? I'd like to create a curtain around her so she's not so exposed to the public, if you know what I mean."

"Of course," he said and ran into his house.

He returned a few moments later. Katie and Mrs. Gilley had arrived with their own sheets and blankets. Maggie directed them to hand each spectator a blanket or sheet. Then she told them all to turn their backs and find two corners of their blanket. They were to keep one in their left hand and take a corner of another blanket from the person on their right.

It wasn't long before there was a nice, wide curtain of blankets and sheets surrounding Beth. Another sheet covered her, and a folded blanket replaced Maggie's sweater as a pillow.

A few minutes later, the doctor arrived and surveyed the scene.

"Nice work," he complimented the crowd before ducking under a sheet to kneel beside Beth.

"How are you feeling, Beth?" he asked.

She didn't have to answer. Her groans answered for her.

"I understand." He patted her hand and got to work.

Ten minutes later, Beth screamed and pushed one last time. A healthy baby's cry followed. The crowd cheered, but not one of them turned around to look.

Maggie smiled and laughed with her friend as the doctor finished the delivery and handed Beth the baby.

"It's a girl," he smiled.

Beth looked down at her baby daughter and her smile became a look of shock.

"She's… she's yellow!" Beth stammered.

The doctor looked at the baby, seemingly unconcerned. "Yes, she is."

"What's wrong with her?" Tears filled Beth's eyes.

"She's a canary baby," he answered, nonchalantly. "You worked in the factory, right?"

Beth nodded.

"I'm seeing a lot of these canary babies from mothers who worked in the factory. It's a side effect of the chemicals you were exposed to. It's not harmful to the baby. She'll grow out of it in time."

"Are you sure?" Beth wasn't convinced.

The doctor smiled reassuringly. "Yes. I'm sure. Now, let's get you to the hospital."

Beth and her daughter were carefully loaded into the ambulance. Maggie watched them drive away, feeling a mixture of joy, concern, and worry. She was happy that Beth's delivery had gone so well, despite having to deliver in the park. She was concerned about Beth's baby and wondered if indeed she would outgrow the peculiar coloring. And she was worried that her own baby might be a canary baby. What would that mean? Was the doctor right? Or were there things he didn't know... or wouldn't say?

When she turned around, Mr. Carlisle had already gathered all the blankets and sheets, and Katie was helping to carry them inside.

"Can I help you wash any of those?" she called. "I'd be happy to."

He turned and smiled at her. "No, thank you. I have a perfectly good helper right here."

Maggie watched as he turned to Katie. "This was the most exciting day I've had in a long time. Washing these will help me remember it all the better."

"I want to remember all the better, too." Katie told him. "May I help you wash?"

He laughed and nodded. "Of course, you may."

What a nice man, Maggie thought, as she and her mother carried their own sheets and blankets home. *What an eventful day!*

Chapter Eighteen

April 18, 1915

Friedrich stepped off the train, his heart pounding. Grabbing his bag, he raced down the street towards Frau Schmidt's apartment. He assumed since Frau Schmidt and Herr Otto were caring for his son, that they'd be there.

As he turned the corner, he was struck by how limp Frau Schmidt's flower garden looked. She was always proud of her garden, and even this early in the season, her flowers should be starting to bloom and looking healthy. Instead, they were wilted and many were lying on the ground, nearly dead.

This alarmed him and he pushed to run faster. Reaching her door, he knocked. "Frau Schmidt," he called. "It's Friedrich!"

No answer.

He knocked again, louder this time. "Frau Schmidt! Herr Otto!" he called, his voice becoming frantic.

No answer.

Finally, he pounded on the door and demanded to be let in. There was no answer from inside, but someone thumped down the stairs and he turned to see who it was.

Frau Schultz glared at him. "Why are you making such a racket, young man?"

Then she peered at him through her thick glasses.

"Oh, I know you," she smirked. "You're the flower thief. Well, you can help yourself. Frau Schmidt certainly can't stop you."

"What?" Friedrich stammered. "Why not?"

"Haven't you heard?" The frau's smirk deepened. "She's had a heart attack. They took her to the hospital a week ago. I wouldn't be surprised if the old bat is dead by now."

Friedrich didn't hear the last sentence, as he was racing towards Kaiserswerth Hospital. It was several blocks away, and he'd run two kilometers from the train station already, but although his breathing was heavy, he didn't notice it.

Stopping at the front desk, he asked, "Which room is Klara Schmidt's?"

The nurse behind the desk referred to her notebook. "Room 17," she answered, "but…"

She didn't have an opportunity to finish, however, as Friedrich was racing down the hall, glancing at room numbers as he ran.

It didn't take long to locate room 17. He had enough presence of mind to stop and try to catch his breath. It wouldn't do anyone any good if he burst in on her and caused her another heart attack.

Licking his lips, he gently opened the door and peeked in. What he saw caused his heart to sink down to his shoes.

The dim room was small with two small beds in it. The first bed held a patient, sleeping on her side, facing the wall. He knew this wasn't her, though, because the other bed had a chair beside it and Herr Otto was sitting there holding Frau Schmidt's hand.

"Herr Otto?" he whispered.

The old man turned slowly and looked at Friedrich. Gradually, recognition dawned and a small smile graced the haggard face.

"Friedrich," he whispered back. "Come in. It's good to see you, my boy."

Friedrich stepped into the room and over to the bed. "Where is he?"

Misunderstanding the question, Herr Otto looked lovingly at his fiancée and replied, "She's recovering, but it's going to be a while."

Although Friedrich was glad to hear Frau Schmidt would recover, that wasn't the question burning most on his mind. He put his hand on Herr Otto's shoulder and asked again, "Herr Otto, where is my son?"

Gustav looked up, a little bewildered, then realization dawned.

"Oh, I'm sorry, Friedrich. They took him away."

"What?" Friedrich's voice rose at the horror of what he'd just heard. "What did you say?"

"They took him away," Herr Otto frowned. "It was all so confusing. The doctor was there, and a policeman, and the grouchy lady from upstairs. Then two men came in with a stretcher to take Klara to the hospital. I started to follow them when the grouchy lady wanted to know what we were going to do with the baby. The policeman said there was no choice. The boy would have to go to the children's home until his father came to claim him. That's you."

Gustav looked up with an almost delighted look. "You're here now, Friedrich! You can go and claim your son."

Trying to restrain himself from throttling the old man, Friedrich merely squeezed his shoulder a little. "Herr Otto, there are several *waisenhäuser* in Düsseldorf. Which one has my son?"

Looking bewildered again, Herr Otto thought, then shook his head. "I'm sorry, Friedrich. I don't know. I followed them to the hospital so I could be near Klara. I didn't ask which one. I'm sorry."

Friedrich took a deep breath and forced himself to let go of the old man's shoulder. He turned and walked out of the room without a backward glance.

A few steps down the hall, he stopped and leaned against the wall. Now what? How was he going to find his son? *It's not a big city,* he thought. How many children's homes can there be? I'll search every one until I find him!

"Hey, Tommy-boy." Someone poked his arm and Thomas groaned.

"Hey, buddy. Wake up." Thomas groaned again, but opened his eyes.

It didn't take him long to recognize the familiar face of his friend, Budgy.

"Budgy!" he exclaimed, trying to sit up.

"Don't get up on my account," Budgy laughed, pushing him back down.

"I thought you might be dead," Thomas said, allowing himself to lie back against the pillows.

"I thought so, too, for a while there. I thought you were a goner, too. When I saw you fly through the air like that," Budgy shook his head. "I was sure you were history."

"Guess we were both lucky," Thomas smiled, then his eyebrows shot up as he remembered. "What about your arm?"

Budgy grimaced, then looked at his shoulder, then at the empty sleeve hanging from it. "Lost the arm, but kept my life."

"Oh man! I'm sorry."

Shrugging, Budgy shook his head. "There are worse things to lose. What about you? Any missing parts?"

"No, I seem to be intact except for this headache that doesn't want to go away," Thomas smiled.

Just then, the doctor and nurse arrived.

"Private Ellis," the doctor acknowledged Budgy. "It's nice to see you up and about."

Budgy looked a little confused. "You asked me to visit Tommy-boy this morning, didn't you, Doctor?"

Pursing his lips, the doctor looked a little nonplussed, but nodded. "I did."

Now it was Thomas's turn to be confused. "Why did you want him here this morning, Doctor?"

Sighing, the doctor pulled up a stool and sat down. "Because I have some bad news for you and I thought it might help to have your friend here for support."

"Bad news?"

The doctor nodded. "Besides the wound to your head, the concussion and skull fracture, you sustained another wound that we haven't discussed yet."

Thomas furrowed his eyebrows, but quickly allowed them to relax when his head began to throb with the movement. "What is it? Everything feels fine to me except my head. I'm a little sore, but that's to be expected, right?"

"Yes," the doctor nodded again, then stood up. Pulling a pencil out of his pocket he moved to the end of the bed. "I want you to close your eyes and tell me what you feel."

Obediently, Thomas closed his eyes. He felt the blankets being lifted off his legs and heard Budgy's intake of breath.

Thomas chuckled, but kept his eyes closed. "My spindly legs caught you off guard, did they, Budgy-boy?"

"Uh… yeah," Budgy agreed. "They're scarecrow legs all right."

Everyone was silent for a few moments, then Thomas felt the pencil pressing against his left knee.

"I feel the pencil on my knee," he said.

"Good. How about now?"

He felt pressure running down the outside of his left leg.

"Now it's on the outside of my leg."

Again, the pressure moved.

"Now it's on the inside of my leg."

The doctor kept moving the pencil and pressing different parts of his patient's left leg until he reached the toes. He pressed each toe separately and Thomas accurately reported each one.

"Good," the doctor said, moving to the other side of the bed. "Now we'll check the other leg."

Starting with the knee, he systematically pressed the same points on Thomas's right leg. Thomas reported each pressure point. Knee, outside leg, inside leg, then… nothing.

"Why'd you stop, doctor?" Thomas asked, tempted to open his eyes.

"Because I'm finished," the doctor said, resignation in his voice.

Puzzled, Thomas opened his eyes and looked into the sympathetic face of his doctor. "You didn't finish yet. I didn't feel my ankle, foot, or toes."

Slowly, deliberately, the doctor raised Thomas's right leg so he could see.

It took a moment for the sight to register. There was his leg, battered and bruised from the knee down, with cuts and scrapes adorning his lanky limb. But that wasn't what drew his attention. At the end of his leg, where his ankle and foot should have been, there was nothing. A gauze bandage covered the stump.

"I don't understand." He shook his head to clear his thinking, and winced as the pain reminded him he wasn't supposed to move his head. A moment later, he continued, "For a week now, I've been bending my legs, exercising my muscles, knees, hips, calves, ankles, and feet. I can feel my foot. I can feel my ankle bend. I can feel each toe. But..." he paused, "why can't I see them?"

"Because they're not there, Tommy-boy," Budgy said, leaning over to look his friend in the face. "It's called phantom pain. I have it with my arm, too."

Thomas looked at Budgy, dazed and uncomprehending. "Phantom pain?"

"Yes," the doctor interjected matter-of-factly. "It's quite common with amputees. Your brain hasn't processed that there is no foot there, so it manufactures sensations that it thinks should be there."

"But..." Thomas started, then stopped, comprehension finally dawning. "I have no right foot... I have no right foot!"

"That's right, my friend," Budgy said, "but you're alive. What's more, you're going home to your sweet Maggie! That's worth a foot, isn't it?"

Closing his eyes, Thomas took a deep breath and tried to understand what Budgy was telling him. He had no foot, but he was going home. But then what? Who was going to hire a cripple? How was he going to support Maggie and the baby? The baby. How was he going to raise a child if he couldn't even run with it, or play ball with it, or jiggle it on his knee?

"I want to be alone," he said, forlornly.

"Maybe you should talk about what you're feeling?" Budgy said. "It helped me when I found out."

"No. I just want to be alone," Thomas said again.

"There are a group of amputees that meet..." the doctor began.

"I said, I WANT TO BE ALONE!"

Silence for a few moments, then the doctor and nurse walked away. Finally, Budgy stood and patted his shoulder. "Just let me know when you're ready to talk, Tommy-boy. I'll be right here."

Thomas stared at the ceiling. At other crisis times in his life, he'd turn to God in prayer. Now, he just stared. He couldn't talk to a God who would let something like this happen.

He tried to think of Maggie singing a song. *That might cheer me up,* he thought. But the song that came to mind was "Daddy has a Sweetheart", the first song he ever heard her sing, and that just made him angrier. Clenching his teeth, he pounded his fists into the bed on either side of his hips as tears began rolling down his face into his ears.

After a few minutes, however, he took a few shaky breaths, trying to calm down, since crying caused his head to hurt again. Finally, he opened his eyes and tried to turn his head to call for the nurse.

He was surprised to see Budgy sitting on a stool a few feet away.

"What are you doing here?"

"I couldn't leave my friend when he's in trouble," Budgy replied cheerily.

Thomas tried to hold back the tears that threatened again. He'd never had such a loyal friend!

"Hey now, Tommy-boy. No more tears. They're not good for your headache."

A wry smile crossed Thomas's face. "That's the truth. So now what?"

"Now, you focus on healing. First, your head. Once it's safe, the doctors, nurses, and orderlies will help you get your muscles strong enough to walk on a wooden foot. By the time your baby is born, you'll be strong enough to chase him around the living room."

"That seems pretty optimistic." Thomas was dubious.

"Maybe just a little. The point is, you'll be able to do nearly everything you could before." Budgy stood and put his hand on Thomas's shoulder. "And I'll be there to cheer you on."

Once again, tears filled Thomas's eyes. "You're a good friend, Budgy. The best."

"I'll do in a pinch," Budgy grinned.

Tears streamed down Maggie's face as she crumpled the unwelcome letter in her hand. *Why?* she thought. *Why?*

Her mother glanced up from her mending, studied her daughter's face for a moment, then set the sewing aside.

"What is it?" she asked softly.

Maggie turned to face her mother. Her face had huge red splotches on it. Tears were streaming from her eyes. Silent sobs wracked her body.

Mrs. Gilley rose and crossed the room, sitting beside Maggie on the davenport. Putting an arm around her, she pulled her close.

"Let it out, Maggie-girl. Let it out."

That was the final straw, and Maggie's silent sobs became vocal. She cried hard for nearly twenty minutes.

Once, in the middle, Katie came in, but her mother's stern look and shake of the head sent her scurrying back to her room.

Finally, Maggie's tears began to subside and her mother handed her a fresh handkerchief from her pocket.

"Now, what's this all about?" she asked kindly.

Her kindness nearly started a new flood of tears, but Maggie gulped hard and bit her lip to keep the tears at bay.

"It's Thomas," she whispered.

"Yes?" Mrs. Gilley prodded gently.

"He's... he..." Maggie stopped, unable to articulate what she'd read.

"Take your time," her mother advised. "The words will come."

Maggie took a deep breath, then another. One more deep breath, then she blurted, "He's lost his leg!"

That announcement sent her into a flood of new tears. Mrs. Gilley held her, stroking her hair and whispering consoling words.

Again, the tears subsided and Maggie took a shaky breath. "What are we going to do?" she asked forlornly.

Her mother cocked her head and regarded her carefully. "Are you ready to hear a real answer, or do you need more consoling?"

Taken aback, Maggie looked at her mother as though she'd grown another head.

"What do you mean?" she demanded.

"I mean you are a grown woman who's facing a very difficult

situation. I am more than willing to keep consoling you, but that's not going to help you handle this in the long term."

Maggie considered this for a moment, then nodded. "I think I understand. I need to face reality so I can be ready when Thomas comes home, right?"

"Exactly. If you have faced the possibilities and have some ideas in your head already, you'll be ready to help your husband as he adjusts to life without his leg."

Staring at the handkerchief in her hand, Maggie's thoughts turned from her own pain to the pain and fear Thomas must be feeling. She looked up again and replied, her voice stronger. "I'm ready to face reality."

Her mother smiled with approval. "Good. Let's start with the hard things first. What's the worst thing you can think of that might be a result of this?"

Maggie thought hard. "He might be in a wheelchair for the rest of his life."

Mrs. Gilley nodded, considering. "That would be hard. What if there are other wounds that he was afraid to tell you about?"

"Oh, I hadn't thought about that. I was focused on the missing leg."

"I know, but even if it was only his leg was physically wounded, there are other wounds that will be unseen. His self-confidence, his feeling of being a whole man, his ability to work...and there might be nightmares that affect his mood and personality."

Maggie's eyes grew wide at the picture her mother painted. "Oh dear," she whispered.

"However," her mother continued, "he may have only some of those problems. He may have no problems at all. That's the challenge of war. Some men come away with very few side effects. Others have many. So, let's talk about some of them and try to formulate a plan for dealing with them."

For the next hour, they talked about different scenarios and came up with a few ideas for handling them. Mostly, they talked about how Thomas might be feeling about it all, and how Maggie could help him.

"Can I come out now?" Katie asked timidly from the hallway.

"Yes, poppet," Maggie smiled, opening her arms to her little sister.

"Oh good. I was getting tired of being by myself," Katie sighed, giving Maggie a big hug. She snuggled herself between her mother and sister, looked at each in turn, then asked, "So, what are we talking about?"

Maggie laughed and ruffled her hair. "We are talking about Thomas and how we can help him when he comes home."

"Help him?"

Mrs. Gilley placed a finger under Katie's chin and turned her face towards her. "Yes, Katie. Do you remember when we learned that Thomas had been wounded in the war?"

Katie nodded, her attention riveted on her mother.

"We just learned that his leg was shot so badly that they had to take it off."

Katie frowned. "So he only has one leg now?"

"Yes. Plus, he hit his head hard and hurt it, too."

Katie's eyes widened, "So he has no head?"

Maggie laughed in spite of herself. "He has his head, poppet. But it was hurt and may give him headaches sometimes."

"Oh," Katie nodded. "So how can we help him?"

Looking at her mother, Maggie took the lead. "Mostly, we love him. We treat him the same way we always have, and if he asks us to help him do something, we do it."

"So, we can still tease him?" Katie's eyes twinkled.

"Yes, I think that would be most appropriate," Maggie chuckled, and her mother joined the laughter.

"Oh good. I don't think it would be fun if I couldn't tease him sometimes," Katie grinned.

"Perhaps that will be the best medicine of all," Mrs. Gilley smiled, hugging her daughter.

Chapter Nineteen

Friedrich closed the door behind him, then leaned against it, closing his eyes. This was the seventeenth children's home he'd checked, but no one knew anything about his son. Oh, everyone had been polite and some even feigned concern, but with dysentery running rampant, and the war taking the lives of so many fathers, there were more orphans than the city could care for, so no one had time to truly care for one little *kleiner*.

He took a deep breath and pulled a list out of his pocket. Only two more left to check. He'd left them until last because they were on the outskirts of town. He hadn't thought it likely that his son would be there.

But when all else has failed, it's time to check out the unlikely, he thought. Pushing off from the door, he started walking down the street.

Two hours later, he found himself looking at a shabby old apartment building that looked as though it should be torn down instead of housing orphans. He truly hoped Karl wasn't here!

Knocking on the door, he looked up at the dirty windows and wondered if his son was on the other side of one of them. In a moment, the door opened to reveal a disheveled, red-haired matron with a faded flowered dress and a dirty apron.

"Yes?" she asked pleasantly, brushing a strand of hair from her face.

"Pardon me," he hesitated, her pleasant manner taking him off-guard. "I am looking for my son. He…"

Just then there was a blood-curdling scream coming from inside.

The woman's eyebrows shot up and she raced back inside. Friedrich followed her, his heart pounding.

They ran down a narrow hallway into a large room with open windows and toys strewn everywhere.

"What's wrong? Who screamed?" the woman asked, her voice stern, but not frantic.

"He did," a skinny girl with dark hair and freckles answered pointing to a boy pouting next to her.

Putting her hands on her hips, the matron frowned. "Heinrich, why did you scream? I thought someone was being killed."

"She took my truck and wouldn't give it back," the boy accused, reaching for the toy in question.

"Is that true, Frieda?" she asked the girl.

"Well..." she hedged. "He put it down and I thought he was finished with it."

"I put it down so I could rebuild the road she spoiled," Heinrich's voice was rising in frustration and anger.

"I see." The matron pursed her lips. "I think the only answer is to put the truck away and clean up for lunch. In addition, I have two words of advice for you two. First, Frieda, you must learn to play nicely or other children won't want to play with you at all. Second, Heinrich, you need to learn when it's appropriate to scream like that. If you or another child is hurt, then it's appropriate. If you are angry, there are other ways to express that anger. Do you both understand me?"

Both children nodded and the matron clapped her hands to get the attention of the dozen or so children in the room. "It's time to clean up for lunch, *kinder*. And there is a surprise in store for you if you clean up well."

"Hurray!" the children yelled as they scurried about putting toys, books, and dolls away.

She watched them for a moment, smiled, and nodded to another woman who nodded back.

Turning to Friedrich, she apologized, "I'm sorry for the interruption. I've found that dealing with such behaviors as they are happening is much more effective than waiting until the child has forgotten what he or she has done."

Friedrich nodded his understanding.

"Now, what can I do for you?" she asked.

"I'm looking for my son," he said simply.

"I see. Come into my office and tell me the story. Let's see if we can reunite you with your son." She smiled and led the way into a small, dingy room with a desk and two chairs. Two boxes sat in the corner with papers and files sticking out from under the lids.

Indicating he should sit, she took out a piece of paper and pencil. "Now," she said, her voice was all business. "How were you and your son separated?"

Friedrich told her about being sent to Belgium and having to leave his pregnant wife in Germany. He told how she'd delivered a healthy son nearly five months before, but she had never recovered and died six weeks later. He related how Frau Schmidt and Herr Otto had cared for Karl, but when she had a heart attack, the authorities had taken his son and placed him in a children's home, but no one seemed to know which one. After relating his experiences at the other homes he'd visited, she clucked her tongue and shook her head.

"I truly don't understand how such places stay open," she announced. "I've been in some of them and they don't care one bit about the children. They're only interested in the money the government pays them to house the unfortunate little ones."

She tapped the pencil against her chin thoughtfully. "I don't recall any babies being placed here under those circumstances. However, there was a fire at a *waisenhaus* across town and some of the children were sent to my friend's place for temporary refuge. She began taking in little ones when her husband was killed in France a few months ago. If your son is there, he's being well cared for. Let me give you her address and you can check with her."

"Fire?" Friedrich asked, suddenly alarmed.

"Yes," the matron nodded as she continued to write. "The kitchen caught fire and the place was filled with smoke. None of the children were hurt, but since they couldn't feed them from a burned-out kitchen, they were placed in temporary housing until the kitchen is rebuilt."

His heart began to slow its frantic beating as he reached for the paper she offered. He looked at it and realized it was only a couple of kilometers away.

"Thank you," he said as he stood and offered his hand. "I appreciate your help."

"It's my pleasure. I hope you find your son," the matron smiled kindly and escorted him to the door.

As he left, he finally had hope in his heart. Breaking into a run, it didn't take him long to find the tidy house the address indicated.

Knocking on the door, he looked at the flowers in the yard, the clean porch, and immaculate windows.

The door opened and a young woman holding a baby smiled at him.

"Can I help you?" she asked.

Friedrich stared at the infant in her arms and couldn't speak because of the lump that suddenly formed in his throat.

When he didn't answer, she tried again. "Can I help you?"

Swallowing hard, he managed to finally speak. "I hope so," he replied, his voice gruff with emotion. He told her an abbreviated version of his story, finishing with, "So, I was wondering if you by chance had my son?"

He looked pointedly at the baby she held. He hadn't noticed, but as he talked, the young woman tried to interrupt several times. Finally, when he finished, she put her hand on his arm. "Is your son's name Karl?"

"YES!" he yelled, startling the baby in her arms. "Is that...?"

"Sh," she admonished, then smiled. "No, come with me."

They made their way to a sunlit room with six cribs lined up against the wall. Each crib had a sleeping baby in it except one. She led him to a crib in the middle and pointed.

"Is that your son?" she asked.

Tears filling his eyes, he admitted, "I don't know. I've never met him before."

"Oh dear," she frowned. "That could be a problem. I don't know how we can prove he's your son, and without that proof, I can't allow you to take him."

Whirling to face her, Friedrich's months of frustration surfaced full-force. "What?" he yelled, then took a deep breath and with great restraint repeated, "What are you saying?"

"I'm saying we need to prove he's your son before I can allow you to take him," she said, her own voice showing frustration.

"How do we do that?" Friedrich asked.

"I'm not sure." She thought for a moment, then her face brightened. "Do you or your wife have a birthmark?"

Puzzled, Friedrich nodded. "My wife had a triangle-shaped birthmark on her right shoulder. Why?"

The young woman's face beamed. "That's good enough for me!" she exclaimed. She laid the now-sleeping infant in the empty crib then reached for the baby in the middle crib, lifting him out gently. She pulled back the blanket and little shirt to reveal a triangle-shaped birthmark on his right shoulder.

Tears filled Friedrich's eyes as he recognized the mark. Reaching for his son, he started to take him, then pulled back. "What if I drop him?" he asked, suddenly afraid.

"You won't," she reassured him, showing him how to hold the baby properly.

Friedrich cradled his son in his arms, kissing his head and stroking his face. After a moment, Karl stirred and opened his eyes. He stared up into his father's face for a moment, then offered the sweetest smile that melted Friedrich's heart.

"Well, I'll be," the young woman breathed.

Looking up for a moment, Friedrich's eyebrows went up quizzically. "What?"

"It's nothing short of a miracle," she replied. "Your son has been distraught since they brought him here. When he's not sleeping or eating, he's crying and fussing. Nothing we did seemed to console him. We've had the doctor here many times to be sure he wasn't sick or injured, but the doctor reassured us that he's healthy, just a very sad little boy. That's the first time I've ever seen him smile!"

Tenderly, Friedrich smiled back at his son. "Do not worry, *mein sohn*. I will be sure you have many opportunities to smile from now on."

He looked up at the young matron. "Thank you…" He paused. "I'm sorry. I don't know your name."

She smiled. "You've had other things on your mind. I'm Ilsa."

"*Danke,* Ilsa," Friedrich returned her smile. "I'll be forever in your debt."

"Would you like to stay for a cup of coffee, or...?" she left the question hanging.

"I think I should get Karl and I settled somewhere," he answered.

Her face fell, but she recovered quickly. "If you're looking for an apartment, there's one open next door."

"*Danke*, again," he grinned. "Perhaps I will stay for that cup of coffee."

The train wheels screeched as it came to a stop, smoke and embers billowed up to cloud the windows of the passenger car.

"Boxmoor and Hamel Hemstead Station," the conductor called as he made his way slowly between the seats.

Thomas allowed the man next to him to stand first, then he rose using his crutches for support. Reaching under the seat for his duffel, he pulled it out, aware that his heart was beating fast and his breath was shallow. He was nervous.

"No need to be nervous, Tommy-boy." Those were Budgy's parting words to him before he got off in London. "Your Maggie will love you whether you have a right foot or not."

I hope he's right, Thomas thought as he made his way down the aisle. He hesitated as he reached the steps leading to the platform. The distance between the last step and the wood of the platform looked very large.

Thomas swallowed hard and put his crutches on the first step, then followed with his good foot, holding the stump on his right leg behind him. *So far, so good.*

The next step was easier, but the step to the platform was farther down. Big breath, crutches, good foot, and...

His stump caught on the last step and he started to stumble forward. Trying frantically to catch himself, he reached too far with his left crutch. It slipped from his hand and he felt himself falling, losing his right crutch as he braced himself for the impact. Instinctively, he closed his eyes.

But suddenly, he felt soft arms sliding under his armpits and a soft bosom preventing his fall. He opened his eyes in wonder and found himself looking into the radiant face of his beloved Maggie.

"Careful there, soldier," she smiled. "Can't have you all banged up your first day back."

Gazing into her eyes, he didn't even realize he was balancing on one leg. "Oh, Maggie," he breathed as he bent his head to kiss her.

She stood on tiptoe and returned his kiss with all the fervor of a lonely army wife. The kiss was everything he'd dreamed about while he'd been in Belgium. Sweet, sensuous, wholesome, and all-encompassing. His heart pounded in his chest as he pulled her even closer, hugging her to him as if he'd never let her go.

After a few moments, the conductor cleared his throat behind them. Reluctantly, Thomas released his wife and looked over his shoulder to see the conductor holding his duffel.

"Is this yours, soldier?" he asked, smiling.

Thomas laughed. "Yes, sir. I must have left it in my haste to see my wife." He looked lovingly down at Maggie.

"I understand. Are you ready to carry it, or shall I leave it on the platform so you can finish greeting her?"

Maggie laughed. "I think we'll finish our greetings at home."

Thomas nodded, reaching for the duffel. He nearly lost his balance as he turned, but Maggie slid her arm around his waist, holding him up. He glanced at her with gratitude, but also felt a little foolish. A stray thought crossed his mind, that maybe she'd have to hold him up for the rest of his life. That didn't sit well in his mind and he frowned.

"What's wrong?" she asked, suddenly worried.

"Nothing. Just thinking." He tried to smile, but the smile didn't reach his eyes. Her expression told him that she didn't believe him, but he wasn't willing to talk about it in public. "Let's go home."

Maggie reached down to retrieve his crutches. It was only then that he truly saw her very pregnant belly.

"Maggie! You shouldn't be doing that," he admonished.

"Doing what?"

"Bending over like that. Won't that hurt the baby?"

She laughed. "Not at all. It's a little awkward sometimes, but our baby is perfectly safe, even when I bend over."

Standing up, she handed him the crutches, then reached for his other hand. Placing it on her belly, she smiled. "I think she's glad you're home. She's kicking like crazy."

Thomas held perfectly still, trying to feel his child moving. His eyes grew wide as he felt the little flutter across the palm of his hand.

"Is that him?" His voice was filled with awe.

"Or her," Maggie corrected. "It could be a girl, you know."

"But we don't know, do we?"

"No, but I like to imagine it's a little girl. I can see her sitting on your knee, blonde, curly head bobbing as she tries to tell you a story. She'll have you wrapped around her finger, you know," Maggie teased.

Thomas laughed. "I'm certain of that, boy or girl!"

Maggie linked her arm through his as he tossed the duffel over his shoulder. She didn't seem to notice the awkwardness of holding his arm as he used his crutches. Smiling down at her, Thomas felt his heart swell with love for this amazing woman and the child she carried within her. *It's good to be home*, he thought.

As they made their way down the street, they were content to be together again. Conversation seemed unnecessary.

Thomas couldn't take his eyes off her, which caused him to stumble a couple of times. After the second time, she grinned up at him. "You'd better watch where you're going instead of staring at me. You're likely to pull us both down when you fall."

The thought of making his pregnant wife fall brought him back to the realities of walking with crutches. He studiously looked where he was walking and found himself noticing the familiar streets, buildings, and tiny gardens. Although most had only begun to bloom, they were beautiful to his sight. He smiled.

"Looks good to you?" Maggie's eyes sparkled.

"Oh yes," he breathed. "It looks very good."

Chapter Twenty

May 15, 1915

The bells on the front doors rang as Katie entered the grocer's shop. Thomas looked down from the ladder, placing the last can on the top shelf.

"Hi, Katie. I'll be right with you," he called down. Maneuvering the steps with a little difficulty, he was careful to step off on his good left foot, rather than the wooden one on his right. He'd learned that lesson the hard way a few weeks back.

Katie didn't wait for him to come to the counter. She ran over and began tugging on Thomas's arm.

"You have to come, Thomas!" she urged. "Maggie's having the baby and you have to come now!"

"Holy smokes!" Thomas's eyes grew wide as her message registered. "Mr. Davies, Maggie's having the baby. I have to go."

"Go ahead," a voice from the back room called. "I'll mind the store."

Thomas and Katie ran the entire way and arrived breathless but excited. They burst through the front door and Thomas called as he made his way down the short hall to their bedroom. "Maggie! Maggie, are you all right?"

"I'm fine, dear," she smiled up at him from the bed. "It hasn't been too bad, actually."

He sat beside her and took her hand. "Truly? You're not in pain?"

She laughed. "I wouldn't say that, but it's manageable."

He smiled back at her. "I'm glad. What can I do?"

She started to shake her head, then a look of great concentration fell on her face. He was immediately alarmed.

"What's wrong?"

Mrs. Gilley stepped forward and placed her hand on his shoulder. "She's fine, Thomas. It's just another contraction. If it bothers you, you can wait in the living room. The midwife will be here shortly."

"No, I want to stay with her." His voice was adamant.

"As you wish." She smiled down at him, then went to collect more linens.

As the contraction passed, Maggie's smile returned. "You don't have to stay, you know. Women have been birthing babies without their husbands present for many years."

"I want to stay, if that's all right with you." His voice was tender and his gaze filled with love.

Squeezing his hand, she nodded her assent.

A mere hour later, Maggie gave one final scream and push as Thomas sat behind her, holding her shoulders close. Suddenly, a baby's cry filled the room and Maggie relaxed against him.

"It's a girl," the midwife announced, wrapping the infant in a blanket before handing her to Maggie.

Maggie enveloped the little bundle in her arms, cooing and kissing the tiny head.

Thomas's finger found its way to the little ear, stroking it gently.

"It's a girl," he whispered, awestruck by what he'd just witnessed. He leaned down and kissed his wife's forehead. "It's a girl, Maggie. We have a daughter."

She smiled up at him. "I know. Isn't she beautiful?"

"As beautiful as her mother," he answered.

October 31, 1915

Baby Karl clapped and cooed delightedly as Friedrich scooped him up from his crib in the corner.

"Come, *mein sohn*," he grinned. "We must hurry, or we will miss everything."

A tall, lanky man looked at himself in the small mirror by the door. "A fine haircut, Friedrich," he commented, then smiled. "As usual."

"*Danke*, Herr Engel," Friedrich called. "See you in a couple of weeks."

Dropping a few coins in the box by the door, the customer put his hat on his head and saw himself out as Friedrich gathered his son's necessities, placing them in a small brown satchel.

"Who would have guessed that one baby would need so many things?" he asked Karl playfully.

The baby babbled and squirmed happily as his father tried to put a coat on him. Once he was dressed for the cool fall air, they left the little barbershop.

Walking down the street towards the church, Friedrich marveled for the thousandth time how blessed he truly was. He had his son, he had the little barbershop he'd always wanted, it was a beautiful autumn day, and he was going to attend a miraculous event. Grinning to himself, he hurried on to the church.

As he entered, he took a moment for his eyes to adjust to the candlelit chapel. Nodding to the few people sitting near the aisle, he found the woman he was looking for. She stood and smiled as she saw him, reaching for the baby.

"Thank you, Ilsa," he whispered.

She smiled back and then settled into the pew, talking softly to Karl.

Friedrich looked to the front of the chapel, but didn't see who he was looking for. An older gentleman sitting near the front tugged his sleeve.

"He's in there," he said, pointing. "Probably worried about his tie or some such nonsense."

Friedrich chuckled, then stepped to the anteroom indicated. He knocked twice, then entered. Sure enough, a very nervous Gustav Otto was frantically trying to tie his tie.

Smiling, Friedrich reached to help. "Here, Gustav," he said. "Let me help you."

"I never could get those things tied right," the old man grumbled. "Not sure why we have to wear them anyway."

"Because the woman you love has requested it," Friedrich smiled.

At that reference, Gustav's face softened. "Oh, right," he said with a small grin.

Once the tie was appropriately fastened, the two men walked into the chapel, standing together at the front.

The organ started, playing softly at first, then building into Wagner's familiar *"Brautchor"*, "The Bridal Chorus". The doors at the back opened and a radiant Klara Schmidt entered, carrying a bouquet of autumn leaves collected from the park. Her pale yellow dress was accented by the color in the flowers beautifully.

"Oh Lord, help me," Gustav breathed. "Just when I think she can't get more beautiful..."

Friedrich's smile held a touch of sadness. "Love does that," he commented. "Makes them more beautiful every day."

The wedding was simple, but the elderly couple beamed the whole way through. Friedrich was thrilled to see his dear friends finally united in matrimony. *They may not have many years left on this earth,* he thought, *but those years will be joyous now.*

When the ceremony was over, he joined Ilsa and his son on the front steps. They cheered and threw rice as the happy couple exited the church.

Helping Klara into the flower-decked cab, Gustav kissed her hand, picked a rice grain out of her hair, and whispered, "No need to worry about how many grains of rice are in your hair, *mein Klara.* We're long past having children, aren't we?"

She laughed, and he hurried around to the other side. Waving at the small crowd, he ducked inside and they were off.

Friedrich took Karl from Ilsa's arms, then turned to watch them depart. "They look so happy."

"Yes, they do."

The smile touching his lips held once more a trace of sadness, his eyes on the cab as it pulled away. "Perhaps we can each find such happiness again someday."

She looked up at him, a subtle warmth in her eyes. "Perhaps... someday."

Epilogue

December 20, 1923
Ypres, Belgium

"Karl, please stop pulling your sister's braids," Friedrich warned. "And Liesel, please stop teasing him. He'll be nicer if you are nice to him."

"But, Papa," the little girl started to protest, "he started it."

Friedrich shook his head and tousled her hair. "Then you be a good girl and end it… peacefully."

The train slowed to a stop. Friedrich and Ilsa gathered their belongings, took the children in tow, and moved slowly down the aisle.

When they reached the doorway, Friedrich jumped down, placing their bags on the platform. He reached for four-year-old Liesel, helping her down, and started to reach for Karl.

"I can jump myself, Papa," he announced with every ounce of nine-year-old pride he could muster.

Friedrich smiled and stepped back.

Karl made the jump with only a little stumble as he landed.

"*Gut*," his father grinned, then turned to the train to help his wife.

She moved slowly these days, as most pregnant women do, but she favored him with a smile of gratitude as he lifted her gently onto the platform.

"*Danke*," she said softly.

He hugged her for a moment, then turned to see where his children were. He saw them standing on the edge of the platform looking out at the village.

"It looks much like home," Karl observed.

"And so it is," Friedrich agreed. "The location is different, as are some of the customs, but these people live much as we do."

The little family carried their bags to the inn at the edge of town. After checking in, as they settled into their room, Karl asked, "When can we see No Man's Land, Papa?"

"Tomorrow. Your mother needs to rest after such a long journey. We will find some supper, then retire for the night. Tomorrow after breakfast, we will go to No Man's Land."

"Is that where you cut the Englishman's hair?" Liesel asked.

"Yes, Liesel," he smiled. "That's where we sang, talked, and played football, too."

"Did he really give you his cap?" Karl asked.

Friedrich grinned and reached into his coat pocket. "You mean this one?"

He pulled out the old cap, stuck his finger into the bullet hole and wiggled it at Liesel. She squealed and hid behind her mother.

"May I wear it tomorrow?" Karl asked, his eyes alight with excitement.

Nodding, Friedrich placed the cap on his son's head.

The next morning, they started out, excitement in their steps. The children had long heard about the Christmas Truce and the Englishman their father had befriended. Today, with any luck, they'd be able to see the very spot where that had happened.

"Those are very tiny houses," Liesel commented, pointing to a group of huts.

"Those are the temporary housing the Belgian government provided for the people after the war was over," Ilsa said, stroking her daughter's hair.

"Why didn't they live in their own houses?" Liesel asked.

"Their houses were broken, silly," Karl answered her. "By bombs and fire and such. Right, Papa?"

"That's right," Friedrich answered. He pointed to a large building with scaffolding around it. "*Schau.* Look. That's Cloth Hall. That's where people used to make the cloth for their clothes."

"Was it broken in the war, too?" Liesel asked.

"Yes, and so was the cathedral," her father said, pointing. "But they are rebuilding it, so it will look beautiful again."

Continuing their informal tour, Friedrich pointed out some of the buildings and landmarks he remembered. His heart sorrowed for the devastation the war had brought to this beautiful little town.

They approached the Menin Gate where so many soldiers had passed on their way to the trenches.

"What are they doing, Papa?" Liesel asked, pointing to some workmen climbing on scaffolding by the gate.

"They are building a memorial and are carving the names of soldiers on it," he answered. "It's a way to say thank you to the soldiers who gave their lives here."

"Then why are we here now, Papa?" Karl asked. "Why didn't we wait until they were finished with it?"

Friedrich regarded his son fondly. "Because Christmas is the time I wanted to remember, *mein sohn*. There will be a special surprise waiting for us in No Man's Land today."

"A surprise?" Liesel began jumping up and down in her excitement. "I like surprises!"

Friedrich smiled at her, then paused, paying his own silent tribute to those soldiers.

After about an hour, they approached what was No Man's Land. As they drew closer, Friedrich slowed, then stopped. There were huge craters throughout the field, filled with brackish water.

Karl pointed to something half buried near an especially large crater. "Look, Papa! What's that?"

Friedrich looked where his son was pointing.

"That's part of an artillery shell. You will see many of them all over this field."

Karl nodded solemnly. Then he saw something that caused a complete change in his attitude. As they stepped over a small rise, they looked out over a vast expanse riddled with smaller craters, long rows of trenches, half-destroyed sandbags, and the wreckage of a large German tank that had been bombed.

"Wow! Can we take a closer look?"

Friedrich was torn between his son's excitement and the sadness that filled his heart at the memory of so many good men lost on that battlefield. Placing his hand on his son's shoulder, he nodded.

"Yes, *sohn*. We can go closer."

They walked down the short slope and skirted the end of one trench to approach the tank. Ilsa held Liesel's hand, and Friedrich kept a firm hand around Karl's.

The boy oohed and aahed over the shrapnel and shell holes in the sides of the tank. His eyes were wide with amazement at the size of the tracks that used to move the monstrous vehicle. When they came around to the front, his jaw dropped when he saw the massive gun poking out.

But Friedrich wasn't watching his son's face in that moment. His attention was drawn to another family approaching from the far side of the war-torn expanse. A father, mother, and three children.

Friedrich dropped his son's hand and began walking again. His walk turned into a trot, then his trot became a run. Soon, the two men were moving into what was once No Man's Land directly towards each other, one at a full run, the other using a peculiar loping, limping pace that looked odd, but that surprisingly covered a lot of ground quickly.

In the middle, they stopped, shook hands, then pulled each other into a hug with lots of back slapping and laughter.

"You came, *kumpel!*" Friedrich announced, unnecessarily.

"Yes," Thomas grinned. "When I received your letter, I couldn't resist. Can you believe it's been five years?"

Friedrich shook his head. "It seems so long ago, yet I remember like it was yesterday."

By then, the children had caught up to their fathers. They stood back, shyly at first, then Karl ventured forward towards the oldest girl.

Bravely, he stuck out his hand. "I'm Karl. That's my papa."

The blonde-haired girl smiled and put her hand out, shaking his. "I'm Molly and he's my father." She pointed at Thomas.

Thomas looked down and smiled. "Friedrich, this is my family. Maggie, my wife, Molly, Michael, and Edward."

Friedrich proudly returned the introductions. "My wife, Ilsa, my son, Karl, and my daughter, Liesel."

At the mention of her name, Liesel pulled at Friedrich's coat. When he bent down, she whispered loudly in German, "Are they the surprise, papa?"

Nodding, Friedrich tousled her hair. "They are. Is it a *gut* surprise?"

She looked at the English family, squinted her eyes, then smiled. "Yes. But I was really hoping for a pony."

Friedrich laughed, then translated for Thomas and his family.

Looking at Karl, Thomas grinned. "I see you are wearing my cap."

Karl's eyes widened. "This is yours?" he asked, awed. The boy reached up and removed it, offering it to Thomas.

"It looks better on you than it did on me, so why don't you keep it?" Thomas smiled.

Karl looked up at his father, who nodded. He looked back at the Englishman, placed the cap back on his head and grinned. "*Danke.*"

"If that means thank you, then you are welcome."

The two families chatted and walked around the battle site, the men pointing out places they remembered, recalling stories of that unusual Christmas. The older children were mesmerized. The younger ones enjoyed playing together. The wives moved off after a while to commiserate about pregnancy and babies while Maggie nursed her baby.

"Life has been good to you, Thomas?" Friedrich asked.

"Yes, we are happy and content. We have a roof over our heads, food in our bellies and peace in our corner of the world. What more could a man ask for?"

Friedrich nodded. "For us, as well. I often miss my sweet Gerdie, but I love Ilsa, too. She is a good wife and mother. We have all we need and some of what we want. *Das is gut, ja?* That is good?"

"It is good, my friend," Thomas agreed.

He glanced over to see Molly and Karl whispering together.

"Would it not be ironic if our children should grow up and marry someday?" he asked Friedrich.

Friedrich smiled. "That would be poetic justice, I think."

Returning from their little detour, Maggie and Ilsa rejoined the group. Maggie reached out and touched Thomas's hand. "Do you think we should continue with our plan, Thomas?"

He smiled. "I don't see why not."

Turning to Friedrich, he explained. "Maggie had the idea that perhaps we should sing *Silent Night* while we are here. That was the song that started the truce, as I recall."

Grinning, Friedrich nodded. "*Wunderbar!* I think that is a splendid idea. We only know it in German, of course."

"No matter. The melody and message are the same."

Maggie started, and the others joined in after only a few notes. Even the older children sang along, each in their native language.

How appropriate, Friedrich thought as the last notes of the hymn died away, *that two soldiers who served on opposite sides of the war should come together in this place and sing together the song that started it all.*

Coming Soon

Winnie's Wish

"Be careful what you wish for."

by

EMILY DANIELS